The Dorset Boy Book 6 - Vendetta

This is a work of Fiction. All characters and stories are fictional although based in historical settings. If you see your name appear in the story it is a coincidence.

Credits

Thanks to Kate from Blondie Marie Editing who edited this book, and to Dawn Spears the brilliant artist who created the cover artwork. My wife who is so supportive and believes in me. Last my dogs Blaez and Zeeva and cat Vaskr who watch me act out the fight scenes and must wonder what the hell has gotten into their boss.

The Dorset Boy Book 6 - Vendetta

THANK YOU FOR READING!

I hope you enjoy reading this book as much as I enjoyed writing it. Reviews are so helpful to authors. I really appreciate all reviews, both positive and negative. If you want to leave one, you can do so on Amazon, through the website or Twitter.

About the Author

Christopher C Tubbs is a descendent of a long line of Dorset clay miners and has chased his family tree back to the 16th century in the Isle of Purbeck. He left school at sixteen to train as an Avionics Craftsman, has been a public speaker at conferences for most of his career in the Aerospace and Automotive industries and was one of the founders of a successful games company back in the 1990's. Now in his sixties, he finally got around to writing the story he had been dreaming about for years. Thanks to Inspiration from the great sea authors like Alexander Kent, Dewey Lambdin, Patrick O'Brian and Dudley Pope he was finally able to put digit to keyboard. He lives in the Netherlands with his wife, two Dutch Shepherds and a Norwegian Forest cat.

You can visit him on his website
www.thedorsetboy.com

The Dorset Boy, Facebook page.

Or tweet him @ChristopherCTu3

The Dorset Boy Book 6 - Vendetta

The Dorset Boy Series Timeline

1792 – 1795.
Book 1. A Talent for Trouble, Mart joins the Navy as an Assistant Steward and ends up a midshipman.

1795 – 1798.
Book 2. The Special Operations Flotilla, Marty is a founder member of the Special Operations Flotilla, learns to be a spy and passes as lieutenant.

1799 – 1802.
Book 3. Agent Provocateur, Marty teams up with Linette to infiltrate Paris, marries Caroline, becomes a father and fights pirates in Madagascar.

1802 – 1804.
Book 4. In Dangerous Company, Marty and Caroline are in India helping out Arthur Wellesley, combating French efforts to disrupt the East India Company and French sponsored pirates on Reunion. James Stockley born

1804 – 1805.
Book 5. The Tempest, piracy in the Caribbean, French interference, Spanish gold and the death of Nelson. Marty makes Captain.

1806 – 1807.
Book 6. Vendetta, A favour carried out for a prince, a new ship, the S.O.F. move to Gibraltar, the battle of Maida, counter espionage in Malta and a Vendetta declared and closed.

The Dorset Boy Book 6 - Vendetta

Contents

The Dorset Boy Book 6 - Vendetta

An excerpt from Book 7

The Dorset Boy Book 6 - Vendetta

Chapter 1: A festive break

Hood's plans for the Special Operations Flotilla (S.O.F.) meant that Marty would have some rare and valuable home time. He was looking forward to it as he felt like he had missed much of his children's early childhood, it was late 1805, and Bethany was now six and James three.

All his ships were being refitted, which would take time as none of them were particularly new, and they had been used hard in the Caribbean. The Alouette was a former French Navy Corvette, the Hornfleur a former French Whaler and now a transport/landing craft for the Marines, the Eagle a Baltimore Clipper and the Tempest an old Jackass Frigate. He had been promised at least a thirty-six-gun frigate to replace the Tempest as the Navy didn't want to buy her back in, but there was no sign of one yet.

His crew were all on leave except the harbour watches on the ships. This was not normal practice in the Navy as sailors would normally run if let ashore. However, all his men were volunteers, that went with the special status of the S.O.F., and while some would decide to retire on the prize money they had made while sailing with him most would come back.

The band of men that were his followers were like an extended family, staying with him wherever he went and were known as the Shadows. This select group had grown over the years and although they had lost a few through death, more had joined. He had also invited any of his crew who had no families in England, and there were many, to stay at his family estate in Cheshire.

Now, as the Christmas season approached, the preparation for the festivities was intense, led by Marty's wife Caroline, the estate team were being tested by the sheer scale of the celebrations.

They needed enough beer, mead, wine and food to entertain three hundred estate workers and Marty's followers and men. To complicate things there were many nationalities as well: Basques, French, German, Dutch, African and even a couple from the Nordics.

Some of the Africans had no idea what Christmas was. They had been rescued before becoming full slaves when Marty had bought them off the block to free them. They had only recently been exposed to Christianity by their crewmates and had never met a priest. The others, who were recruited from the slums in Jamaica, had been converted to Christianity before they had joined Marty.

Marty wasn't overly religious and, like many sea captains, had a pragmatic approach to religion at sea, but as the Lord of the Manor he had to set an example and made sure he attended services at the estate church. This was greatly appreciated by the local vicar, the reverend Iain McQuat, who had been appointed by Bishop Majendie of Chester, whose diocese they fell under.

The Reverend caught a dose of holy zeal, took the conversion of the Africans as his personal mission and determined to bring them to God. However, the boys soon proved they were not the ignorant savages that he presumed they were. To start with they had all learnt English, the version used on ships, and were, to a man, intelligent. They sat in a semicircle facing him as he read parts of the scriptures to them.

It soon became apparent that they already knew some of the scriptures and certain church rituals. Marty had a strong suspicion about who had taught them. They asked questions about baptism, the eucharist and confessional. All Lutheran traditions. *I will have to have a word with Ackermann,* he chuckled to himself as he saw the Right Reverend struggling to sell his version of Christianity.

That apart, the preparations were going as planned, a veritable convoy of carts were pulling up the drive delivering everything a good party would need. He watched a flock of geese, bred on the estate, being herded into a pen by a well-trained border collie.

Earlier Blaez, who was in his prime, had occasion to challenge a younger drover's dog who had the temerity to pee on a post in his territory.

A challenge was thrown down and accepted. The combatants threw themselves into the fight with enthusiasm and murderous intent!

Fur flew and teeth clashed to a background of blood curdling snarls and ended with the dogs being dragged apart before they could do any real damage to each other.

Blaez was banished indoors until the deliveries had been completed and once released made a beeline for the post, well and truly washed it down then scratched the ground around it with stiff legs to say, "MINE!"

The weather turned and it started to snow which was a new experience for those brought up in the tropics. Samuel ran into Marty's study, eyes wide in amazement,

"Boss, the sky is falling!" he cried pointing out of the window.

Marty looked out and saw the large white flakes drifting to the ground and restrained a laugh,

"it's alright Samuel, that's just snow," he explained and when Samuel still didn't understand, "it's just frozen water."

"Don't look like the ice on the pond," Samuel insisted.

Marty opened the window and put his hand out to catch some of the flakes and show Samuel that they melted to water on his skin. Once he saw that, he put his own hand out and tried it for himself, a look of awe on his face. Later Marty had to laugh when he heard him say to some of the other Africans,

"It just frozen water, didn't you know that?"

Tom had finally asked Marty if he could marry Amara, the Indian servant that had stayed with them after they left the sub-continent. Marty and Caroline were her surrogate parents while she was with them. She was a Christian already so that made things easier, but the vicar still had reservations about the mixed-race nature of the union. Marty who had immediately given the marriage his blessing, had a quiet word with the Right Reverend and made a substantial donation to the church of a pair of large gold candlesticks which turned him into an enthusiastic supporter immediately.

Marty's family wouldn't join them for Christmas as Cheshire was just too far from Dorset to travel that time of year. They did, however, receive a delivery of ten firkins of good Dorset scrumpy as a gift from one estate to the other. Scrumpy was made from apples and was almost as strong as wine. That made it dangerous as the temptation was to drink it like beer that was a quarter the strength. The Basques absolutely loved it as it was reminiscent of the Sagardoa they drank at home, but, as Tom pointed out, "that stuff is bloody lethal and if you drink it don't fart 'cus it turns your guts to water!"

Christmas eve arrived and after a hearty breakfast the family attended midday mass with the children at the local church. After the service Marty and Caroline oversaw the distribution of gifts to the poor of the parish. Pragmatic as always, they ensured the gifts would ease their lives at least for the Christmas season. They also attended midnight mass which meant Marty had been to church more times in that week than the whole of the rest of the year.

Christmas day was spent with the family, Caroline's parents arrived in time for lunch which started at two o'clock and continued until five. Presents were exchanged and games played. It was a most enjoyable and relaxing time.

Caroline's sister Julia arrived on Boxing Day with her husband and children giving them more presents to open. Her husband Frederick was a post captain in the Navy and gifted Marty with one of the new brass framed sextants. These precision instruments were replacing quadrants as their production became easier and their size decreased. He in turn gifted the good captain with a set of solid gold buttons for his dress uniform.

The big party started in the afternoon. Two of the barns were commandeered and set out with tables of food laid out down one side with benches and tables filling up all the rest of the space. Marty and the family had the top table, naturally, the managers and senior staff sat closest to them with the rest of the estate in reducing level of rank further away. The barns were heated with braziers burning charcoal which gave good heat without too much smoke.

During the dinner, Marty and Caroline took a walk to the second barn to wish the people there a Happy Christmas and make sure they had plenty to eat and drink. Most of the ladies who worked in the dairy were in this second barn as they had only low worker status. Their husbands, who Marty had pressed because they were drunkards or abusive were still serving in the Navy, but the women seemed to be thriving and well satisfied with life.

Once the food was finished the tables were cleared away and the benches were put around the sides of the main barn. A group of musicians gathered and started to play popular tunes for everyone to dance to. Marty and Caroline got things moving by dancing a Reel which soon had many couples up and moving.

Outside after dark a huge bonfire was lit in a paddock behind the barns and many people danced around it even though the temperature was well below freezing. The party wound down as midnight approached and the revellers staggered back to their homes or just wrapped themselves in their cloaks and slept in the barn.

They left for London on the twenty-seventh of December as Marty wanted to visit Chatham and see how the work on his vessels was progressing. As usual it took two days and involved stopovers at their favourite coaching inns. The Shadows accompanied them without Tom who was honeymooning with his new wife in their new cottage that Marty and Caroline had gifted them. The rest of the crewmen would stay until the ships were ready. Tom would keep an eye on them and make sure they didn't cause any trouble.

Just south of Birmingham, as they passed through the black country with its smoke, soot and poverty, a group of hapless, sorry-looking ruffians blocked the road and attempted to rob them.

"Boss, you better see this," laughed Samuel from up top as the coach stopped. Marty stepped out and took in the ragged clothes, the array of mismatched weapons held ineptly, and the way the men clumped together for mutual support.

"Who is your leader?'

A slightly more determined-looking man stepped forward.

"What do you want?"

"We want yeow to give us yeow weapons and hand over yeow mooney," he said in a distinct black country accent with all the authority he could muster.

Marty made a show of thinking about that.

"Well if you want either you will have to take them," he said in a worryingly calm voice.

His pistols appeared in his hands and with a ripple of clicks the rest of his people followed his lead.

The look of surprise on the faces of the desperadoes was a picture when they realised, they were suddenly facing an array of weapons held professionally by every adult member of the coach party, including the women. Worse, several men had managed to get behind them, and they were surrounded.

"Up to now, no one has gotten hurt and no money has changed hands." Marty smiled at them so reasonably that some even looked hopeful. "Now if you would be so kind as to pile your weapons there," he indicated a spot beside the spokesman, "we can resolve this without any of you getting killed."

Samuel stepped down off the carriage and put the weapons in a cornsack he had found on the roof. He would later toss them over the side of a bridge as they crossed a river.

"If you are hungry and want a job because, to be frank, you aren't cut out to be highwaymen, then make your way to the Royal dockyards at Chatham in Kent and ask for Captain Stockley. If you make it there, I will give you a place on one of my ships as a landsman." The pistols disappeared and he pulled out a purse.

"Here are two shillings each. I pay better than the King's shilling. Make it to Chatham and there will be a sovereign waiting for each of you there." He walked amongst them and handed each of them their coins. When he was finished, he got back in the carriage and they continued their journey, leaving the astonished men behind them. Blaez opened one eye in greeting from his place on the floor; he hadn't bothered to even get up to look during the whole episode.

"That was very generous, Sir," Mary, their nurse complimented him.

"Not really," Marty replied, "half that set out won't make it and the ones that do will have shown the resourcefulness that I want in my crew. In the end, I win."

London was cold and wet, the snow they had enjoyed in Cheshire hadn't settled in the warmer Southeast and instead the whole city was wreathed in a persistent drizzle mixed with smoke. They got settled into the house and sorted through the social invites that had been delivered in case they made an appearance.

One stood out from the rest as it had the royal seal on the envelope. They had been invited to the Royal New Year's Eve Ball, ostensibly by the King but more likely by the regent. There was a separate note from Hood saying that, should they be going, Marty should be in uniform as his exploits against the Spanish treasure fleet in the Caribbean had been published in the Gazette and he was somewhat of a personality.

"I suppose they need something to take the public's mind off the death of Nelson," Caroline guessed.

As he only had to put on his best uniform with all his honours Marty had time to take one of their coaches down to Chatham. Caroline was in a frenzy of dressmaking and Marty was glad to be out of the way.

Samuel and Blaez came along for the ride and to provide a bit of added protection. When he got there, he was shocked to see the yard was still full of ships waiting to be repaired after Trafalgar and was told in no uncertain terms his little ships would have to wait. It was a cold, slow trip back to London.

Chapter 2: Georgie's Confession

He was dressed in his best dress uniform with its gold epaulette on his right shoulder, the gold watch and chain that Caroline had given him hung across from one pocket of his waistcoat to the other, the cross of the Knight of the Bath was pinned to his left breast. Tempted as he was to conceal a few weapons he restricted himself to his dress sword and a barker in his overcoat pocket.

Caroline was in her element; she had run her dressmaker ragged and appeared on the night in a dress based on the latest fashion made of the finest silk from India. Low-cut in the bodice and high-waisted it flowed down her body and out behind in a short train. She ignored the flouncy lace trims that many women favoured but had it decorated with seed pearls sown in an intricate pattern across the bodice. It was at once simple and extremely elegant and would cause a sensation.

She wore a diamond tiara that had a centrepiece of a blue-white diamond of twenty carats matched by a diamond necklace of unsurpassed quality. On her left breast she wore the leaping tiger given her by the Peshwa Baji Rao, its gleaming ruby eyes warning everyone she was dangerous as well as beautiful.

They had aimed to arrive after most of the other guests but when they pulled up in front of Kensington Palace their coach was ushered to the front of the line.

"What's this all about?" Marty pondered out loud.

"I don't know," Caroline replied, "it's not normal." They were, after all, the lowest rank of aristocracy as Baron and Baroness and they were being ushered past at least one Viscount.

A footman in royal livery placed steps at the door of their coach and Marty exited first so he could help Caroline down. She had to be careful to neither trip over her dress nor get the train snagged.

A herald led them up through the huge main double doors and to the entrance of the ballroom. Another herald met them inside and announced their arrival in ringing tones. They stepped forward into a maelstrom of greetings and eventually made their way to the end of the receiving line to be greeted by the Prince Regent.

Prince George was dressed in his usual flamboyant style with yet another new consort on his arm and when he saw the pair of them were next in line, he beamed a smile and greeted them in a loud, friendly, German-accented voice that was incapable of pronouncing the letter *r*.

"My dea' Marty and Cawoline, what a pleasure it is to see you," he fairly boomed, "my dea' you look absolutely wavishing!" and then sotto voice to Marty, "how do you sleep at night?"

Marty put on a smile and replied, "Oh quite well, eventually, you know."

Which caused his Royal Highness to guffaw with laughter. He then leaned towards Marty and said quietly,

"I need to speak with you on a matter of some sensitivity, please meet me in the games woom at ten o'clock."

He then stood back, shook Marty's hand and clapped him on the shoulder like they were old friends.

Slightly bemused but intrigued, Marty and Caroline worked their way out through the crowd to find a quiet corner. Caroline smiled dazzlingly throughout, especially at those women who were openly admiring her new dress. The smile took on a slightly feral look when she noticed women eyeing Marty speculatively.

"What the hell is all that about?" Marty exclaimed in a loud whisper.

"I wish I knew," Caroline replied.

"Has there been any gossip lately?" Marty asked.

"He's got himself a new woman, but that's nothing new and the old one apparently wasn't too impressed." Caroline offered.

"Phht, nothing new, that man leaves women lying behind him like discarded clothes," Marty replied. "Who was the old one?"

"An exiled French aristocrat named Marie Fortin. A minor Contessa I believe." Caroline answered.

Just then Hood walked up to them.

"Good evening you two," he greeted them, "have you spoken to the Prince yet?"

Even though Marty tried to get his superior and mentor to talk, Hood wouldn't say anything to enlighten them. They were sure he knew something of what was afoot but deftly changed the subject whenever either of them tried to question him.

At precisely ten o'clock he was led discretely to the games room by a liveried servant who suddenly appeared at his elbow. He was left waiting on his own for about ten minutes and started knocking the balls around on the billiard table. Eventually the Prince entered through a concealed door that otherwise would be taken as part of the bookshelves.

"Sowwy to keep you," Prince George said as he shut the door behind him, he looked flustered. "Admiwal Hood said you might be able to help me with a small pwoblem I find I have." He went to the door Marty had entered by and checked the corridor was empty. Marty noticed that his speech impediment had gotten more pronounced now they were alone.

Marty was beginning to feel worried about what was coming, but he held his nerve.

"I am at your service, your Highness. If there is anything I can do to help, you need only to ask, but please tell me what is wrong so I can consider what could be done."

The Prince looked at him for a long moment and then sighed.

"You saw that I have a new lady attending me this evening."

"My wife noticed that and mentioned it, yes."

"Lady Cawoline is very astute, you are a lucky man. Well my former consort has wun off with something that belongs to my family," the Prince admitted.

Marty waited. The Prince looked increasingly uncomfortable,

"And, I may have let slip a couple of things that I shouldn't have in a moment of passion," he said in a rush.

"Pillow talk, your Highness?" Marty said without much sympathy.

"Yes, well, she knows some things she shouldn't."

"So, you want me to retrieve this object and eliminate the chance that she could divulge the information to someone she shouldn't," Marty said, cutting to the chase.

"Concise and to the point," Prince George said with a grimace, "but there is a small pwoblem."

Marty looked at him and waited.

"She has bolted and left the country. I'm led to believe that she has fled to Spain with a view to making her way to her homeland."

"France," Marty stated.

The Prince nodded.

"How long ago?" Marty asked

"Did she leave?" the Prince asked and when Marty nodded replied, "thwee days ago."

Marty sat on the edge of the billiard table and thought for a moment. The Bethany was still in port and was the fastest thing on the water, but a three-day head start?

"Do you know where she was heading in Spain?" he asked.

"She has welatives in a place called Almewia. I believe she would head there initially," the Prince replied looking hopeful.

"Initially?" Marty noted and then asked, "Where do you think she will go after that?"

"She will twy and hurt me as much as possible so I think she will head to France and twy and bargain the information for permission to stay and get her family lands back," the Prince replied.

"And what was the object she took?" Marty asked.

The Prince blushed and examined the green baize of the billiard table but eventually said,

"I let her borrow my wife's state necklace to wear in bed when we were, you know, intimate."

"The one with the four sapphires the size of pheasant eggs, and about twenty diamonds?" Marty asked, recalling an image of the princess he had seen in a portrait.

"Yes, that one."

"That would keep the good Contessa in comfort for the rest of her days," Marty frowned. "And the information?"

"She was vewy interested in the defences we had prepawed in case Napoleon invaded. She was tewified she would be caught and executed, and I just wanted to weassure her!" the Prince explained in a miserable voice.

Marty looked at him for a long moment and then shook his head in disbelief,

"I will get started first thing in the morning," Marty told him as he stood, bowed and left the room. This was turning into a mission of national importance

"I need to use the Bethany. Is she in India dock?" Marty asked Caroline as he hugged her and gave her a kiss on the cheek after he returned to the ballroom. She raised an eyebrow in query. "Georgie's been a mite indiscreet and has asked me for help," he said as he moved in again for a second kiss.

"Aah the French courtesan?" she asked from behind her fan which she used to shield the kiss from prying eyes.

"Quite," Marty replied through a smile without moving his lips.

The rest of the evening went smoothly. They spent time with Admiral Hood and his wife and the Count and Countess de Marchets, circulated with the other guests and danced. They left at an acceptable hour but as soon as they got home messages were sent to prepare the Bethany for sailing in the morning. The Basques, Samuel, and Rolland were also given the heads up to get ready to leave. Marty gave them the option to stay behind as they were going into territory where, if they were caught, they could be executed out of hand. Not one declined.

At midnight there was a knock at the door and a servant showed in a courier who delivered a package which Marty had to sign for. It contained a portrait of Marie Fortin and a detailed description of distinguishing marks that could only have come from someone who had an intimate relationship with her, or her mother. It also contained the names of all her known family, their last known whereabouts and a picture of the necklace. He looked at the portrait; there was something very familiar about the woman, but he just couldn't put his finger on it.

Marty calculated that if she had taken a regular cargo ship, she would need at least fourteen days to make the trip to Almeria. The Bethany could do the trip in half that if they were lucky. She had a four-day head start so if they were really lucky, they might just get there at the same time she did.

But when they got to India dock the Bethany wasn't going anywhere, during an inspection they had found a series of loose planks around the bow which would have to be repaired before the ship went anywhere.

"It was that big bastard of a cannon we had fitted in the Caribbean," Tarrant, the Bethany's captain reported, "it shook the bow to pieces. It's a wonder we got home!"

"How long to repair it?" Marty asked.

"At least a week," Tarrant replied.

"You have three days," Marty told him. "I don't care what it costs, get this ship ready for sea."

They returned to the house and John Smith unexpectedly showed up. When Marty asked him what he was doing he told him,

"I heard you was off on a mission and there aint no way I be letting you go without me

The mystery was solved when Caroline admitted to having sent for him as she thought him an indispensable member of the team.

"Why don't you just hire another ship?" Caroline asked him as they lay in bed that night.

"A normal ship would take the same amount of time as hers and we would still be four days behind her. If the Bethany sails in three days we will still catch up a day or so, if we are lucky, and be that much closer," he explained.

The next morning Admiral Hood paid a visit at breakfast time and tucked in with relish when Marty invited him to join him. . Marty suspected the old fox had heard that Rolland was at the house and knew he made the most exquisite croissants, which he was devouring one after the other.

"When we heard about the delay, Wickham recalled Linette, she was just finishing a survey of the troops encamped along the French coast and he had those Deal fellows fetch her back. She should be here in time to go with you."

Caroline, who was sitting with them and sipping a cup of tea asked,

"does she know the Contessa?"

Hood wiped the crumbs away from his mouth,

"I believe they have met a couple of times," he replied, slightly hesitantly.

"Then she will be able to positively identify her?" Caroline persisted.

"I should think so," Hood replied, "a positive identification will make life easier for you."

Marty glanced at Caroline who was eyeing Hood with a distinctly suspicious look. *There's something he's not saying,* he thought, but he chose to wait and see rather than try and force the issue.

Impatience drove Marty to visit the docks to see how things were going and he was amazed to find the carpenters from the Tempest, Alouette, and Eagle all working on the Bethany along with their mates. He found Fletcher on deck next to Tarrant.

"I wondered where you had gone," Marty said as he walked up to him, Blaez at his heel. He nodded to the men clustered around the bow and on the dock, sawing timbers to length to replace those that had split, steaming them, then bending and hammering them into place. "Your idea?"

"Didn't think it would hurt," Fletcher replied with a smile.

"And you found a supply of teak. Thought there was a shortage at the moment?" Marty observed as the Bethany had been built in India.

Fletcher didn't answer that, as the source of the wood probably didn't know it had left his possession yet. He would square the account with him later.

With the extra hands and Fletcher making sure that everything they needed was supplied in time they were making better than expected progress.

The Dorset Boy Book 6 - Vendetta

Fletcher had joined Marty to avoid the retribution of some gentlemen of dubious distinction and violent tendencies who felt that he had cheated them. He had used his prize money to pay them off when they returned from the Caribbean. He could have returned to his prior life and business, but that would be boring now he had experienced the excitement of sailing with Marty.

The Admiralty and the Government had argued over how to treat the treasure that Marty and the others had captured from a Spanish treasure fleet in the Caribbean. The Government wanted to take all the treasure as 'Droits of Admiralty' and just pay what was effectively a salvage fee. The Admiralty had argued that it should all be treated as prize money. In the end they compromised, and they treated half as Droits and the other half as prize money.

Marty had his bank, Coutts, look after the distribution of the, still very large, prize to his men and to the freelancers, many of whom chose to open bank accounts rather than take that much money in cash and make themselves targets.

Chapter 3: The Hunt for Marie

With the extra hands and Fletcher greasing the wheels the work was finished in two and a half days. Unfortunately, the tide was against them and there was no way Tarrant was going to try the Thames and estuary in the dark, so they had to wait until the next morning's tide to sail.

Linette arrived at dawn with Ryan. They had managed to grab a night together, and their arrival signalled it was time to go.

"Keep chasing those idle bastards at Chatham," Marty called to Fletcher as the gangplank was sent crashing to the dock.

"Will do, Captain!" Fletcher called back as they warped away from the dock and the lightermen waited to take up the tow to get them out onto the river.

As they slid downstream, the team gathered on the main deck out of the way of the sailors to check their equipment. Tarrant was astonished at the array of weapons that appeared as the team, including the French girl, laid them out to sharpen or service them. Some he recognised, an array of knives, daggers, stilettoes, punch knives, knuckle dusters, pistols and crossbows. He didn't recognise the blackjacks or garrottes, as he had never seen them before, or the latest innovation from the Workshop which was an explosive device sealed in a cast iron cylinder with a clockwork timer fitted in one end. John Smith had a box of them which he was showing to the others and explaining how to use them. He decided that he was better off not knowing.

He turned his attention back to getting the Bethany safely down the river to the estuary. Once out into the English Channel he made the best of the Northeast wind and steered to take them almost due West to a point off the isles of Scilly where he would turn a point West of due South to clear Brest and stay out of the Bay of Biscay. The Bethany flew, this was her element and she revelled in it. The Atlantic rollers presented no challenge at all and she seemed almost to skate over them, only occasionally spearing through an exceptionally big one.

They arrived at the Straights of Heracles in what must have been record time and shot through with neither a 'by-your-leave' nor 'thank you' to the Rock of Gibraltar. But their progress didn't go unnoticed and a report was sent to the Admiralty of a clipper under British colours racing through the straights at 'a reckless pace as though the devil himself was after them.'

They arrived in Almeria just seven days after they left, flying an American flag, the crew tired from keeping up the relentless pace day and night. The merchant ship the Contessa had taken was still anchored in the bay flying a Danish flag and would be the first point of call for Marty and Samuel.

Almeria wasn't much more than a fishing village with a small wooden dock normally used for offloading the catch. The bay was bordered by a village of fisherman's huts and further inland, as the land rose, were several grander looking houses surrounded by olive and orange groves.

The visit to the merchantman confirmed that they had indeed carried a French lady to this port and yes, she did go ashore but no, the captain didn't know where she went after that. She had paid in gold for them to get there as fast as they could, and they had done the trip in twelve days, which he was very proud of, after which she had left as soon as they had docked. They were only two days behind her!

Back on the Bethany he called the team together.

"We need to move fast so only Linette, Ryan, Matai and myself will go," he announced. Samuel looked like he was about to object so Marty forestalled him by saying,

"You don't speak Spanish or French and you don't ride well. You need to stay here with the rest of the men and make sure we can get out of here when we get back.

Linette coughed to get his attention and said,

"I can go ahead and see if she is still at her family's holiday home, I have been there before and know where it is."

Marty readily agreed; there was no point in shaking up a hornet's nest if they could do this quietly, Ryan would go with her. *He doesn't need to pretend to be her paramour,* he grinned inwardly.

Linette and Ryan left immediately the meeting broke up and were rowed ashore. Marty gave Tarrant papers, created from a genuine set they had commandeered sometime in the past from an American ship. Their resident forger had carefully erased the names of the ship and the captain by scraping away the ink with a razor and had filled in new details, so they now looked to be an American ship out of Boston.

Marty suggested they make it appear that they were looking for a cargo of olive oil. To give him his due Tarrant accepted his role without question and said he would wait until they returned, or Marty sent a message otherwise.

Ryan and Linette stepped onto the dock and strolled along it to the beach. She wore a simple, but elegant dress and had her hair covered by a bonnet. He was dressed in the Spanish style in a well-cut jacket with a high collar, white silk shirt and cravat.

"I will talk to the housekeeper alone," Linette told him, speaking Spanish.

"Why?" Ryan asked.

"They don't know you and they will not want to speak of the family in front of you," she replied and, when he went to object, turned to him and placed her hand on his cheek. *"Trust me, I know these people."*

Ryan knew she wasn't telling him something, but she was a spy after all, so he let it go and agreed.

They approached the large, grand gate set in a high wall. There was a coat of arms on a plaque in the centre of each of the gates which were intricately made of wrought iron. He looked twice at the coat of arms; there was something familiar about them.

Linette asked him to wait in the garden until she had spoken to the staff, so he wandered off to look around. The gardens were typical of the area, a mixture of brightly flowering shrubs with blooms that looked like trumpet horns in various shades of red and white and tropical trees like he had seen in the Caribbean. In between were strategically placed rocks, one caught his eye.

He walked over and knelt to examine it. It was the coat of arms he had seen on the gate and he studied it carefully. There was a shield divided diagonally from top right to bottom left. On the right-hand side were three fleurs-de-lis in a triangle, on the left a horse rampant. Above the shield was a centaur. It was bounded either side by two lions rampant. He guessed the owner was a chevalier, the French equivalent of a knight.

Something was nagging at him, a memory of something he had seen at some time that looked similar but try as he might he couldn't pull it back.

Linette returned,

"They told me Marie came here two days ago; she was very upset about the way the Prince just dropped her for another woman and is determined to have her revenge. She left for Madrid yesterday at dawn in one of the family coaches. One of the grooms is driving her. They will make good time as there are many places to change their horses on the way."

Ryan knew that Marty needed this information as soon as possible so hurried them back to the dock and whistled up the ship's boat.

"So, she should arrive in Madrid in around three days," Marty stated as he looked over a map. "Any idea who she will visit there?"

"I think she will go to the French embassy to try and get permission to return to France," Linette replied.

"That could take a while if the embassy is typical of others I have seen," Marty said as he thought out loud. "Where would she stay?"

"There is one family in Madrid who were friends with the Fortins. She may stay with them or she could be at a hotel," Linette added.

"Well sitting here thinking about it won't sort this out we need to get moving," Marty stated decisively.

"I could sail you up to Valencia if that helps," Tarrant offered.

"No, you are better off staying here. The Bethany would be too conspicuous in Valencia, it's far too busy a port. We need horses."

Linette told them she knew where to get some and went ashore with Ryan. An hour later they returned with four saddled horses and four remounts.

They rode hard, switching horses every two hours. It was getting dark as they entered a town called Huéneja and found a place to stay. They were all sore as none of them had ridden in anger for a while and their muscles just weren't used to it.

After a good night's sleep, they were back on the road at dawn. They continued to rotate the horses every two hours and apart from a short break for lunch didn't stop until dusk. They rode into Madrid after three hard days. Both the horses and riders were exhausted.

Ryan knew Madrid and led them to a good hotel not far from the French embassy. They put the horses in the stables and got another good night's sleep so they could start the search for Marie in the morning.

Marty sent Matai and Ryan to watch the embassy while he and Linette went to find the home of the family who were friends of the Fortins. Linette said the patriarch was Don Louis de la Venta or something like that. They asked a couple of passing people who turned out to be visitors and couldn't help at all, then an army officer who was strutting down the road like a cockerel showing off his plumage.

"Ahh Don Louis! Yes, he lives in the Retiro, it is not far from here I can show you the way," he told them while leering at Linette.

He led off at a stroll walking in a way that made it obvious he was out to display his new uniform.

"You have been a lieutenant in the Army for a long time?" Linette asked innocently causing Marty to have to cough to hide a laugh.

"I have been in the army for two years and made lieutenant just one week ago," he told her with a proud tilt to his head.

"Oh my!" She cried in admiration. *"You look so handsome in your uniform I was sure you must be an officer of some renown."*

The young man grew an inch, as the praise of such a beautiful girl pumped his ego even bigger.

Marty grunted as Linette's elbow dig into his ribs as she had felt his body shaking as he silently laughed behind the handkerchief he had taken out of his pocket.

They soon came to the gates of a large house that was set back off the road. The lieutenant, who had introduced himself as José Santiago, offered to walk them to the door but Linette politely declined.

"You have been so gracious senior; we cannot use any more of your valuable time as I am sure the Army needs you." She held her hand out for him to kiss in farewell, then made their way towards the ornate front door.

Once they were sure he had moved on they quickly ducked behind a low hedge and started to make their way around the outside of the house peeking into each window as they passed them. Seeing nothing of interest they made their way to the back of the house to the stables.

There was only one groom visible, currying a large black Arabian blood stallion, who was a beauty! Marty estimated he was a good sixteen and a half hands tall with a long flowing mane that hung down the side of his neck. He held his head high and proud and his tail swished back and forth keeping flies at bay.

They waited until the groom finished his work and led the horse back into the stables. They moved quickly to the coach house and slipped inside the door. There were several carriages, but none had the Fortin family coat of arms on the doors. Their quarry's coach wasn't there.

They quietly exited the coaching house and worked their way back to the front of the house and out of the gate.

"It doesn't look like she is here," Marty sighed; he had been hoping she would be.

"She may have sent the carriage back to Almeria," Linette said thoughtfully, "although I am sure we would have seen it if she had."

"Well, we need to be sure," Marty stated.

Just after midnight, two figures made their way through the gardens of the house of Don Louis de la Venta. They were dressed in black close-fitting outfits and wore black hoods that covered their heads and only showed their eyes. They crept up to one of the windows on the side of the house that was in the shadow cast by the moon and couldn't be seen from the road. The taller of the two slipped a long strip of spring steel between the window and the frame. A little wiggle and the catch lifted allowing them to open it just enough to gain entry.

Once inside they closed the window before crossing the room silently and trying the door. The latch clicked gently as the handle was pushed down and the door cracked open. A gentle push opened the door fully allowing them access to the hallway.

They waited, listening for any sign that their entry had been heard. Hearing nothing, they crept across the tiled floor on their soft leather soled shoes making no noise. They were at the bottom of the grand staircase to the second floor where they guessed the family slept. They paused and listened again before slowly climbing the stairs, testing each step before putting weight on it.

They reached the hallway and split up, going in opposite directions. Again, they tested every step they took before committing their weight, avoiding any loose floorboards that may squeak and give them away. When they reached a door, they listened carefully before trying the handle.

The shorter one came to a door that was slightly more ornate than the rest and listened. The sound of snoring came from inside and, if she wasn't mistaken, the louder was a woman.

She opened the door and slipped inside, treading carefully in case clothes had been left on the floor. There were two people in the bed, a thin old man with a magnificent moustache who's waxed ends were held against his face by a fine cheesecloth strip tied around his head and a very large woman lying on her back and snoring loud enough to give the devil a headache.

The two met back at the top of the stairs before making their way back down and left the house the same way they had come in.

In the hotel the four of them met in the suite Marty had rented as a base. Ryan and Matai shared one bedroom while Linette had another (her choice much to Ryan's surprise) and

Marty the third. It was just after dawn and they sat around the table eating churros for breakfast.

"She definitely isn't at the family house," Marty told them, "we looked in every room and the only people there were the Don, his wife and what could be a spinster sister of hers as they were both of a size."

Ryan looked at Linette who puffed out her cheeks and imitated an extremely fat woman making them all laugh.

"Any luck at the Embassy?" Marty asked.

"They certainly have enough room for people to live there," Ryan stated. "The place is imposing, and that is intentional I think as they also behave like they own the town when they walk around."

"Did you get around the back?" Marty asked

"Yes, we found the back gate, but is guarded by at least two soldiers at all times so we couldn't get in."

"I think it's time we played this game differently," Marty concluded with a frown.

Chapter 4: A game of seek

Around mid-morning, Marty staggered through the front door of the embassy, dressed in torn clothes and sporting a black eye and split lip. Matai had not enjoyed giving his captain and friend a beating, but Marty had insisted as his cover story depended on being absolutely convincing.

He approached the receptionist's desk and almost collapsed across it alarming the neatly dressed man sat behind it.

"You must help me! They robbed me and stole all my money!" he wailed as his legs folded.

On hearing a distinctly Toulon accent, the clerk jumped up and ran around the desk to help him into a chair.

"Sir, please slow down and tell me exactly what happened." He gently instructed, his face showing his real concern as he beckoned over a messenger.

"Please ask Mr. Aubele to come," he instructed the young man, *"then bring a brandy for Mr.--?"* He looked at Marty in question.

"Mr. Bernaux, Pierre Bernaux. I am a merchant from Toulon," Marty told him.

A tall man in a black suit arrived and Marty immediately tagged him as a security officer. He pulled up a chair next to Marty and sat down.

"I am Cedric Aubele head of security here at the embassy," he introduced himself, *"please tell me who you are, what you are doing in Madrid and what has happened."*

Marty spun them a tale about how he was a merchant and had taken ship to Valencia to come to Madrid in search of luxury goods he could import into France.

"I arrived here this morning and was set upon as I entered the city. They knocked me down and stole my horse, luggage

and money. I am left with nothing," he cried, putting his heart and soul into the performance.

The messenger arrived with a glass of cognac. He took a big gulp of it and coughed as the fiery spirit hit his throat.

"Can you describe your attackers?" Aubele asked.

"Spaniards, peasants, ruffians," Marty replied, *"five of them armed with clubs and knives. Had those strange floppy hats they wear."*

"Local rebel militia," Aubele concluded with a frown.

"Can you put me up in a hotel overnight and loan me some money so I can get home?" Marty pleaded.

Aubele looked at the clerk and asked,

"Do we have any of our guest rooms left?"

"The minister is in the royal suite, we have the Contessa in the blue suite, the small guest suit is free," he replied.

"Put him in there and get someone to see to his wounds," Aubele ordered as he stood to leave. *"We will have a further talk when you have recovered sir."*

The clerk detailed a messenger to escort Marty to his rooms and he was taken to a garret on the third floor.

"Are all the guest rooms up here?" Marty asked.

"Oh no sir, the Royal Suite is on the second floor and takes up most of the West end and then there is the smaller Blue Suite at the east end. The kitchens are in between. Doesn't stop the Contessa from visiting the minister though," he gossiped. *"She is a beauty and rich to all accounts, word is she is looking to get back to France, I think she will sleep her way there, if you know what I mean."*

I love servants, Marty thought as he listened to the wealth of information the man gave up without thinking, *he just wants to have someone to talk to.*

After the man had left Marty checked the view from the windows and was pleased that one overlooked the street in front of the building. He looked through the cupboards which were all empty then. He quickly removed his hidden weapons and tools and hid them in one. He threw himself on the bed as he heard footsteps coming up the stairs.

There was a knock on the door, and he bade whoever it was to enter in a weak voice. A scholarly-looking man came in carrying a black bag and introduced himself,

"Good day, I am the embassy's physician."

He proceeded to give Marty a cursory examination; it was obvious he wasn't really interested in what he was doing. He quickly checked the bruising on Marty's face and body, didn't ask about any other wounds and pronounced that he would heal with nothing more than time.

Marty thanked him and let him find his own way out, then settled down to wait. The messenger came up with a tray of soup and fresh bread for his lunch and Marty encouraged him to sit and chat while he ate it.

"Do you wait on all the guests?" he asked.

"Why yes, I am the only one with any experience of service on the staff, so I get to look after all the guests," the little man whose name was Bernard, replied making 'service' sound like a rare skill.

"I bet you could tell some tails," Marty laughed.

"Oh, you bet I could," he boasted, *"you wouldn't believe the goings on. You take that Contessa and her visits to the minister late at night."*

"Really? Do they .... you know?" Marty asked, pretending to be scandalized.

"At it like rabbits judging by the noises that come out of his suite, and him in his sixties and married!" he confided.

"Well, I never, and I thought members of the government were above that," Marty gasped.

Once the messenger had left and locked the door behind him, he started to think things through and look at his options. Ideally Marie should accompany him willingly, failing that he would just have to kidnap her. The question was how to finagle things, so she wanted, or had, to go with him.

At midnight he let the rest of the team know all was going to plan. He took a candle and went to the window overlooking the street and placed it in the window then, using his hand, shielded it and exposed it in the pattern short, long, long, which was the pre-agreed signal for 'stand by, all alright'.

He fell asleep with the problem running around in his mind. He woke suddenly in the wee small hours with the answer clearly laid out in his head. He got up collected his tools and knives and slipped out of his room.

The next morning, he woke to absolute pandemonium. There was shouting from the floor below and then the sound of footsteps on the stairs. His door was unlocked and slammed open. Aubele stepped through holding a pistol. Marty sat up in bed and the sheets fell back exposing the network of bruises on his torso.

Aubele sent two men in and they searched every cupboard, every nook and cranny. They even tipped him out of bed and stripped the covers off. They found nothing and Marty sat in a chair with a sheet wrapped around him asking what was going on.

"The Minister has been murdered in his sleep. It must have been done by someone in the Embassy and we are checking every room," he told Marty who squawked his innocence and said he hadn't moved from the room all night!

A man came to the door, beckoned Aubele to him and whispered something in his ear. Aubele's eyebrows shot up and he barked an order to his men who left abruptly.

"You will stay here. You are not to leave this room," he snarled at Marty with a look that said if he didn't obey, he would be sorry.

Marty dressed and waited, after an hour his friend the messenger arrived with his breakfast.

"What the hell is going on Bernard?" Marty asked.

"Oh sir, terrible things happened in the night, the Minister was murdered in his own bed!" François confided in a quivering voice. *"They say it must have been someone who was staying in the Embassy and they are tearing the place apart looking for clues."*

"How did it happen?" Marty asked, naïve and wide eyed.

"A knife through the heart, so they say. A very ornate knife it was the type the rich use to open letters."

"They were here!" Marty told him with a worried look. "*Almost tore the room apart,"* he said indicating the dishevelled bed.

"Don't worry you are in the clear," François reassured him. *"They found something in the Contessa's room that they think is suspicious, they are questioning her now."*

"She is an aristo, they cannot be trusted," Marty snorted.

"True but such a beauty!" François replied, *"but now a bird in a gilded cage, she is under house arrest in her suite."*

Marty also knew he was effectively under house arrest as they kept his door locked, but apart from that he was left alone. He was patient, waiting until dark before sending another message with his candle to the watcher across the street.

He retrieved his weapons and tools from the gutter outside the window where he had hidden them after the alarm was raised. The lock on his door was easy to pick and he relocked it behind him as he crept down the stairs. The corridor on the second floor was dimly lit by candles that guttered and smoked as they needed their wicks trimming.

The royal suite was unlocked and unoccupied but still had all the minister's possessions in place. Marty quickly searched it and found an attaché case under the bed, which he took.

He went back into the corridor and made his way along to the kitchen that separated the royal suite from the blue suite the Contessa was locked in. He checked for another exit and wasn't disappointed when he found a set of stairs leading down to the back of the house. Satisfied he had an escape route he made his way through to the door which led into the corridor to the Contessa's rooms.

Marty put his ear to the door and listened. There was no sound from the other side, so he gently pressed down on the handle and pushed it open. The corridor was empty which surprised him as he expected there to be a guard.

The lock of the Contessa's door was no more a problem than the one to his room and he entered the suite which was dark apart from faint moonlight that came in through the un-shuttered window. The Contessa was asleep on the bed muttering in her sleep as she had a dream. Marty walked quietly up to the bed and sat on the edge.

Marie woke with a start, sensing someone was in the room, as her eyes opened a hand gently covered her mouth and masculine voice said,

"please do not cry out, I am here to help you. Do you understand?"

It took a second to get over the surprise and then she nodded. The hand was removed but she got the impression it would return if the intruder needed to silence her. She could see he was a young man and wondered who he was.

"They are going to send you to Paris to be tried for the murder of the minister, it is a forgone conclusion that you will be found guilty as the evidence is compelling," he whispered. *"The sentence will be death."*

She tossed her head and said,

"I have information to bargain for my life," she replied with more confidence than she felt.

"The plans for the British defence against invasion? Useless as Napoleon has abandoned his plans to invade after the disaster at Trafalgar," he told her.

"How did you know?" she started to ask.

"You mentioned it to the minister. He told the security staff and I have a friend on that staff. They were laughing that you were trying to trade something that was worthless. Now you are going to be used as the scapegoat for the assassination of the minister," he told her with a sad voice.

"What can I do?" she asked.

"I can help you escape the embassy and get to the coast where you can buy passage on a ship to a neutral country. You do have funds, don't you?" he asked.

"Yes, I have assets I can use to pay for a passage."

"Gather them and pack a bag quickly, then dress for travel, we must leave immediately."

She signalled him to move away. He rose and backed into the shadows. She quickly dressed behind a screen then threw clothes and her necessaries into a bag. Last, she collected her box of jewels and placed that in her bag as well.

He led her out of the room into the kitchen, to a door at the back and down a staircase to the ground floor. At the bottom was another door that was locked. Her rescuer knelt at the lock and fiddled for a few seconds then stood and eased the door open. It led into the courtyard behind the embassy and he led her confidently across it to the gates.

She was terrified, if they were discovered it would be the end and she didn't want to die.

Marty lifted the bar on the gate, eased it open and stuck his head through the gap. The first thing he saw was a guard who turned toward him and grinned.

"Hello Matai," he grinned in greeting.

The two guards had been disposed of silently and bloodlessly by Matai and Ryan, timed so they would be on station around the time Marty had signalled with his candle. They had stripped them of their uniforms, hidden the bodies then taken their place at the gate. Now they quickly changed back to their regular clothes and returned to the hotel. The horses were already saddled, and a dog cart was harnessed. Linette was ready to drive it with her cloak's hood covering her head. They bundled in the Contessa and left town by the road to Valencia. Once they reached the outskirts, they took a side road to the south towards Almeria.

Everything had gone to plan so far and now they needed to get to the Bethany and out of Spain as fast as possible. The sun came up and they had travelled for three hours so they stopped to change horses.

"Hello Marie," Linette said as she dropped the hood.

Marie froze then slowly turned to look at the figure beside her.

"Louise?" she said surprise writ plain on her face.

"Who else?" Linette replied.

"What the hell are you doing here?" Marie asked her voice rising in pitch and volume.

"Stopping you from making a huge mistake as usual," Linette snapped back.

Realization hit Marie like a hammer,

"You were behind the murder of the minister?" she shrieked.

"No that was me," Marty said from beside the cart where he had approached to find out what the noise was all about, "*and if you two don't keep it down I will bind and gag you both!"*

Marie turned around and now they were side by side, Marty could see they were almost identical. There was a gasp from Ryan as he saw them for the first time as well.

"It's time for an explanation I think," he said giving Linette a hard look.

She had the sense to look contrite and took a deep breath.

"My real name is Contessa Louise Fortin, and this is my younger sister, Marie."

"You killed Robert? You fool! He was going to take me back to Paris with him," Marie shrieked.

"That is precisely what got him killed," Marty said calmly. *"I couldn't take the risk that you had told him any details of the plans for the defence of London."*

Marie's hands flew to her mouth as the import of what Marty had said sunk in.

"Who are you? Who are you all?"

"That, my dear lady, is irrelevant, what is, is that you are now wanted for murder by the French state, and if we are captured, I will plead that you seduced me to help you escape."

Linette started to chuckle and when they all looked at her, she said,

"this is one mess she can't sleep her way out of

Marty raised an eyebrow in question,

"You have Caroline, Ryan is mine and Matai is smitten with Tabetha."

At the look of surprise on Marty's face she explained,

"He hasn't stopped talking about her the entire trip."

Marty looked over at the handsome Basque in surprise.

"Well I never."

Marty took Marie's bag from the dogcart and slung it from his saddle with the attaché case. Without the jewels and cash, she couldn't go anywhere.

"They really are sisters then," Ryan said to Marty while they walked the horses to give them a break.

"That would seem to be the case, yes," Marty replied. "They chose quite different paths to survive the war."

Ryan was quiet for a few moments and then said,

"I don't know whether its right to condemn Marie for sleeping with men to survive."

Marty swivelled in the saddle and looked at his young compatriot in surprise.

"She is neither the first nor last woman who has," Marty replied.

"It must be hard," Ryan added, looking thoughtful.

Marty cocked his head for him to continue.

"Well men can fight, or start a business, or fall back on a trade. Women, especially aristocratic ones, are expected to be above all that so when it all goes wrong for them, they have little to fall back on. It is hardly just."

They rode on for a few more minutes and then Ryan sighed.

"now do I call her, Linette or Louise?"

Marty chuckled. "I am sure she will let you know."

They got back to Almeria and as soon as they rode onto the beach a boat was sent over to collect them. They untacked the horses and let them go, they would in all likelihood make their way back to the original owner.

Marty locked the attaché case, jewels and cash in his arms chest. Linette insisted she and Marie shared a cabin so she could keep an eye on her.

"As if I could swim ashore even if I wanted to!" Marie complained.

Once they were out to sea and the Bethany was kicking up her heels and making a dozen or more knots, they all relaxed a little. Marty found himself on deck with Marie, who was dressed in one of Linette's spare gowns.

"Who are you?" she asked as he turned to greet her. "Louise won't tell me anything and I feel I have seen you before."

Marty laughed. "You have at least twice to my knowledge. I was dressed in very different clothes the first time and wore a sash with my rank, the second time I was in the uniform of a Lieutenant of the Royal Navy. Both times I was accompanied by my wife, Caroline."

The penny dropped and Marie looked at him in amazement.

"Lord Candor?"

"Took you long enough," he laughed.

"Georgie talked about you, he was convinced you were a spy or something."

"Was he now? I wouldn't spread that rumour if I were you," Marty said seriously.

"Don't worry. I don't expect I will get the chance once you get me back to England."

"Why do you think that?"

"Well, they will throw me in prison for stealing the necklace and running away with the secret plans."

Marty looked at her.

"What?"

She looked at him in surprise.

"The plans?"

Marty nodded.

"I took a set of the plans."

Marty looked at the heavens and took a breath to steady himself. "And where are they now?"

"I gave them to Robert."

Marty excused himself and went straight to his cabin. Once inside he found the attaché case he had taken from the minister's room and, saying a short prayer, picked the lock.

The papers he took out of the first compartment were just French government letters. The second was a small stack of large sheets of paper that had been carefully folded. He opened them and let out his breath in a whoosh!

They were plans of a new mansion the minister was going to have built in Paris.

The plans for the defences were not there.

Chapter 5: Unfinished business

"She had copies of the plans?" Linette screeched in disbelief.

"Calm down! Yes, she did, and they were somewhere in the minister's things, unless he gave them to the embassy staff for safe keeping," Marty replied.

"What do we do now?" Ryan asked.

"As I see it there are two possibilities," Marty concluded.

"One, the plans are still at the Embassy and if they have them, they need to be recovered or destroyed. Two, the plans are still hidden amongst the minister's things, which by now will be on their way back to Paris with his well pickled body and need to be recovered or destroyed."

Marty was alluding to the fact that the body of the deceased would be transported back to Paris in a keg of brandy to preserve it.

"A good fire should eliminate the embassy," Ryan said with a grin.

"Yes. You and Matai need to get back to Madrid, torch the place and make sure that the head of security hasn't got the plans at his home. It's unlikely that anyone else would be trusted with them. If he gets damaged in the process so be it. Linette and I will go to Paris and find out where the minster lived and try and intercept his belongings."

Marty looked at them for acknowledgement and then turned to Tarrant. "Where can you put Matai and Ryan ashore?"

"Malaga is probably the best place. We will be there in an hour or so."

"Right! Ryan go and find Matai and get your things together, take some of the new bombs and a couple of spare timers. Once you have completed the job make your way up to Bilbao and wait for us. The Bethany will pick you up in three weeks, which gives you enough time to get to Madrid, do the job and then get to Bilbao without killing any horses."

Ryan left and Marty looked at Linette. "Are you alright?"

She sighed, sadly. "Yes, my sister brings out the worst in me," she said, then took a deep breath and stiffened her back. "What is your plan for Paris?"

"The good Captain will take us to Le Havre, and we will go to Paris in style," he replied with a smile.

"No more horse riding?" she asked hopefully. "My backside is a ruin already."

Marty laughed. "Your backside is as pert as ever and we will get a carriage," he reassured her.

She gave him a coy look. "If Caroline heard you say that you would be sleeping in separate rooms for a month."

"Just repeating what Ryan told me," he laughed again. "I couldn't possibly notice!"

To say it was a flying stop at Malaga would almost be an understatement. Tarrant backed the foresails to bring her to a halt, a boat was launched, and Ryan and Matai put ashore. As soon as the boat returned, they were off again.

The trip up to Le Havre was rough with contrary winds and big seas. They pulled into the harbour during a storm wearing an American flag. Marty and Linette walked down the gangplank to find Samuel waiting for them.

"No, I am not stayin' behind," he said before Marty could utter a word. "I promise Tom I look after you and dat is what I am gonna do!" Marty looked over his shoulder and Antton, Franco, Garai and John Smith were stood waiting as well.

Linette lent in and whispered in his ear. "You won't stop them; you know they will just follow us."

Marty sighed, looked up to the sky, and shrugged. "Well, come on then. We will just need to hire a bigger carriage."

He did, however, detail Franco to stay aboard to keep an eye on Marie and to deliver a written report to Hood, but it was largely a gesture to regain a bit of authority as Tarrant was taking her straight back to London.

Meanwhile, Ryan and Matai were entering Madrid. They were posing as a gentleman and his servant and stopped for the night at taverns or hotels. Once they entered the town, they made straight for the area where the Embassy was located and found a hotel that suited their cover story.

A quick inspection of the outside of the Embassy showed that security had been increased and the guards on the back gate doubled. They decided to tackle the head of security first.

From their previous visit they had noted that he always left the Embassy at seven in the evening and it was a simple matter to wait for him and follow him to his home. The house was a modest townhouse a block from the Embassy with the front door right on the street.

As he opened the door Matai hit him from behind shoving him through. Ryan followed closely, shutting the door behind them.

Cedric Aubele didn't know what hit him and Matai didn't let him regain his equilibrium, dragging him to his feet and pushing him through a door into the sitting room.

Ryan quickly searched the rest of the house for servants or family and found nothing except a pot of stew simmering on the stove. It smelled good! When he arrived back in the sitting room Matai had Aubele tied up and gagged and was closing the curtains.

Ryan had learnt from Marty that the most intimidating things can be the most mundane, and he carried two bowls of stew and a stick of bread into the room and put them on the table. He invited Matai to sit and eat.

Matai looked over at Aubele, who was hogtied in the most uncomfortable way imaginable.

"Excellent stew! You must give your cook my compliments." He said in French. They had agreed it would

be better for Matai to lead the interrogation as Ryan's French was rudimentary.

They finished their meal and wiped their mouths.

"Now let's talk about the murder of the Minister," Matai opened in a friendly way and signalled Ryan to remove the gag.

"Who are you?" Aubele asked.

"You don't need to know that," Matai answered. *"Why did you murder the Minister?"*

"I didn't kill him! It was that bitch of a Contessa!" Aubele winced as the ropes bit in as he tried to move.

"That's what you want us to think. You killed him and framed her."

"I didn't! I was trying to help them both!"

"Liar! You wanted her for yourself and killed him to get him out of the way!"

"No, that's not true! She is beautiful, yes, but I didn't want her for myself. She had information that could get both me and the Minister promoted."

"So, you killed him for the information?"

"No! I didn't kill him at all. Why don't you believe me?"

"What was this information that was so valuable?"

"Plans! Plans of the British defences against invasion from France."

"Pffft. Highly likely," Matai said with ample scorn. *"How would a woman get hold of those?"*

"I don't know," sobbed a now desperate Aubele. *"But the Minister had them hidden in his rooms. He showed them to me but didn't let me have them."*

"Where in his rooms?"

"I don't know. Please, I am innocent!"

Matai stepped forward, replaced the gag and looked to Ryan. Ryan tried to think like Marty, what was it he said? 'Never leave a live enemy behind you.' He stiffened his resolve and nodded to Matai.

He tried not to look at the pathetic figure lying in a pool of blood as he tossed the lantern into the corner, setting fire to the house on his way out.

The trip to Paris was uneventful and, like his last journey down this road, he snoozed. The last time he had only a half a head of hair and was dressed as a French Lieutenant. That mission hadn't worked out anywhere near as well as they hoped when Napoleon, with the help of his brother, had finessed a coup-de-tat and taken power.

Now the two-day trip was just tedious. They couldn't talk in front of the coach driver and John Smith resorted to a macabre game of charades. He mimed blowing things up, cutting throats and hanging treasonous spies. Marty ordered him to be still in the end, as he could see Linette was getting annoyed. He was missing Blaez, scratching his ears always made him calmer.

Paris was as loud, smelly and exciting as it always was. The boys had never been there before and gawped at the sights out of the windows of the coach.

Linette directed the coachman to a hotel she knew in the centre of town and they debarked at the entrance. Once registered Linette went clothes shopping for all of them, dragging Antton with her as her mule. She had an exceptional eye for size and had 'measured up' each of them with a glance.

Marty got them a floor of rooms, much to the hotelier's joy as it had been a quiet month and he knew anyone with Linette would pay handsomely for him to forget they were there.

He went to the office of the Moniteur and asked where the Minister's house was. The bored clerk knew as the news he had been assassinated had reached Paris a couple of days before and he had sent a reporter.

"The editor is a man of little patience and it is more than my job's worth to hold up the news!" he told Marty. When asked how the story went, he gave him a free copy.

Marty read the article to everyone when they were all back in the hotel.

Minister Robert de Chambre foully assassinated in Madrid.

The body of the story was sensational and a mostly fictional account of how a beautiful émigré had returned to exact revenge on the country and men who had exiled her and then been spirited away with the help of a weak-willed merchant who had fallen under her wicked spell.

"What a load of bollocks," Marty guffawed as he read the last line. They hadn't mentioned the fact that he had to have had help to dispose of the guards. Linette wasn't impressed and pointed out that the Monitor printed what the Government wanted it to say so they were just using at as a rallying call against the Royalists.

Marty sobered at that thought, he knew what a well-orchestrated mob was capable of and shuddered to think of what would happen if the Government decided to use this as the match to light a fuse.

Now they had an address, Marty and Linette went scouting with Samuel in tow. John Smith stayed at the room, forging new identity documents from a set he had 'lifted' from a passer-by. He needed to replace the ones he had made on the Bethany, which were in an out of date style. The rest of the team went out around the city to pick up as much information as they could.

The house of the family de Chambre was in a good part of town not far from the centre and had a French flag flying at half-mast in the small front garden. The front door was bedecked in black ribbons.

"They are making a big play on his death," Marty observed. *"That flagpole has been put up recently."*

A servant came out of the front door and walked up to the gate.

"If you are waiting for Mr. De Chambre to arrive, he is not due for another two days," he told them with a harried look on his face.

"Oh, that is a pity, we were wanting to pay our respects," Linette said. *"We have just returned from Martinique and heard the terrible news. It is a horror!"*

"Martinique? That explains the black man. Is he a slave?" he asked.

"Yes, he is our house slave, but we intend to free him soon," Linette replied.

"Wouldn't bother myself," the man said peering at Samuel who just looked right back at him *"they are only savages, after all."*

With that ringing in their ears they moved on to find the street the house backed onto.

"Did dat man call me a savage?" Samuel asked once they were certain not to be overheard.

"You caught that did you?" Marty replied. "He doesn't know you like we do."

"I am a civilised savage," Samuel declared.

Marty looked at him in question.

"A savage who speaks English," he grinned.

"There are more than a few of those!" Linette quipped.

The back of the house backed onto a narrow lane. Marty got Samuel to make a cup with his hands so he could be boosted up to look over the wall. There was no coach house, which was unusual, but there was a stable. The rear of the house had a large, well-stocked garden and a courtyard which was completely empty. He could see one person pottering around who looked like an elderly gardener.

"We need a map so we can figure out the most likely route for the body to come home by," Marty stated as they walked back to their hotel. Linette said she knew of a shop and they made a diversion to buy one.

In Madrid, Ryan and Matai stood in the shadows across from the Embassy. It was midnight and there was a guard on the door, which was closed and four more around the back. Every ten minutes one of the four would make a circuit of the building.

"They are not making it easy," muttered Ryan under his breath.

"It will take the guards at the back around fifteen minutes to realise that the patrolling man hasn't returned and get around to the front to investigate. That gives us enough time to set the place on fire and leave a couple of surprises for anyone who tries to put it out." Matai stated after counting three laps of the guard.

"Right. We go the next time that guard is level with the sentry," Ryan decided.

There was the double twang of crossbows and the two guards crumpled to the ground, stunned by the heavy bolts. A quick examination showed one would never wake again having been hit in the temple, the other was alive but unconscious. A quick search got them a set of keys.

In the entrance hall of the Embassy they split up to find good places to start a fire. Ryan headed down to the basement and Matai went up to the first-floor kitchen. Lamp oil was liberally splashed around a pile of wood used for the ovens along with anything else combustible he could find. A small pile of priming powder was poured from a powder flask on a pile of paper. A clockwork timing device was set for two minutes and set atop the powder; its wheel-lock primed.

Ryan had been doing the same in the cellar and the two met in the hall. Ryan placed one of their new bombs under the clerk's table and set the timer for ten minutes. Matai took a second and set it near the entrance set for five minutes, a third was set on the stairs set for fifteen minutes. Satisfied, they left through the front door, closing and locking it behind them and replacing the keys in the guard's pocket.

It had taken just over ten minutes and they waited close by to be sure they had done a good job. There was the faintest of whumps and the flickering light of a fire on the first floor could be seen through the windows.

A guard came around the corner from the back of the building looking for the overdue sentry. He was just bending over the prone guards when the bomb by the door went off. The doors burst outwards and the right-hand door tumbled down the steps narrowly missing the three guards. The left hung drunkenly from one hinge.

The smoke from the open doors first billowed out and then was sucked back in as the fires in the basement and kitchen drew it in to feed themselves.

The third guard dragged the unconscious, but alive guard away from the door and was yelling at the top of his voice. Another guard arrived and recklessly ran through the doors into the hallway. After a couple of minutes, he appeared in the door shouting 'FIRE!' at the top of his voice. It was the last thing he ever said as the second bomb went off under the desk and blew him across the street. The blast was bad, but it was the shards of iron from the bomb casing embedded in his back that killed him instantaneously.

Five minutes later, just as a small crowd had gathered to see what was going on, the third bomb detonated effectively, persuading everyone to stay out of the burning building. An hour later with it well ablaze and the roof about to collapse, Matai and Ryan headed back to the hotel, collected their horses and left for Bilbao.

In Paris, Marty and Lynette poured over the maps they had bought on their way back to the hotel. It didn't take long to narrow down the possible routes the minister's body and his baggage would take.

"We know that they sailed the cargo from Valencia to either Marseille or Montpellier. I'm betting on Marseille, but we need to cover both options. Antton, John, and Linette will cover the road from Orleans. Sam, Garai, and I will cover the other route. If we find the cargo, we stop it and search it. If we find the plans, we destroy them. Don't try and bring them back. It's too risky."

He looked at each of them in turn.

"Don't take any risks, we just need to make sure the plans are either not in his belongings or, if they are, they are destroyed. Be stealthy, crafty, and careful."

They split up and headed out of Paris along their respective routes. The plan was to travel until they were a day's cart ride out of town, find a likely stopping place and find out if the carts had passed. As the carters would stop for the night and there were only a few villages on the route with places that they could stay, they just had to check each in turn until they found them.

Marty and his team stopped two hours before sunset at the type of hotel that carters would stay at, took a table overlooking the road, ordered some drinks and waited. No carts appeared and chatting to the landlord they found out that no one had passed, "the road has been quiet all day."

They finished their drinks and tossed some coins on the table in payment, mounted up and headed south to the next potential stopping place. Again, nothing. This time they didn't wait but moved straight on.

It was dark by the time they reached the third and they were greeted by an empty courtyard and stable. There was nothing else for it but to stay the night and try again further south in the morning.

Marty was edgy and grumpy and Garai tried to cheer him up.

"It's alright, boss. If they aren't here, they must be running late, and we will find them further down the road."

Marty wasn't consoled. He had a phobia about failure and the thought made him feel physically sick. He was also terrified that, despite all his successes, he would be revealed as a fraud. It was what drove him, and it was a relentless task master. It was Samuel who snapped him out of it with a half whispered, half rumbled comment.

"Dese Frenchie's aint got no idea about doin' anything on time. Dey is more interested in eatin' cheese an drinkin' wine. The minister fella is in heaven en if dey have him in a barrel of brandy, he be greetin' Saint Peter wid a bad head!"

Marty almost snorted the mouthful of red wine, he had just taken, out of his nose and had a coughing fit on hearing that. All the same, he slept badly and had them on the road as soon as the sun came up. He wouldn't have been any happier to know that Linette and her team hadn't found anything either.

They rode south at a trot, which Samuel hated as he had just learned to ride, and the constant posting made his thighs ache as he hadn't gotten the hang of it yet. He was mightily relieved when they came to the next stopping place and there was a pair of heavily laden carts in the courtyard with a hogshead sized barrel tied securely in the centre of one of them.

The drivers were finishing hitching up the horses and Marty was going to move in when a squad of Lancers trotted around the corner and formed up in front of the carts. The minister had a military escort!

They had no choice but to let the carts move ahead and follow at a discrete distance. Marty chewed his lip as they rode and tried to keep his urge to charge in and try and take the carts by force under control.

"At the speed they are going they will stop again before they enter Paris," Garai, ever level-headed, pointed out. "They must be paid by the day!"

Marty chuckled at that as it relieved the tension. Garai was right! The wagons and escort pulled up to a tavern at midday and spent a leisurely two hours over lunch and a nap. The carts were left unguarded but not out of sight of the Lancers who lounged around at the front of the building.

Mid-afternoon they set off again and trundled along until four o'clock when they stopped again well before dark. This time the horses were unharnessed and rubbed down before being fed and watered.

Marty, Garai, and Samuel took a very cheap room over the stables, had a passable supper and settled down to wait. Around two AM Marty rousted them out and led them down to the courtyard. All was quiet and they made their way over to the carts.

As they approached, they heard a loud snore come from the cart with the hogshead barrel in it. Samuel's eyes went wide, and Marty could clearly see the whites in the starlight. He put a hand on his arm to reassure him and moved over on silent feet to see who was in there.

Laid out across the driver's seat was one of the Lancers. He was fast asleep. Marty pulled a small bottle from his pocket and put several drops from it on a cloth. Careful not to breath any of the vapour, he gently placed the cloth over the nose and mouth of the Lancer and held it there for thirty seconds.

After he removed it, he pinched the guard's cheek and tweaked his nose. He was out cold. Samuel looked over his shoulder and grunted something on his native tongue and prodded the Lancer in the chest. When he got no reaction, he grinned at Marty, showing his brilliant white teeth. *Damn,* Marty thought. *You can see them for a country mile!*

Garai was checking the baggage cart and had already undone the tarpaulin covering it, He began opening boxes and carefully sorting through them. Luckily, the starlight was enough for them to see by, the concern was that it was also bright enough for them to be seen.

Marty joined him after posting Samuel as a sentry and saw that there weren't that many boxes and chests to work through, but, all the same, it was four AM when Garai tapped Marty on the arm and handed him a sheaf of folded drawings. It was too dark to make out what was on them, so Marty went back to their room and lit a candle.

By its flickering light he saw that they had found what they were looking for, well, mostly. Having unfolded three sheets he realised that one was missing. He had a plan of London and its immediate surrounds, another of the Eastern approach to it covering the Thames, Medway, and down to Hastings, and a third that started around Brighton and covered the southwest approach. He didn't have the one which covered the area from Brighton to Hastings.

He took the drawings to the fireplace and carefully tore them into shreds and fed them into the fire, stirring each piece to make sure it was fully destroyed. Matai came back to the room, followed soon after by Samuel. He hadn't found any more sheets.

Marty sat and thought about it. Would he have handed over the full set? The answer to that was a definite no! He would want some insurance that he was going to be treated fairly. So, he could assume that Marie had held on to at least one sheet. After all, she was vengeful, not stupid.

Chapter 6: A Prince's Gratitude.

They met up with Linette and the others back in Paris and took a coach back to Le Crotoy, where they were to meet the Bethany. Tarrant had been waiting for them out of sight of the coast and a fishing boat was ready to take them out. Ryan and Matai were already aboard with Franco.

"Who came to collect Marie?" asked Linette once they were all in the dining room.

"A pair of palace footmen and four guards dressed in black tunics with red piping and letters," Franco replied.

"Yeomen Warders," John Smith stated, "they be from the tower."

"Did they state where they were taking her?" Marty asked.

"One of them, the older one, told her she had been very foolish, and she would have to explain herself to the Prince and plead for his forgiveness," Franco replied.

"Zat will not go well," Linette frowned, her accent slipping.

"I will talk with the Prince, see what is going on and what their plans are," Marty stated trying to stop the conversation from going any further.

"Well they only send traitors to the Tower," John Smith said with a knowing look then yelped as Marty kicked him in the shin under the table.

It only took the Bethany a few hours to sail up to the Thames Estuary and then she had to be reined in to make the passage upstream to India Dock. Once they got there, he went straight to St James' Palace and requested an interview with the Prince, only to be told to go to the Tower and that he was expected.

He got a cab to the Tower and was greeted at the gate by a Yeoman who escorted him to the Beauchamp Tower and up several flights of stairs. They passed carved names and other graffiti left by the myriad of noble prisoners who had spent their last days there, to a suit identified by the Yeoman as Anne Boleyn's rooms.

Oh Christ! he thought as the symbolism hit him. Anne had been beheaded for treason by Henry VIII and had spent her last hours in these rooms. The Prince Regent wouldn't have her tried for treason, would he?

He entered and was struck by the austerity of the rooms with the bare stone walls and wooden floors, heavy oak furniture and dim, dirty windows. His guide led him through to another room which was furnished with some more contemporary furniture and there he found Marie and the Prince sat opposite each other in lounge chairs.

She was dressed in a plain dress with her unbound hair falling over her shoulders. She looked the twin of Linette like that and he had to remind himself who she was and what she had tried to do. The look she gave him spoke of both defiance and fear.

He bowed to the Prince and said,

"Your Highness, I have returned to report on my mission."

"Oh, come and sit-down Martin, no need for all that stuffiness here," replied the Prince and gestured for him to take a seat in a chair to his right.

Marty sat and a servant came in and handed him a glass of port.

"I must say you have lived up to your weputation and have done an admiwable job!" the Prince chirped happily.

"It went well, your Highness, but there is one thing that has eluded me," Marty confessed. The Prince raised an eyebrow in question and nodded for him to continue. "We found the plans in the Minister's baggage and I personally burnt them."

"Oh, well done!" cried the Prince with relief.

"But," Marty continued, "there was one missing." He looked at Marie. "Your insurance?"

She gave him a dirty look and huffed as she turned away.

"You didn't have it on you when we took you from the embassy in Madrid, Linette would have found it. Did you hide it in your rooms there?"

Marie spun around eye's blazing, "yes, and you will never find it. Only I know where it is, and it will stay there until some Spaniard discovers it or I remove it myself after I have been given a guarantee I will not be put on trial

The Prince's eyes went wide, then dangerously narrow, and was about to say something when Marty held up his hand. "Please do not worry, Your Highness. That segment of the plans has been destroyed."

"But you said you hadn't found it!" he exclaimed in exasperation.

"We didn't," Marty replied. "But we did burn down the embassy and everything in it."

Marie looked shocked. The Prince looked amazed, then burst out laughing.

"My God! You don't do things by half do you," he chuckled. "Now, my girl we can start our little discussion over again!"

"Your Highness, may I make a suggestion?" Marty asked.

Prince George looked at him shrewdly and nodded.

"We have managed to prevent any harm from being done but some punishment must be meted out. However, both the court and government would be extremely sensitive to the scandal that a trial would generate. Not to mention the public reaction. May I suggest that Marie be presented with a stipend and passage to St Lucia? She can live there in exile until it is safe for her to return to France. We can monitor her whereabouts and behavior through the garrison on the island."

Marie looked at him in horror.

"The alternative is that you disappear the other way, no trial, no chance of appeal, no future. Just an unmarked grave."

"Louise would never allow you to . . ." she gasped.

"She would never know," Marty lied, hoping that his bluff wouldn't be called.

The Prince looked at him in shock, Marie in horror. Marty just sat back and exposed the handle of one of his stilettoes by pulling back his sleeve an inch.

"I don't have a choice, then," Marie concluded bitterly.

"Not really," Marty replied, pulling his sleeve back down.

Martin accompanied Prince George back to St James' Palace where he sent a message to Linette telling of her sister's fate and asking her to pack her wardrobe and necessities for the voyage. He added that she would have enough funds to live comfortably there until the situation in France enabled both of them to return to their homeland safely.

The Prince took Marty to his private apartments and invited him to stay for supper as he wanted a full report, which he got, Navy-style.

"I must say it all sounds dashed exciting," he exclaimed as Marty concluded. "That team of yours sounds like a dastardly bunch of scoundwels."

"I am sure they would be flattered by such a description," Marty replied with a hint of a smile.

"I suppose I should weward you," Prince George said with a sly look.

Marty sighed inwardly; this could get awkward if he wasn't careful.

"Not at all your Highness," he replied after a sip of wine.

"Please call me George when we are alone," insisted the Prince.

"As far as I and my men were concerned it was a mission in defense of our country and our duty to carry it out to the best of our ability."

"Nevertheless, you have done me a great sewvice and I will take a pewsonal intewest in your progwess from now on," George continued.

"I am flattered, uh, George," he said to the beaming Prince, while thinking that was the last thing he needed.

"I heard from Hood that you were off to Gibraltar to sow havoc with the Spanish."

Did you now, Marty thought.

"That is the plan, but we need to get our ships refitted and a replacement for the Tempest first," he said.

"And how long will it take for the refit?" George asked.

"They tell us it will be our turn once the Agamemnon is repaired. She took a fair amount of damage at Trafalgar," Marty told him. "Once they start, each ship will take six weeks to two months, but they tell me they will have two drydocks available by then so we shouldn't have to wait more than three to four months for all three. Once we have the first two, we can move most of the team down to Gibraltar and the other can follow later."

"And you still don't know whether you will get a weplacement for the, what was it, Tempest?"

"No, unfortunately not," Marty admitted.

The rest of the evening went well. The food was excellent, as one would expect, and the company was charming. No more was said about Marie or Marty's upcoming mission.

Two weeks later, Alouette and Hornfleur entered drydock to begin their refit and the bribes started to flow. New extra thick copper, rigging, replacement masts, where they were damaged, soft planks in the hull replaced and new stronger knees fitted so they could fit bigger guns.

Then Marty received a package from the Admiralty by courier.

"By the Commissioners for executing the Office of the Lord High Admiral of Great Britain &c *and of all His Majesty's Plantations.*

To Captain Martin Alfred Stockley hereby appointed Captain of His Majesty's Ship Formidiable.

By virtue of the Power and Authority to us given We do hereby constitute and appoint you Captain of His Majesties Ship Formidiable willing and requiring you forthwith to go on board and take upon you the Charge and Command of Captain in her accordingly. Strictly Charging and Commanding all the Officers and Company belonging to the said ship subordinate to you to behave themselves jointly and severally in their respective Employments with all the Respect and Obedience unto you their said Captain; And you likewise to observe and execute as well the General printed Instructions as what Orders and Directions you shall from time to time receive from your superior Officers for His Majesty's service. Hereof nor you nor any of you may fail as you will answer the contrary at your peril. And for so doing this shall be your Warrant. Given under our hands and the Seal of the Office Admiralty this 20th day of March in the one thousandth eight hundredth and sixth Year of His Majesty's Reign.

By Command of their Lordships

It was accompanied by a second letter telling him that the ship was in Portsmouth Harbour with half a crew and that he was to make up the other half himself. He was to make sail in accordance with his standing orders from Admiral Hood.

"Well, bugger me!" he exclaimed as he finished reading both the letters.

"Good news darling?" Caroline asked from across the table where they were eating breakfast.

"They've given me the Formidiable!" he told her with a grin. "They must have brought her back to England for repair."

"She was fairly well bashed around when we finished with her," Caroline commented as she picked up young James who had crawled under the table and was about to try and take Blaez's bone from him. The children's nurse was visiting her brother while they were in London and Caroline had decided to look after the children herself.

"Oh, that was all mainly superficial," Marty said thoughtfully. "It was mainly her transom and port side that took most of it."

"And the mast?" Caroline asked.

"They probably just fitted whatever they had at Port Royal and patched up the rest to get her back here. She will have been fitted with a new one. I need to get word to the Tempests." he replied and went to his study to write some messages.

Caroline sighed and held young James tightly, her man was about to run off and do what he loved most, exercising his talent for trouble.

That night she reminded him of what he would be missing, he got very little sleep.

Chapter 7: A Rainy Month in Portsmouth

Marty arrived in Portsmouth on the first of April 1806 and went straight to the harbour. There, swathed in a fine mist, two hundred yards offshore was the Formidiable, yards crossed, harbour gaskets fitted. She looked different from the first time he had seen her.

Her hull was the same but now she sported bigger gun ports to take the twenty-eight, eighteen-pound longs the Navy had fitted. She had a pair of thirty-six-pound carronades fitted on the fore deck and four massive sixty-eight-pound carronades on the quarterdeck. He also knew she had a pair of twelve-pound longs as fore chasers and another pair in his cabin as stern chasers. She was classified as a thirty-six as she would normally have four twelve-pounders on the quarterdeck, but the big carronades were far more effective at close range.

Her rigging was, however, totally different. She was now fitted with a taller main mast than before that had a jaunty rake to it and her sail layout was purely English. She was three years old and quite a bit of her was much younger than that.

"She is prettier than the last time we did see her," Sam commented. He was now officially Marty's Cox as Tom had decided he preferred life in Cheshire with his wife. Blaez nudged his hand as if to say, *come on let's get on with it.*

"Call us a boat Sam, the others will be here soon," Marty said without taking his eyes off her. The 'others' were the rest of the Shadows, his followers, who weren't going to let him go anywhere without them, and Fletcher, who had volunteered to be his purser and had somehow bribed, or blackmailed more likely, someone on the Navy board to give him the position at very short notice. They were following in a pair of carts containing his luggage and furniture.

Sam gave a piercing whistle and a boat manned by an old man and a teenage boy pulled up at the steps. Blaez jumped straight in scaring the boy but Sam quickly followed and reassured him, but the boy hadn't seen a black man before and Sam was very fierce looking so all he succeeded in doing was scaring him even more. Before the whole thing dissolved into a farce Marty stepped down, commanded Blaez to lay down and sat between Sam and the two boatmen.

His presence calmed them, and they pushed the boat away from the steps and started to row across to the frigate. There was absolutely no wind, so they didn't attempt to raise a sail. The drizzle was persistent though and soon Marty's boat cloak was dripping water.

There was a hail from the ship, and the boatman replied, "Formidable!" which was close enough and indicated the Captain was approaching. Marty asked him to row around the ship once before hooking onto the chains by the entry port. It gave him a chance to look her over and the crew onboard to organise a reception committee.

From the papers he had been given he knew he had new second and third lieutenants, a pair of midshipmen, the usual warrants, less a purser, a division of Marines and half a crew already on board. Ackermann was his First and he was expecting him in a couple of days with Shelby, the ships physician/surgeon.

She was a beauty! Spanish built to a French design she was long at over two hundred and fifty feet on the gun deck, forty feet wide at the beam and drew a tad under fourteen feet fully laden. The gingerbread on her stern had been picked out in gold at some time and looked a bit scabby now with all the repairs and she had a brand-new rudder.

The circuit completed, the teenager hooked onto the chains and Marty stood ready to board. He moved his sword to a place where it wouldn't trip him, stepped onto the first batten and gripped the side ropes, which he noted were freshly whitened. Up he went and as his head cleared the deck the Spithead nightingales started to sing their song.

His two new lieutenants were there to greet him, fresh faced, neither was more than twenty-two years old.

"Captain Stockley, welcome aboard the Formidiable," his new second lieutenant said and touched his forelock after Marty had doffed his hat to the quarterdeck.

"Phillip Trenchard, Second Lieutenant at your service," he continued as Marty locked eyes with him. *Christ, he is intense!* he thought, caught by Marty's very direct look.

"Any relation of Captain Trenchard of the Poseidon?" Marty asked.

"My uncle, sir," he replied. "What the hell?" he exclaimed.

Marty turned to see Sam's head appear over the side with Blaez draped around his neck. He twisted so the dog could reach the planking and then tilted his shoulders, so he slid off on to the decking.

Blaez looked around his new domain stepped forward, sniffed Trenchard's groin then took up position on Marty's right. Sam took the time to get up onto the deck and position himself just behind Marty's left shoulder.

"My cox, Samuel, and my dog, Blaez," Marty said in introduction then looked at the third lieutenant who was nervously moving his weight from foot to foot.

"May I introduce Third Lieutenant Andrew Stamp," Trenchard said, getting the hint and moving down the line. Marty shook hands then moved on down the line, forcing Trenchard to keep up.

"Please assemble the men so I can read myself in," he said as the introductions finished.

He walked up the steps to the quarterdeck and positioned himself by the rail. He took his commission from his pocket and read it out in a clear strong voice. At the end he cast an eye over the ship. It looked in good order, despite just coming out of the yard, then looked across the crew. He didn't recognise any of them.

Dammit! I suppose I had better say something.

"I don't know what you were told when you were ordered to join this ship but if you are here you are a volunteer. Pressed men have no place in the work we will be doing." A muttering ran around the men and he waited until it stopped. "You will be joined shortly by the crew of my last ship; they will tell you what you need to know and if you decide you don't want to be part of our happy band then you can leave. The Formidiable is the lead ship of the Special Operations Flotilla and will be involved in dangerous, sometimes profitable, and always interesting missions. Mr. Ackermann, our First Lieutenant, will join us in a couple of days, as will the rest of the crew. In the meantime, we will continue to provision and prepare the ship for sail. Dismiss the men, Mr. Trenchard."

Marty had been looking around the faces as he spoke and had seen curiosity, amusement and caution but no fear. *They'll do,* he thought.

"I will carry out a ship-wide inspection in twenty minutes," he said quietly to Trenchard. "I will expect to meet all the officers, mids and warrants on my way around."

He entered his cabin to find it sparsely furnished. There was a cot suspended by ropes from the ceiling in his sleeping quarters and an old desk and chair in his day room. The room was bigger than he remembered it when he had been a prisoner, when the Spanish captain had furnished it with a lot of chunky chairs and tables. He was going to have to go shopping.

There were the two twelve-pound stern chasers tied down securely either side against the hull ready to be run out if the need came upon them. He would need a cover for them as well.

Sam came in from the direction of the steward's cabin, he was going to need one of those as well. *Shit! I am unprepared for this,* he thought in panic. Forcing himself to calm down he grinned at his cox.

"A bit bigger than we're used to isn't it," he said.

"You can give de dog a room of his own if you got too much boss," Sam replied with a grin.

Marty ignored the incorrect honorific as Sam only used it when they were alone and looked up when there was a loud bump of what sounded like a heavily laden boat hitting the side and then there were shouts of alarm.

"What the hell?" he said and made his way up to the quarterdeck.

It was chaos. They were being boarded over both sides, screaming men swarmed over the sides grabbing the crew and shoving them into a huddle amidships. Some screaming a war cry – AY, AY, AY AY, AY, EEEAAAAH. Any that didn't move fast enough were kicked and pushed; a group of half-naked black men with white markings painted on their bodies waved broad bladed spears and danced a macabre dance of death. Samuel started to chuckle; the Tempests had arrived.

Marty fought hard to keep a straight face as Ackermann, resplendent in his new uniform, walked out of the group and up to the quarterdeck.

"The Formidiable has been secured sir," he reported as he saluted, "and I wish to inform you that the ship is now at full strength."

"Thank you, Mr. Ackermann," Marty replied, touching his hat in return. "You may release the prisoners and meet me in my quarters to explain how you got here two days early with the entire crew of the Tempest."

Ackermann grinned, saluted, and started shouting orders. A team was already reeving tackles to sling baggage up from a large barge that was tied up on the larboard side. Marty walked over, looked down, and saw Antton in the stern.

"I hope you didn't damage my hull with that arrival," he called down. Antton made a show of inspecting the hull and gave him a thumbs up with a broad grin.

Down in his cabin Sam was overseeing the placement of the few pieces of furniture Marty had taken out of the Tempest. It was woefully inadequate, but at least he had a couple of chairs, a table, and a more suitable desk. His weapons and sea chests had also been carried down. A familiar face was unpacking.

"Adam Cooper! What are you doing here?" Marty asked in surprise at the sight of one of the footmen from his London home.

"Lady Caroline said you would be needin' a steward milord and I volunteered. I always fancied goin' to sea."

Marty was astonished and welcomed him aboard; he was a top rate footman and valet. Ackermann arrived and Marty invited him to join him in the dining room as that was the quietest place for them to talk.

"Now tell me how you rounded up all the Tempests and got down here so quickly," Marty asked after the usual pleasantries.

"Fletcher got word to me by fast courier. Me and him had come up with the idea, before we disbanded everyone, to choose one man from each of the places the boys lived and make him a point of contact. Then all we had to do was send messages to nine people and they round up the ones in their area and got them to assembly points. Fletcher arranged for wagons and coaches to be provided and they shipped all the men to a place just outside of Portsmouth called Eastleigh. Once we were all there, we moved on to the docks and got boats organised to take us all over."

"Commendable! It was well done. Whose idea was it to treat it as a cutting out exercise?"

"I have to give credit to Wilson for that, sir. He thought we should give the new men a taste of what's to come, and I agreed."

"Well it certainly shocked them," Marty grinned then got down to business.

"We have around one hundred new men, all volunteers and seasoned sailors. I want a watch list made up that mixes up the Tempests and the new men. I don't want any divisions or favouritism in the crew because some have been with me longer than others."

"Aye aye, sir. I will have it ready by the end of the week. Oh, and by the way, Mr. Shelby will be joining us tomorrow. Fletcher is already aboard, and I believe Wilson is now rated Bosun."

"Yes, and John is quartermaster, Garai captain of the afterdeck, Antton captain of the mainmast, and Matai of the fore mast. Yeovilton is gunner and his friend still his mate," Marty listed off what Ackermann already knew. "Do you know when Captain la Pierre will arrive?"

"Last I heard he was in Portsmouth, weeding out the men he doesn't want in his brigade."

"You mean the honest ones?" Marty joked.

"Probably," Ackermann replied with a laugh. "And to break in his two new lieutenants. They will relocate to The Farm once he is happy."

"Well get to it. Let me have the watch list as soon as you have a first draft and we will go over it together. Now, I would like to inspect my new ship."

They started on the rigging. Marty changed into a set of slop trousers, old shoes and his old midshipman's shirt and jacket. He only wore his fighting knife on his left hip and a pistol clipped to the back of his belt.

They started with the mizzen and checked every rope, block and stay. Then moved on to the mainmast and at the top yard they separated to check either side. That's where Marty met Arnold Fuller, a topman from the new men.

"You one of them blokes from the Captain's old ship?" he asked Marty, who replied using his best Dorset drawl.

"That I be."

"What be he like? We heard all sorts of rumours but all of 'em be too wild to be believed."

"I dunno what you 'erd but 'e aint yer normal cap'ain," Marty drawled.

"Did 'e really capture a treasure fleet wiv one hundred tons of gold?" Fuller asked. "And what about them savages? Where did he get them from?"

"Well it were only five and twenty ton o' gold and fifty of silver, an' them 'savages' be all freed slaves."

At that point Ackermann clambered across from the other side. Fuller immediately got back to work and froze halfway through tying off a gasket when Ackermann said,

"All's well that side Captain. Anything over here?"

"All seems to be in order," Marty replied. "Gaskets seem to be well-tied."

Ackermann looked at Fuller, who was staring at Marty in horror.

"Make sure the rest are just as good," he said.

"Aye aye, sir!" Fuller replied and, with shaking hands, finished the knot.

At the foremast, Matai was waiting for them. He had seen Marty and Ackermann climbing the other masts and guessed what they were doing.

"Captain," he greeted Marty, who responded with a nod.

"Race you to the top" and threw himself into the starboard ratlines. Matai didn't need a second invitation but threw himself into the ratlines on the other side. The two of them raced up the mast, Marty slightly ahead but Matai had the agility of a monkey and was catching him rapidly. The men were watching their new captain in surprise and when the Tempests started to cheer on one or the other, they joined in.

Marty knew Matai was gaining and threw everything he had in a burst of speed over the futtock shrouds, hanging out at forty-five degrees. His foot missed a hold, hitting a vertical rope instead and his body swung away from the shrouds, hanging vertically. There was an audible gasp from the men below. He pulled himself up with his arms alone, hand over hand, until he could swing his legs over the edge and climb up on the platform.

Matai hadn't waited and was already climbing the top mast. Marty knew he was beaten but gamely set off in pursuit. He had just gotten his head level with Matai's feet when Matai touched the cap, winning the race. Marty finished the climb and patted Matai on the shoulder congratulating him.

There were cheers and groans from below as men won and lost bets. Ackermann grinned up at the two of them and then bellowed orders for the men to get back to work.

Once back on deck after checking the foremast rigging Marty went over every inch, personally checking every rope and eyebolt. He made sure he met the men who were working in each area and chatted with the warrant or midshipman in charge. Ackermann had produced a notebook and was as vigilant as his captain noting down every fault, damaged item, deficiency or shortage.

They progressed to the guns and Yeovilton joined them. Marty noticed there were a few comments about the gunner's appearance from some of the new men, that were rapidly squashed by his old hands.

The big sixty-eight-pound carronades on the quarterdeck could be swivelled through over ninety degrees on the wheel and track at the rear of the mount around the azimuthal pivot. Recoil was taken up by the slide which also made loading them much easier than a long. Marty had the crew swing them through the full range to get an idea in his mind of how he could use them.

If the marines thought they would get away without an inspection they were mistaken. He had them fit swivels on all the available mounts and discovered they were deficient in both mounts and guns. However, the ordnance they wanted to keep from the Tempest would soon be brought aboard, which would solve the shortage of guns, and installing more mounts was just a matter of time and effort.

They checked each of the eighteen-pound longs in the main battery and the four twelve-pound chasers. Then they went through the orlop, holds and bilges.

Back in his cabin Marty, Fletcher and Ackermann went over the list and when Yeovilton joined them discussed the armament.

"Could we replace the two thirty-twos on the foredeck with one sixty-eight with a swivel that could track say two-hundred and forty degrees?" Marty asked.

"There's room for two sixty-eights with mounts like that placed in line on the centreline if we lose the two forward most eighteen pounders," Yeovilton suggested.

"Now that is an idea I like," Marty replied with a happy smile at the thought of the devastation the big smashers would cause.

"Can you get us a couple more sixty-eights?" he asked Fletcher who was making notes of what he needed to procure.

"Certainly, from the Navy or privately?" he responded without looking up from his notes.

"Let's get the Navy to provide them," Marty decided. "We will keep the eighteens in the hold, they will help trim the ship if we store them towards the stern," he added.

"Where are we storing the ordnance from the Tempest?"

"She has been stripped of all the guns and they are waiting at Chatham. The swivels and small arms have been sent down to the Farm," Fletcher reported.

"And the big guns from the Bethany?"

"They are on a barge in India Dock and will be shipped down to Chatham as well."

Marty was pleased to hear that as he owned the guns off the Bethany as well as a couple of the guns off the Tempest.

"How long before we can sail," he asked Ackermann.

"We can leave for Chatham now and I think once we have the new guns fitted, we can probably be ready two weeks later as we are still missing some sails," he replied after pondering for a moment.

"I need to have a word with the provisioning officer about the age of some of the salt beef they are trying to palm off on us if you will excuse me," Fletcher added and stood to leave.

Alone once more Marty thought about how lucky he was to have such good men helping him. Cooper brought him in a cup of tea, put a bowl of water down for Blaez then left him alone to catch up on the paperwork that the Navy demanded from all its captains.

A week later at Chatham a heavily laden barge was moored up beside the Formidable and the crew were setting up the tackles to raise the carronade mounts up on to the deck. The two forward most eighteen pounders had been moved down into the hold to a point aft of the centreline that had been calculated to counterbalance the weight of the carronades. That had been the hard part as the two-and-half-yard-long, two-ton barrels were awkward and if not handled carefully could develop a mind of their own. With true Navy ingenuity the mounts, then the barrels were raised up and fitted into position.

There had been a steady stream of new men join. Some had sailed with Marty before and had retired once from active service. There were a number who had sailed as freelancers in the Caribbean and had gotten bored with life ashore or had been duped out of their prize money. There were even three from the black country that had never sailed before, the only survivors of the group that had tried to hold up their coaches at the beginning of the year.

Marty was just about to go back down to his, still sparsely furnished cabin, when Blaez stood with his forepaws on the rail and barked towards the shore. Marty walked over and put his arm around the dog's shoulders to see what had gotten him excited. There was a coach on the dock that looked familiar and stood beside it were the unmistakable figures of his wife and children.

He was about to order his boat to be sent over when he saw Sam climbing down into his barge which was already manned and John Smith organising a chair to lift them on board. He sighed, even though he really appreciated how his men used their initiative he wished they would let him tell them what to do sometimes instead of just doing it.

Blaez was almost beside himself with excitement as the barge was rowed back to the ship and Marty had to stop him from jumping into the sea to swim over to it.

Caroline was hoisted aboard, managed to look stunningly elegant throughout and was greeted enthusiastically by Blaez until the kids came up in the arms of Samuel and Antton, which sent him into paroxysms of joy.

He hugged and kissed his wife on the cheek in greeting and was acutely aware of the stares of the new men. There was suddenly the sound of a fist contacting some part of a head and a thump of someone's rear hitting the deck. A glance showed one of the new boys sitting on the deck with blood coming from a split lip and one of the Tempests rubbing his knuckles. He didn't ask but assumed something had been said which was deemed inappropriate.

They all retired to his quarters and when she entered Caroline was dismayed.

"Is this all you have?" she asked sweeping an arm around to take in the whole cabin.

"Well, I have been a little busy!" Marty protested feeling the wind picking up.

She looked at him with a soft look on her face then hugged him, which turned into an extended kiss. When she came up for air, she had a determined look on that Marty knew all too well.

"We'll be going shopping then," he said.

And shop they did, new comfortable chairs and sofa, dining room table and chairs, sideboards, desk and chair, wine cabinet and even a checkerboard canvas for the floor and curtains for the transom windows, a dinner service and cutlery, bedding and tablecloths. It was all carted to the dock where it was barged over to the ship. Then there were his private stores which, after Caroline had checked them and deemed them totally inadequate, were topped up locally and would be further supplemented by a large order she sent to Fortnum and Maison's to be delivered to the Farm.

When they got back aboard, they found their son James being entertained by the Shadows. They had made him a wooden sword scaled to his size and Matai was sparring with him. Beth was sat over to the side with Blaez and his steward Cooper playing with a doll but watching James carefully.

"Is Shelby on board?" asked Caroline.

"Yes, he has been building a dedicated surgery on the orlop deck, you will probably find him down there. I have to attend to some things before dinner, will you be able to find him, or do you need a guide?"

"No, I can manage," she said and made her way to the stairs.

Marty went down into his newly re-furnished cabin and settled at his desk. He had letters from Lieutenants Campbell and Thompson. James Campbell and Ryan Thompson had been with him for years now and had joined him as midshipmen. Ryan was in command of the Eagle and James the Alouette. James reported that the refit of the Alouette and

Honfleur were going well and he expected that another three weeks should see them back at sea and another week after that they should be at Deal.

A new mid had been given the Honfleur, he was twenty-year-old Angus Frasier a dur Scott from Aberdeen according to the letter from Thompson. He wrote that Frasier had been sent by Hood and according to his service record had been denied a lieutenancy for telling his previous commander he was an ass. Apparently, the commander had decided to force his ship through a number of French fishing boats, causing two to capsize. Frasier had taken him to task over it resulting in him being beached.

A man of principle then, well we will see how he fits in with this bunch of pirates.

Caroline joined him an hour later and sat down on the settee waiting for him to finish with his work and when he put down his pen for the last time and stretched his arms she said,

"I have some news darling,"

"Hmm?" Marty said as he stood and stretched his back.

"I am pregnant again."

He froze mid-stretch and looked at her. "How far along?"

"According to Shelby, three months."

Marty dropped to the settee beside her and gathered her into his arms and kissed her. Beth and James chose that moment to come down and the four of them celebrated the moment together.

Marty stayed with Caroline on shore for the next two nights and during the day they went back aboard. The second day, around mid-morning, a lookout reported that an ornate carriage had pulled up on the dock and the escort was signalling to the ship.

Marty went on deck and immediately recognised the carriage.

"Mr. Ackermann! Please have my barge manned immediately and send it over to pick up the Prince Regent from the dock. Have Mr. Trenchard command it in his number one uniform!" he added spotting the second lieutenant dressed in working rig.

Fifteen minutes later the barge with smartly dressed crew in matching white trousers with blue and white striped shirts and second lieutenant, in full dress, was heading to the dock.

Ackermann had a full side party assembled and Caroline was in a panic as all her dresses were ashore and James had gotten tar on his clothes. Marty assured her she looked fabulous.

They had a bosun's chair rigged and the Prince was brought aboard with all due ceremony. As soon as his feet hit the deck he stood and walked towards Marty with his arms outstretched. Marty had no choice but to accept the hug and kiss on the cheek in front of the entire crew.

"My dear Martin! I just couldn't wait to come down and see if you liked my gift to you." he crowed joyfully, holding Marty at arm's length so he could look him in the eyes.

Marty realised he must be talking about the Formidable. "She is wonderful, Your Highness, the perfect ship for the tasks ahead" he extemporised.

"I had a little word in the ear of some of my friends in the Admiralty and as you captured her it was only just you get her!" He turned to Caroline. "Lady Caroline, you look absolutely radiant!"

Marty gave the Prince a guided tour.

"Is the Captain really a Lord?" asked Stan Wilkins, a bosun's mate who had volunteered for special duty as it paid better than normal Navy pay. He had eight kids and two wives to support in two ports.

"He certainly is," Wilson told him. "Lord Candor, he's got a big estate up in Cheshire and another down in Dorset."

"The old hands say they get paid in cash, not slips."

"That we do," Wilson confirmed.

"And he's a friend of the Prince?"

"Looks like it dunnit," Wilson said in a voice that ended the conversation.

Prince George stayed to a sumptuous lunch prepared by Roland du Demaine and played with the children, luckily Blaez took to him and just watched to make sure all was well. He left at three in the afternoon and invited them both to visit when Marty was back in London the next time.

Chapter 8: Shake down to Gibraltar

Slightly over crewed, provisioned and in all respects ready for sea, the Formidiable came up to her anchor and as it broke loose fell off to the wind as her sails filled. The wind was fresh from the Southwest and the sea was slight. The rain had stopped, and the clouds parted to allow the sun to glint off her brightwork and newly gilded gingerbread.

She heeled over as more sail was set and made a fabulous sight as she stayed close to the wind and made her way out of the Medway. Marty watched his family recede into the distance as Caroline and the children stood on the dock to wave him goodbye.

Marty intended to use the trip down to Gibraltar to get the ship shaken down and the new watches bedded in. To add a little spice, he intended to enter the Bay of Biscay and look into Bilbao on the way.

Before they had left, he had sent a signal to Hood by semaphore that they were preparing to sail, and he had got one back three hours later telling him that there would be an extra passenger joining them. Francis Ridgely made it on board with an hour to spare and presented Marty with a letter of introduction from William Wickham, the head of British Intelligence.

“So, you are our pet spy then,” Marty said after he had read the letter.

“Well officially your ‘Intelligence Officer’ but the description is apt,” grinned Francis, who was a scholarly looking chap with a shock of brown hair that refused to be tidy no matter what he did. He had dark brown eyes behind round glasses, that Marty wasn’t sure actually had anything but plain glass in and was dressed in a non-descript dark grey suit.

"When we get to Gibraltar, we need to organise shore accommodation and a base of operations like I heard you had in Deal," he commented.

"Too much to ask that someone had already done that I suppose," Marty grumbled.

"Admiral Hood suggested that we look at Rosia bay, it's away from the main docks and has a number of warehouses that could be requisitioned and adapted," Francis suggested as Cooper served them with tea. "It would also keep us out from under the eyes of the Port Admiral and Governor."

"Did he now?" Marty said, pulling out a map of Gibraltar and taking a good look.

They made as much westing as they could so that they were able to run just a little West of South to stay out of the Bay of Biscay if they needed to.

Marty stood on the windward side of the quarterdeck as was his right and watched the crew lowering the topmasts. It was blowing hard and was ideal training weather. Ackermann shouted encouragement, insults and praise in the same breath and the men looked to be working in good humour.

He asked Antton what caused the new man to get a punch in the mouth. All he would say was he made a crude suggestion about what he would like to do to Caroline. Marty left it at that, trusting the justice of the lower deck to sort it out.

After the exercise with the mast, he had them exercise the guns, no dumb show on this ship, they practiced live firing. The gun crews were all experienced but unfamiliar with each other. They didn't start too badly, but he wanted better, so an hour's practice followed. In the end he was confident that with an hour or so of practice every day they would soon reach his target of three rounds every two minutes.

The bay lived up to its reputation, the wind swung around to the Northwest and increased in power to a howling gale. There was no way they could look in on Bilbao as it was as much as they could do to maintain their course West of Southwest to clear the point at Viveiro. The effort involved, Marty decided, was about the same as picking the ship up and carrying it.

Throughout it all, Ridgely was as sick as a dog, sicker in fact, as the rough weather didn't faze Blaez at all, who either lay down or stood with all four legs braced out at angles to keep him stable. The spy was so sick that Marty sent him down to the orlop deck with Shelby where the pitching and rolling and corkscrewing weren't as bad, and the physician could keep an eye on him.

The bad weather lasted until they turned into the Straights of Heracles and they shot into the harbour at Gibraltar under topsails only, swinging her into the wind in a spectacular fashion and dropping the hook with relief as the gunner finished the salute.

The Flagship was in port and a signal soared up the mast requesting Marty's presence aboard. He got dressed in his best uniform and checked the latest issue of the gazette he had picked up before they left. Yes! Collingwood was Commander in Chief Mediterranean Fleet. Marty had met him on the trip back from Jamaica when Nelson had invited him to dine, and saw Collingwood as the natural successor to Nelson, he just hoped the Navy did.

His boat crew did him proud, decked out in their matching clothes and hats, Samuel stood at the stern dressed the same but in a blue jacket with silver buttons. They arrived smartly and as soon as they hooked onto the chains Marty ran up the side.

He was surprised to see York as Flag Lieutenant. "Hello York!" he greeted him, "didn't expect to see you here. Managed to escape English Harbour then."

"Good afternoon Captain Stockley. Yes, my father managed to get a replacement commissioner sent out post haste and I was sent to Admiral Collingwood, joined him just after Trafalgar. Please follow me the Admiral is expecting you."

Marty was duly announced and entered the great cabin, Collingwood greeted him as one Baron to another, which surprised Marty and after the usual pleasantries and a glass of cool, dry white rhenish, said,

"I didn't see you at Nelson's funeral, he thought highly of you, you know."

"One of my greatest regrets my lord," Marty replied, "but I was sent to Spain and France on an important mission and was not in England at the time. I did, however, pay my respects at his tomb as soon as I returned."

"I don't think I need to know what that was all about, and I can guess who was behind it, the Formidable was earmarked to come to my fleet when it was diverted by royal 'request'!"

Marty did his best to look contrite.

"I suppose you are here under the command of Lord Hood?" Collingwood asked.

"Yes, I am to transfer the Special Operations Flotilla to Gibraltar and set up operations here," Marty replied, knowing full well that Hood would have informed Collingwood in advance.

"How many ships in this flotilla?"

"Four Sir. My frigate, a former French sloop of war, an American Baltimore Clipper, and a converted French Whaler."

Collingwood looked thoughtful and then asked.

. "You take on difficult or, let us say, clandestine missions and all your men are trained accordingly, am I right?"

"You are well informed, my lord," Marty replied with a nod.

"Excellent! And as you are in my backyard if I were to pass you the odd, aah, opportunity, then I could rely on you to take care of it?"

"Certainly, my lord, as long as I am still able to fulfil my orders from Whitehall," Marty replied cagily.

Collingwood laughed and then grimaced as something caused him pain.

"Are you well my lord?" Marty asked, rising to assist him.

He was waved back to his seat.

"You can't, but I believe you have a physician on board that is of some note?"

"I will have Mr. Shelby attend you at your earliest convenience."

And with that the meeting was over.

The next day, Shelby returned to the frigate after spending a whole morning with the Admiral. Marty didn't ask what he had found but the look of worry on his face spoke volumes.

Marty, Ridgely and Fletcher, with Blaez and Sam in attendance, went ashore to look at potential bases for the Flotilla, Fletcher had been ashore procuring stores and making sure that before they left, they would be able to replace the one and a half tons of powder and shot they used in gunnery practice on the way down. He had put the word out they were looking for buildings and he had been tipped off that there was a disused barracks with storerooms, owned by the army, behind Rosia Bay. Marty wanted to have a look at them before he met with the Governor, James Drummond, that evening for dinner.

As it turned out there was a small, fortified barracks, big enough for a division of cavalry plus horses sitting empty and falling into disrepair one and a half cables from the shoreline. It was ideal as there was a forge, that must have been the Farrier's which the 'tool shed' could take over. Plenty of sleeping accommodation for the marines and sailors to spend time ashore, a quadrangle for training and a range to practice musketry. Not to mention a fairly large officer's quarters with space for a kitchen and extensive stables that could be used as storerooms.

At dinner that evening at the Governor's Mansion, in the company of Collingwood, his flag Captain and Lieutenant, General Henry Fox the Commander in Chief of the Army and two of his aids. Marty was introduced both as Captain Stockley and Lord Candor, which made life difficult as it confused the social order, but it also meant he was given more gravitas than a mere captain of less than three years seniority could have hoped for.

He decided to make the best of it and asked about the disused barracks.

"Hasn't been occupied since before the fevers," Fox stated, referring to the epidemic of yellow fever that had decimated the garrison up to as late as the year before. "Used to belong to one of the cavalry units but we don't have much cavalry here now, except in transit to somewhere else and they stay at the main garrison."

"So, the buildings can be taken over by Sir Martin and his men?" Drummond pressed.

Fox looked like he had sucked a lemon, the army didn't like giving up anything to the Navy, but acquiesced with a nod, albeit reluctantly.

"Good that's settled then, we can move on to desert," Drummond smiled.

Marty detailed forty sailors under Midshipman Hart and ten marines under Sergeant Bright to start cleaning up their new home. Fletcher volunteered to stay and provision the place with furniture and goods. Ridgley went ashore and disappeared into the town after telling Marty he would find a place to set up shop away from the barracks. That settled Marty set sail back to England to rendezvous with the

Alouette and Hornfleur and bring back as many men and supplies as they could without the Eagle.

They had changed the watches to compensate for the men they had left behind, and something wasn't working as intended. A day or so out he sensed there was a problem, it was the slightest of changes in the rhythm with which the ship ran but he picked up on it and decided to investigate.

He watched each team in turn and finally he spotted it. The larboard watch contained six of the black ex-slaves, four of which were working as landsmen hauling on the mainmast sails when trimming, the other two at the foremast.

When the mainmast men lined up on a halyard to haul, four of the white sailors were jockeying for positions where they didn't have to be next to them. That was slowing down the trimming of the sails and disturbing the rhythm of the ship.

"Mr. Ackermann, I would be obliged if you would bring those four men to the quarterdeck once their watch is finished," he said, indicating the four men in question.

The bell rung and the watch changed, four very nervous-looking men climbed the steps to the quarterdeck behind Ackermann.

Marty made a show of reading the log then checking the chart, looked up at the sails and sniffed the wind. Then he called Sam over and, putting his hand on his shoulder, asked him something. When Sam answered he laughed and slapped him on the back as he turned towards the four waiting men.

He stood in front of them and looked each carefully up and down then walked behind them and looked again.

"Gentlemen, you have bemused me," he said as he came around in front of them again. "You don't look different from the other men, or smell different, so what is it that stands you apart?"

The men looked at each other in confusion.

"Well there must be something as I have noted you deem yourselves too good to stand beside our African crew members on the line."

They all suddenly looked defiant and one even a little angry.

"Please go ahead and tell me," Marty said to the angry man.

"Start with your names."

"Jedidiah Dollond, and this be Gambier, Garrick and Minet," he said with a faint French accent," Marty got an inkling of the problem.

"We don't associate with heathens and blacks be the worst heathens of all."

A light went on in Marty's mind.

"You are all Huguenots aren't you. Do you see black people as less than you?"

"They are only fit to be slaves or servants, not to stand alongside God's people."

Marty looked at the four men one by one and saw only stubborn defiance. He knew when he was on a hiding to nothing when confronted with prejudice like this as it was too deeply ingrained, so dismissed the men to go to their dinner.

"Mr. Ackermann, those men are disrupting the smooth running of my ship," he said as if in passing, "split them up between the watches and put them in work crews that do the meanest jobs. Once we get back to England, pay them off and put them ashore."

He was angry. He was all for religious tolerance and he firmly believed in the equality of all men. Prejudice that was blind and fuelled by one man's conviction that he was superior to another because of his race or colour was just anathema to him. Especially as in this case the Huguenots had been persecuted by the Catholics in France and forced to flee to England to have religious freedom, and here they were doing effectively the same to the Africans. He couldn't understand it.

Chapter 9: Moving House

They dropped anchor in the Downs and Marty and Blaez took the barge up to the Farm. The Alouette was tied up in front of the faithful old Lark and the Hornfleur. The dock was a hive of activity with piles of stores being prepared for loading in nets. He was expecting to hear about the status of the Eagle once he got to the Farm

Paul la Pierre, Captain of Marines was shouting orders and chivvying men to pile stores in the right place. There was no shortage of men, the extra marines had arrived and were mucking in with sleeves rolled up.

The Barge tied up and Marty stepped ashore. Immediately the call went up,

"Captain on deck!"

And every marine snapped to attention. *There are disadvantages to wearing a uniform,* Marty thought as he was always uncomfortable with this type of reaction. Paul la Pierre walked over to him and snapped a salute with a grin. Marty shook hands with him in greeting and said,

"I suppose you want me to inspect your band of rogues, thieves and murderers?"

"The men would appreciate it, if you don't mind."

Marty sighed, then grinned. "Form them up Captain la Pierre."

Paul nodded to a lieutenant who was stood nearby, who bellowed,

"Marines! Form up for review!"

"George Fairbrother, loudest voice at Chatham," Paul commented sotto voice.

Marty schooled himself to be serious and, as soon as the men had replaced their jackets and ranks were formed, followed Paul to the end of the first line. They progressed slowly and Marty greeted marines he knew by name. At the end of it, the two captains moved to a pile of crates and Marty climbed on top of them and called for all the men to gather around.

"As you know we are moving from here to Gibraltar. We have found a base and a team of sailors and marines is there getting it ready for your enjoyment." He looked for the three marines who made up the tool shed,

"there is a forge you can use as a workshop," he indicated the rest of the marines,

"a quadrangle so you marines can march up and down," that caused a laugh and a few disparaging comments about the lobsters from the sailors,

"a range where you can all practice your musketry," disparaging comments from marines about the ability of sailors to 'hit a cow's arse with a paddle.'

"Once there and settled in, we will resume our effort to cause pain and confusion to the French and their allies," there was a growl of agreement and he let it peter out,

"and of course, prizes and prize money for all!" which caused a huge cheer.

He called his officers together. James Campbell of the Allouette, with his midshipman, Archibald Davidson, Midshipman Angus Frasier of the Hornfleur and Captain Paul la Pierre and his two lieutenants, Edward Griffin and George Fairbrother.

"Are we fully up to strength?" he asked and got confirmation that both ships and the marines were.

"Good, then we will load as much as we can onto the ships we have at our disposal. Use the Lark to ferry stores and equipment to the Formidiable, she draws too much water to get up the river to here. Ackermann is ready and waiting for them so get that started straight away. Any news on the Eagle?"

"She will be in dock for another three weeks and will need another week to re-provision and take on powder," James reported on Ryan's behalf.

"Good! We will leave their share of the stores and equipment here to collect along with their marines. Mr. Griffin, I believe you command them?"

"Sah!" Edward Griffin replied in a parade ground bark causing the other to laugh.

"We're not on parade, a simple 'Yes Sir' will do," Paul admonished him in his relaxed manner causing the red-haired and freckled lieutenant to blush furiously.

"James, how long until we will be ready to leave?" Marty asked.

"Three days should see everything stowed away and us ready to go," he replied then added, "will you take Will Barbour with you?"

"I had forgotten about him!" Marty admitted. "I have most room so yes that makes sense, he can run the officer's wardroom on the shore base once we get there."

After taking care of a few other minor questions he dismissed them and walked to the Farm. Blaez was delighted to be back and hunted the hedgerow for rabbits and terrorized the birds. He was greeted at the door by Will and was slightly saddened by the empty echoey rooms where he and Armand had planned and executed so many adventures. He told Will to get himself and his baggage over to the Lark and then saddled one of the horses. They would be left at Deal for Armand to either keep or dispose of.

He rode with Blaez trotting by his side, tied the horse to one of the hitching rings set into the front wall of the Wagon and Horses and walked in through the front door into the dimly lit bar. He had forgotten he was in full uniform and the room went silent as he was silhouetted against the light from outside.

Then with a squeal Susie, Armand's wife came around the bar and wrapped him in a huge hug,

"Marty! We didn't know you were back!" she cried after kissing him soundly.

Marty returned the hug then held her at arm's length so he could see her. "It's a flying visit, can you put me up for the night?" he laughed.

Armand came out from the back room to see what all the fuss was about and stepped up to hug him and kiss him on each cheek, French-style, in greeting.

"Mon Amie! Look at you! Captain Martin Stockley! Where is your ship?"

"Anchored in the Downs, she's too big for the dock."

"Wickham said you had a Frigate. He joked that you used royal connections to get it."

"No joke, Prince George intervened on my behalf, he thought as I had taken it, I should have it."

"Friends in high places indeed but be careful my friend he can turn in a moment," he cautioned. Blaez went outside with Susie and Armand's daughter, Jessica, who was old enough to play ball with him now.

They sat to chat over an ale and Bill Clarence, the head of the Deal smugglers joined them. The chat became an extended drinking session, when Bill's son turned up, that went on long into the night. When Marty woke up the next morning, he had the mother and father of all hangovers.

The ride back to the dock was, to say the least, uncomfortable as every jolting step the horse took rattled his poor aching head and turned his stomach over, but he wouldn't have changed last night for anything!

He didn't have to say anything when he finally rode up to the dock, the wince he made at every loud noise said it all. Private Dibble from the tool shed team found a hammock and slung it for him in one of the empty store houses where he could sleep it off.

His headache was still with him on the trip back to the Downs and Sam took great delight in singing a hymn in his deep tenor to set a rhythm for the rowers that vibrated through Marty's skull as if he was inside a drum. He climbed the tumble home and winced as the bosun's pipes welcomed him home. A quick word with Ackermann and he concluded the ship was looking after itself without his interference and went to find Shelby.

"A modicum more ale than you are used to?" Shelby asked with a completely straight face. It was true he hadn't ever drunk that much ale in his life, preferring wine, so he just nodded miserably.

Shelby mixed some powder with carbonated water from a bottle with a strangely shaped neck with a marble in it. He looked at it closer and saw that the marble was forced up the neck by the gas and sealed itself against the neck. When Shelby wanted to pour some out, he inverted the bottle and pushed the marble down with his finger releasing the water under pressure.

"Drink this, it's an infusion of willow and when mixed with the carbonated water has good pain killing properties," Shelby informed him.

Marty drunk the bitter potion.

"Christ! I don't know if the cure is worse than the malady," Marty sputtered.

"If the cure was nice to drink people would be more encouraged to get ill," Shelby quipped.

With that nugget of wisdom ringing in his ears Marty went to his cabin.

Morning dawned and they prepared the Formidiable for sail. She was loaded with all the stores they could get aboard while still having room for an extra forty marines. They waited until the lookout called down that he could see the Alouette and Hornfleur approaching.

They came up to the anchor, sails were set and as they took the wind John Smith at the wheel caught her and steered Southwest. The Hornfleur fell in next in line with the Alouette bringing up the rear. Marty didn't want to get into any kind of fight with the ships so heavily loaded and manned, so he took them well out into the Atlantic to the West before turning South to clear Ushant by a healthy margin. That had the unfortunate side effect that the seas were rough, and he had a lot of sick passengers.

It was with a real sense of relief that they sailed into Rosia Bay where they were greeted by a gun from the barracks and their skull and crossed pistols flag, which was run up as they anchored.

"That will annoy the admiral," Ackermann noted with a smile that said he didn't care.

"Probably, but pretty much anything out of their control is annoying to them," Marty replied, "let's get this ship unloaded so we can get on with business."

Rosia Bay was where they had towed the Victory after Trafalgar so they had a good depth of water to work with right up to the old stone dock where they could moor one ship at a time. There was a road that sloped up to the barracks and Fletcher had managed to get a couple of four wheeled wagons pulled by oxen to move the heavier stores.

They unloaded the Formidable first, then the Alouette and finally the Hornfleur. It took four days to get everything in and the men settled.

There was a tower in one corner of the barracks where a lookout could be posted but it wasn't very high. Marty had a wooden platform built on top of it with a railing, to raise it another twenty feet, and set a lookout.

A scruffy urchin of a boy turned up at the newly made and hung gate and asked for Marty. When he was let in, he demanded in a broad Eastend of London accent that he get a shilling.

"Why should I give you anything except a clip around the ear?" Marty asked.

"'Cus I got a message from Mr. Ridgley fo' ya! An' he said you would give me a shillin' if I give it to yer person like," the wretch replied cockily.

"Well when you have given it to me you can have this," Marty replied, holding up a sixpence.

"That aint no shillin!" he squawked indignantly.

"Are you sure?" Marty said, "look closely," and when he peered at it, he performed a simple magician's switch and the sixpence turned into a shilling.

"Cor blimey! How'd you do that?"

"Work for me and I will show you, now what was the message?"

"Oh, right! He said he is set up at Devil's Tower Road in number 17b. He has made contact wiv somebody called Enreekay."

Who Enreekay was Martin had no clue, but he must be someone significant, it was time to go and visit their Intelligence Officer.

"What's your name young man?" Marty asked as he twirled a florin across his knuckles. It was an exercise he used to keep his fingers supple and dexterous.

"Billy Hooper, Owdoyoudothat?"

"Well, Billy Hooper, show me where 17b Devil's Tower Road is and I will show you."

Sam turned up with Blaez. Billy looked at him with his mouth open and his eyes wide and when he saw Blaez ran behind Marty.

"It's a bleedin' wolf and a giant!" he squeaked.

Marty laughed and knelt so Blaez could nuzzle him and lick his nose.

"It's just my dog, Blaez, and my cox, Samuel. They will be coming with us."

Billy edged his way to the door, keeping well away from both of them.

It was around a forty-five-minute walk and the last part up hill. Marty's calves were burning by the time they reached number seventeen. Billy was now walking between Blaez and Sam, strutting like he was the king of the walk knowing he was totally safe for one of the few times in his short life. Marty had shown him how to shuffle a coin across his fingers and back again and had given him a penny to practice with.

Billy led them in through the door and up a flight of stairs to an upstairs apartment. He banged on the door and pushed it open before there was an answer.

Marty looked around; Ridgely obviously didn't slum it; the apartment was furnished with expensive comfortable chairs and a well-made dining room table and chairs. There was a fireplace in which a merry fire burned, and the room was pleasantly warm. There was a small kitchen to one side through an archway. The big windows at the front led out to a balcony from which he had a panoramic view to the border between Gibraltar and Spain and across the bay to Algeciras. He had an enormous telescope mounted on a tripod on the balcony.

Ridgely came through a door set into an alcove on the far side of the room and Marty caught a glimpse of a large four poster bed.

"Thank you, Billy," he said and flipped him a shilling which disappeared as soon as it was caught. "I will call when I need you." Billy tugged his forelock and left giving Marty a wink and Blaez a pat on the head.

"Captain Stockley! So pleased you could visit," he smiled and held out his hand. The grey suit had disappeared, and he was dressed in a pair of black trousers and a cotton shirt with a ruff down the front, open to his chest. Around his neck he had a gold chain with an odd looking pendant and the glasses had disappeared.

Marty shook his hand and looked him up and down. "I assume you have taken a new persona to cover your activities?" he asked.

"Absolutely, rake in exile, father is so disgusted with my behaviour back in England he sent me out here to learn restraint!" he grinned, "but I expect you will want to see where the work is done."

He took Marty by the arm and led him to a bookshelf. He took the pendant, pressed a stud and a sprung loaded key swung out. He inserted it into what looked like a knot hole in a shelf and turned it. There was a click and a section of the bookshelf swung open revealing a staircase to what must be the attic.

They made their way up after the door was closed behind them, light filtering down from above. Marty noticed the walls were lined in cork and the stairs covered with thick sound deadening carpet. They emerged into a loft with skylights letting in light but with thick black material fixed so they could be covered at night. The walls were also covered in cork and the floor had more of the thick carpet, the room was soundproof. Lamps stood in a row on a shelf waiting to be lit.

There were maps pinned to the walls and a rack of charts in one corner. A row of cabinets with numbered and labelled drawers were lined up along one wall and the end wall was covered in an array of weapons that Marty would have been happy to have in his chest. A desk with clerk's chair, a sofa and two comfortable chairs provided a workspace and somewhere to sit.

"Made yourself at home then." Marty observed.

"Absolutely! Cup of tea?"

Marty nodded and Ridgley went to a corner where there stood a samovar with an oil burner under it, a wisp of steam escaping the lid.

"I have something for you already, it came from Admiral Collingwood," he told them as he served the tea.

"Good! By the way who is Enreeekay?" Marty responded.

Chapter 10: Scouting

The Formidiable coasted along under minimum sail just North of Sicily following the Calabrian coast. They were passing Tropia and swinging more East as they made their way towards Pizzo. The smell of the land drifted out to them, a mixture of dust, olive trees and dry grass. Marty was struck by the clarity of the air and the way the light played on the rocky coast casting different colours.

It was an hour past dawn, and they were heading for the estuary of the river Maida where they would put a team ashore to perform an advance scouting and mapping exercise. In the process they would also contact local partisans who were rebelling against the French occupation.

Marty had been briefed that the Army, with Major-General Stuart in overall command, and Navy, with Admiral Sir Sidney Smith commanding the fleet, were planning on landing an expeditionary force of over five thousand troops to take on the French General Jean Reynier. It was estimated he had a force of around five and a half thousand based somewhere near Maida.

Their mission was to scout the landing area, map it, locate the French army and estimate its size and make up.

Marty had brought Lieutenant Ryan Thompson, who spoke Italian, to lead the landing party. They would meet a contact called Francesco, who was a Sicilian and would introduce them to the partisans. Marty would stay with the ship and patrol off the coast until it was time to pick his men up after five days or so.

Ryan had his hand-picked landing party assembled on the main deck. Six marines with appropriate skills. Three of the marines were scouts, ex-poachers or countrymen who knew how to move silently through the land, two were close combat specialists and were bodyguards for Ryan and the sixth member of the team who was an artist and cartographer. He could have taken more but in this case he though less was best.

None of them wore uniforms, the bright red jackets of the marines would have stood out like beacons in the brown and green landscape, instead they wore non-descript grey jackets and trousers and could pass for locals at a distance. They would forage for food so each only carried a pack with ammunition, emergency rations for two days and a canteen of water. Ryan checked that the canteens only had water in them as he didn't want anyone smuggling alcohol ashore. They also carried French muskets rather than their own rifles.

"All set?" Captain la Pierre asked him

"Yes, we are as ready as we will ever be," Ryan replied

"Corporal Evans don't let the scouts get too far ahead, they are there to warn not to engage and no messing with the local women," la Pierre warned.

Marty was watching the shoreline and comparing it to drawings the Master, had in his extensive records. He had sailed the gulf of Santa Eufernia in the past and like all good masters had made sketches and watercolours of the coast for future reference. The Amato Estuary came abeam, and he ordered the sails backed to bring them to a halt.

"Man the barge!" he ordered and Ackermann shouted the orders to get it pulled up alongside and manned.

He stood at the starboard rail and scanned the shoreline with his telescope, then checked the time with his watch. It was six AM. They were on time according to the instructions that Ridgley had given him. He scanned again and saw a man step out of a copse of trees on the north side of the estuary. He looked up and down the beach before walking down to the shoreline and waved.

"The contact is on the beach," Marty told Ryan. "Ridgley said we can trust him but be careful. I don't want to have to find a new commander for the Eagle."

Ryan grinned and shook his hand before following his men down into the waiting barge.

"We will be back for you at dawn on the sixth day and return at dawn for the following three days if you aren't here or get a message to us," Marty called down to confirm the arrangement.

Ryan waved and gave a thumbs up as the barge pulled away. Marty watched as they disembarked, the scouts disappearing rapidly into the tree line. Their contact was shaking Ryan's hand and then all of them walked up the beach with one marine sweeping out the footprints with a leafy branch.

"Make way Mr. Ackermann, if you please," Marty ordered as soon as the boat had tied on, "they are on their own now."

He had complete confidence in Ryan and knew the men he had with him were solid and the best for the job. They had a week to gain as much information as they could and to map out the area so that Stuart could choose where he would meet the French.

Marty intended to use the time to patrol up the Italian coast to Naples and beyond, pick up a prize or two if they presented themselves and to have a look into the bay to see if there were any French country ships there.

He flew a Spanish flag and cruised under topsails and royals making around eight knots. It was about one hundred and forty miles to Sorrento, and he was timing it so they would be there around dawn the next day.

He retired to his cabin for breakfast and Cooper served him bacon, procured in Gibraltar, and fried eggs from the hen coop, washed down with coffee, black and unsweetened like the French took it. Blaez was fed some dried meat and ships biscuit which he chewed vigorously giving forth with a satisfied belch after he finished it.

He had just settled down to read a book he had picked up in England when there was a shout from the lookout closely followed by the rattle of feet on the ladder and an announcement by the marine guard at his door,

“Midshipman Williams Sah!”

At least he didn’t bellow it, Marty thought as he called for the youngest of his Mids to enter. He had been educating all the marines that they didn’t need to use a parade ground bellow to announce visitors.

Williams was twelve years old and the fourth son of a business associate of Caroline’s. His father was a wealthy trader from Liverpool and the boy had a pronounced Liverpudlian accent.

“Mr. Ackermann’s compliments Sir, and there is a sail to our Northwest. He thinks it’s a snow,” he announced pronouncing snow as snew.

“Thank you, Mr. Williams, and how are your lessons progressing?” Marty asked.

“Mr. Grey says my Navigation is improving. I was only twenty miles off on the last sighting!” Williams replied with enthusiasm.

“Lucky we were in the middle of the Mediterranean and not close to shore then,” Marty observed. “You need to work on that. Ask Mr. Stamp to help with your mathematics.”

“Aye Aye Sir!”

“Now, please go and ask Mr. Ackermann to set a course to intercept and I will join him in a few minutes.”

He smiled as the boy left, he was showing promise and Marty took a particular interest in all his young men as he saw them as the future of his peculiar branch of the service.

Sam came out from the steward’s galley and took Marty’s weapons harness from his weapons chest.

Suitable attired in a silk shirt, his third best uniform coat and his weapons harness complete with pistols, fighting knife and hanger, Marty came up on the quarterdeck. He checked the log, said good morning to the helmsman then spoke with Ackermann.

"Looks like a merchant ship, heading North making about five or six knots. He's hull up now and we are catching him without setting more sail."

"Good, we don't want to spook him too soon," Marty replied, "please get the ship to quarters but don't run out."

Over the next hour they gradually caught up with the snow and could see it was heavily laden.

"He's not going to be able to run, make all sail," Marty ordered.

With all sail set, they soon overhauled their prey, and a shot aimed to pass along their side and land just in front of their bows had her sails flapping as she hove to. Lieutenant Stamp was sent over with a boarding party and he reported she was heading to Rome and laden with olive oil from Calabria. Fair game then. A prize crew was put aboard under Midshipman Hart and she was dispatched to Palermo They would pick them up later when they called on the fleet.

They resumed the trip North but saw nothing else of interest and ran into Salerno Bay the next morning. Apart from a few merchant ships there was nothing there, so they turned and sailed down the Amalfi coast to Capri. The French flag flew over the island that was fortified with batteries but still managed to give the impression it was half asleep.

Marty sailed close to it and wasn't challenged so he took his time and decided to make a record of all the fortifications and defences that they could see.

"Mr. Ackermann I would be obliged if you would send two men who can draw with bring-em-nears to the top of the mainmast and have them sketch every fortification, battery and lookout they can see. Mr. Grey, I am sure you have sketches, maps and paintings of the island in that vast repository of yours. Please make copies so we can overlay what the lookouts come down with."

He also had men counting ships, or masts if that was all they could see, and took note of the depth, currents and tides as they progressed. He was surprised that they still weren't challenged and took the whole morning to make detailed notes. When he was satisfied that they had seen all they could they made their way into the Bay of Naples.

This time things looked a bit more interesting; there were two twenty-eight-gun French corvettes anchored in the bay and a thirty-eight-gun frigate being careened on a beach. He studied the corvettes, they appeared to only have harbour watches on board. He scanned the shore and saw that they were both under the protection of the guns of shore batteries.

"Mr. Grey, what is the state of the moon tonight?" he asked.

"No moon Sir, it sets at a half past eight." The Master responded without looking in the almanac.

Marty looked at his watch, it was a half past three in the afternoon.

"I want those ships pinpointed on the chart then take us out to sea Mr. Ackermann, I've seen enough."

He called his lieutenants and midshipmen to his cabin. Once they were assembled, he began,

"It is my intention to return to the bay tonight, cut out those two corvettes and burn the frigate. Mr. Trenchard and Mr. Stamp, you will lead the cutting out crews, with thirty men each. Mr. Stamp I want you to take the corvette that is furthest into the bay."

He had a chart of the bay laid out on the table and they all lent over it. The two corvettes and the frigate were marked along with all the shore batteries they had noted.

"We will sail in to as close to this point here as we can," Marty said and pointed to a point on the map some two cables from the corvettes. "I hope the corvettes will have harbour lights burning and we can position ourselves from them. If not, we will get as close as we can by dead reckoning. Once the boats are away, we will take the Formidiable back out to sea. Now we need to get those two corvettes before we fire the frigate, or we will just light up the bay and make ourselves targets. The team that will burn the frigate will leave fifteen minutes after the cutting out crews. That should give you enough time to get aboard, cut the anchor rope and get them underway." He thought for a moment, frowning. "The problem is we only have four boats, which is enough for the cutting out crews but that leaves us short for the frigate."

He left the problem on the table for them to discuss and soon the suggestions were getting more fantastic by the minute. Then he heard the rumble of Sam laughing and looked over to see him pointing out of the transom window. He followed his gaze and saw a fleet of fishing boats making their way out to sea. He grinned back at him; problem solved.

Marty bought a boat off one of the fishermen, it was the oldest and shabbiest in the small fleet and he paid at least the price of a new boat for it after an extended haggle. The old fisherman was happy and neither he nor his fellow fishermen would go running to the authorities.

They chose the cutting out crews and allocated them to the boats. It would be crowded with up to fifteen men in each, but they would also row, so it was doable.

It was fully dark by nine o'clock and Marty wanted to be into the bay at ten, so they started their approach as soon as the sun set. The residents of Naples were very obliging, and several large houses had lamps outside that they could steer a course by and there was the dull red glow from Vesuvius. It was a nervous approach in the pitch black of the night even so and they felt their way cautiously in. The corvettes had harbour lights burning much to his relief.

Multiple bearings on the corvettes, Vesuvius and harbour lights got them on station and hove to, the boats pulled around and the blacked-up men loaded.

There were so many variables he was convinced something had to go drastically wrong and his nerves were jangling. *Damn but I would rather be in the cutting out crew,* he admitted to himself. He made a decision.

"Mr. Ackermann I will command the fishing boat," he announced to the First Lieutenant and was aware as soon as he said it, he sounded faintly ridiculous.

Ackermann was obviously holding back a grin as he gave the orders for the cutting out crews to get on their way. Once they were gone, he called up the fishing boat. Marty climbed down and was immediately assailed with the smell of rotting fish and seaweed that was ingrained into the wood. They spent the next fifteen minutes piling combustibles into the centre of the boat and a pair of shuttered lanterns were hung from the mast with the doors closed.

He looked around at the crew and knew that most of his followers were present. John Smith was at the tiller; the Basques manned the oars and he could faintly see someone in the bow?

He checked his watch and saw that the boats had been gone for fifteen minutes. They needed to go.

Phillip Trenchard steered the barge towards the bow of the nearest of the corvettes, the second boat in his team was heading for the stern.

Damn but it's dark! He thought as he steered the boat by the harbour light of their target. They had twenty yards to go and his men were preparing to climb on board as fast as they could. He had a combination of agile sailors and less agile marines; all were armed with either boarding pikes or cutlasses. Two men in the bow had crossbows in case a sentry revealed himself as they approached. Every man carried a billy club or blackjack to deal silently with the harbour watch.

They hooked onto the bow with the faintest of bumps and the sailors shot up the side. A few seconds later ropes were dropped over and the marines went up followed by Phillip.

The men moved down the deck silently, on bare feet or soft soled shoes. The occasional thud indicating they had found a sentry and put them to sleep. Then, as they met the men from the second boat they split into two groups. One to go below and take care of any crew that were still aboard and the other to get the ship under way.

The first thing they did was to step a mast in the corvette's boat and moor it to the anchor cable. Then they mounted a hooded lantern on the mast. They had to extinguish the harbour light on the corvette's mast and uncover the lantern in the boat at the same time so that from shore it would look like the corvette was still there.

From below came the sounds of a struggle and then a stifled scream. He waited until someone appeared beside him and whispered that all was secure.

"Raise the foresail and courses, cut the anchor cable," he ordered sotto voice.

Marty, meanwhile, was navigating by compass towards the frigate on the careenage beach. Every twenty seconds or so he cracked the shutter on one of the lanterns just enough to see their heading, but then he realised that there was a light from a house just to the right of where he wanted to be and could steer by that. He looked back at the frigate but couldn't see it and then across to where the corvettes were. The lights didn't look as if they had moved but he was sure they were lower now.

The beach suddenly appeared as a line of phosphorescence as the small waves broke on the sand and he heard the gentle swoosh of moving pebbles.

“Ship oars,” he whispered, “prepare to land.”

The oars came silently inboard and the two men in the bow got ready to jump over as soon as the bow grounded.

There was the faintest of scrapes, Matai and Garai dropped over the side to steady the boat and Franco jumped over the bow onto the sand to run the mooring line up the beach to secure it.

The rest of the men unloaded the combustibles and piled them on the beach. Marty got ashore and looked for the Frigate that appeared as a dark lump against the lights of the houses, they had landed one hundred yards too far to the East!

He immediately sent Antton and Matai to check for watchmen and got the rest of the men organised to move the flammables. Paul la Pierre appeared beside him, picking up and carrying with the rest of them

The ship was lying on its starboard side and secured with ropes, so it was a simple matter to access the deck and make a bonfire.

Marty made one last check of his watch then opened a lantern and lit the fuse chord that they had laid to a pile of powder in the middle of the heap. He had thirty seconds to get to the boat before it went up. He was about halfway there when there was a challenge!

“Ehi, che ci fai lì?” Aa gruff voice shouted. Marty stopped and turned to see a lantern approaching him. He held his hands out to the side’s palms down.

“Non sai che questa è una spiaggia riservata?” the man said as he walked towards him. He held the lantern high and a pike in his right hand.

Marty stepped towards him with a smile. His right hand hung loosely at his side and then whipped forward. The watchman’s chest sprouted a throwing knife handle just to the left of centre and he folded to the ground with a groan. Marty turned and ran.

They pushed off and turned the fishing boat to seaward when they heard the muffled sound of the powder igniting.

Marty watched the frigate intently. There! A dull glow gradually getting brighter as the fire took hold. It took another ten minutes for the fire to really get going and start spreading. He heard an alarm and shouting from the shore, then an explosion. He could see by the flash that it was between the ship and the sea wall.

"That will discourage them!" laughed Paul.

He had planted one of the timed bombs near the steps to the beach.

"Wait for it!" Paul crowed.

Another bomb went off around the stern of the ship, in the light of the flames they could see men running back up the steps to the road.

In another few minutes the fire had spread throughout the ship, flames were leaping into the air and up the bone-dry rigging illuminating the bay.

Marty could see the corvettes were gone, there was no sign of them or the Formidiable. That was expected as Ackermann had strict instructions to get the ship out of the bay and out of range of the shore batteries before they torched the frigate. He got John to steer them due South, they would find the others in the morning.

A vengeful soul manning the battery on the Castell dell'Ovo fired on them with a pair of twenty-four-pound cannon. Probably on the assumption that any boat in the bay had to be guilty of theft, if not arson. Luckily their shooting was off and didn't even get them wet.

Six days after dropping off Ryan and his team the Formidiable was again hove to a half mile off the Amato estuary and the barge was pulled up on the sand. They waited an hour then rowed back to the ship.

Marty was not overly worried. Scouting missions rarely went to schedule as any number of things could delay the men's return. As soon as his men were back aboard, they slipped back out to sea and rendezvoused with the two prizes. He had decided that the corvettes should stay with them rather than sail down to Palermo and they formed up in line astern to loiter over the horizon until they went back into the bay the next day. Marty gave the crew a make and mend day so they could relax.

Dawn the next morning saw the barge approaching the beach again and, once again, it was devoid of life. They waited the requisite hour and were starting back when there was a shot from the tree line. One of their marines was stood on the beach waving his arms frantically. They turned back.

Marty was watching from the quarterdeck and was aghast when he saw the party come from the trees and down the beach. They looked to have been in quite a fight and three of the men, including Ryan Thompson, were being helped by their mates. There was no sign of Francesco.

As soon as the barge landed the men were at the side and the boat crew helped their shipmates aboard. They were almost all on when a line of blue uniforms emerged from the tree line and started firing.

The Formidiable was at quarters as a matter of routine and Marty quickly ordered the main guns to support the shore party by laying down a broadside on the treeline. That would involve some accurate shooting as they didn't want the shot to fall short onto the barge.

Wolverton himself commanded the guns and Marty watched with a certain amount of pride as the broadside crashed into the trees sending the French running for cover.

Back in Marty's cabin, Shelby was checking Ryan over.

"Well, young man, apart from the musket ball I've just extracted from your buttock, which I might say you were lucky was almost spent, you seem to be fine," the physician told him.

"How are the other two?" Ryan asked through gritted teeth as he pulled his trousers up.

"One will be fine after a couple of weeks rest. The other, I'm afraid, will take much longer if he recovers at all. The musket ball hit him in the abdomen, and I had to stitch his intestine back together. The prognosis is never good for those type of injuries."

Marty knew the man was lucky as Shelby was skilled in his art not like most of the butchers acting as surgeons in the fleet. He would stand the best possible chance of not dying of the stinking rot of anybody in the Navy.

Ryan lay face down on Marty's sofa as he gave his report.

"It all started rather well, we followed the river inland, mapping as we went, until, after three days, we came to the foothills. Maida is off to the south of the river on the top of a line of hills. It seems, the people around here have a thing about building their towns on the top of hills not in valleys. We didn't encounter any French patrols, but we did see signs of their passing, mainly burnt out farmhouses and fresh graves. They are stealing all the food, leaving the locals with nothing. The poor bastards are starving. We had a hard time finding food.

I decided we needed to establish the strength of the French force for ourselves, so we got Francesco to guide us to their camp. We found an olive grove on a hill that overlooked it and settled down to count tents and the like. While we were there, we were joined by some of the Partisans. They hate the French with a passion and are ready to send the country up in flames.

That is, all but one of them. We were betrayed but we spotted the patrol being led right to us by one of the men we had met the night before. After that it was a running fight to get back to the bay and get picked up. I copped a ball in the arse as we were just entering a big olive grove about a mile inland and the other two got hit covering my retreat. It was all a bit of a mess really."

"You did well," Marty reassured him, "not many would have been able to lead their men out of that situation. What happened to Francesco?"

"He went back to find our betrayer. I wouldn't want to be in his shoes when Francesco finds him. He was very angry, and those Sicilians take revenge very seriously."

They sailed into Palermo to find the harbour full of British warships and transports. The flagship, Pompée flew a signal with their number and 'captain repair aboard.' He took Ryan with him and was rowed over.

The two came to attention as they came aboard and saluted the quarterdeck, they were immediately taken down to the Admiral's cabin.

Sir Sidney Smith and Major General Stuart were sat at the table waiting for them.

"Captain Stockley. Welcome," Sir Sidney greeted him. "is your lieutenant wounded?" He asked as Ryan limped over from the door.

"Shot in the course of performing the reconnaissance Sir," Marty replied. "He caught a musket ball in a rather awkward place."

Smith called for his steward and had several cushions brought to ease Ryan's discomfort and when they were all settled asked Marty to introduce himself and their mission to Stuart.

"I command a specialist flotilla under the command of Naval Intelligence, and it is our job to reconnoitre, infiltrate, disrupt and otherwise inconvenience the enemy at every opportunity," Marty told him. "Lieutenant Thompson commanded a small team who have spent a week in the Gulf of Eufemia scouting the lands around the Lamato river up to the town of Maida, where the incumbent French Army are camped."

They now had Stuart's full attention and Marty bade Ryan make his report, which he did, explaining the maps they had made, the temper of the people and the numbers and types of troops they had seen before being chased out.

At the end Stuart sat back with a satisfied gleam in his eye, but Smith looked at Marty and asked,

"While all that was happening, I think I can be safe in assuming you didn't just sit around and wait for the good lieutenant and his men to return?"

"No sir, in accordance with our standing orders we made a nuisance of our selves taking one cargo vessel, two corvettes and burnt a frigate."

Smith's eyebrows went up. He had seen the corvettes but burning a frigate?

"Pray tell," he said with a slightly disbelieving look.

Marty recounted the attack on Naples Harbour, keeping it factual and leaving nothing out. He concluded by passing the written report to the Admiral.

Stuart sat back in his chair and laughed.

"It would seem, Sir Sidney, that our friend has removed all possible opposition to our landing," he guffawed.

"And as he's under Hood's orders, I don't get to see a penny of the prize money!" Smith grumbled.

Chapter 11: The Swedish Knight

Admiral Sir Sidney Smith invited Marty to dinner. Marty couldn't refuse, so at eight o'clock on the dot he entered the Admiral's sitting room and accepted a glass of Madeira. Stuart was there, Smith's Flag Captain William Tremayne, a Cornishman originally from Falmouth and, to his surprise, Captain Turner.

Turner greeted him warmly and introduced him to Tremayne who was a florid faced, slightly overweight man of about five feet seven. Sir Sidney and Stuart were in deep conversation, so they were left to chat. Things seemed to be going well until a small man with a shock of sandy hair came in and whispered something in Sir Sidney's ear whose head spun around as he looked at Marty in surprise.

"Oh bugger! I think our host just found out something I would have rather kept quiet," Marty said quietly to Turner who had also observed the exchange.

They were saved from further speculation when the steward announced,

"Dinner is served, gentlemen, if you would be so kind to make your way to the dining room."

Smith looked concerned and Marty pointedly sat below the other two captains in strict order of military rank. Turner took his seat with a smile and Tremayne looked confused.

"My clerk has told me you are rather more than just a captain," Sir Sidney broached the subject from the other end of the table, "a Baron and a Knight of the Bath as well."

"That is correct," Marty confirmed. "But in the service, I am just Captain Stockley. It avoids awkward incidents." He continued with a smile.

"Quite, quite," Sir Sidney agreed though it was obvious he was having trouble with the idea that the young captain at the other end of the table outranked him socially.

Tremayne looked surprised and looked across the table at Turner who just grinned back at him.

"How are Caroline and the children?" Turner asked Marty by way of diverting the conversation to something more mundane.

"They are well, and last I heard they were down at the farm in Dorset," Marty replied and then a look of realisation crossed Tremayne's face.

"Damned if I don't know you now!" he cried, "you're that chap who married Lady Candor!"

The evening, Marty thought, had reached its low, that was until Turner gleefully recounted his adventures in Toulon. Then it hit rock bottom.

Marty and Ryan were summoned to the flagship again the next day and this time all the commanding officers of Stuart's army were in attendance. Ryan was asked to give his report again and copies of his maps were distributed. At the end, Stuart announced that the landing would take place on the thirtieth of June meaning, they would embark on the twenty-seventh.

The majority of the troops were in Messina so the whole fleet would up-anchor and sail there with the tide on the morrow. Marty was 'invited to attend' as an extra frigate would do no harm. This meant he would have to leave his prizes in Palermo, he needed a full crew if he was going to have to fight.

So far, his first encounter with Sir Sidney Smith hadn't gone at all well in his estimation. The admiral had a reputation of being sensitive about his status and about how long it had taken the British to award him a knighthood. He was still known as the Swedish Knight because the Swedes were the first to award him the honour. His British one had come much later.

He left the prizes with harbour watches on board and set sail, the Formidiable was ordered to scout ahead and warn the fleet if there were any hostile craft on the route to the landing. He took his time and made sure he was fully replenished with fresh before leaving as the slow-moving fleet had to get to Messina, embark the troops and their equipment and even with the best organisation in the world that would take a couple of weeks.

A week later, they were patrolling along the invasion route, they sailed up as far as Naples and then back down to Sicily. When they saw the island, they turned around and repeated the exercise. Apart from the usual fishing boats and the odd coastal trader they saw nothing of interest.

They would make a Southward leg to arrive to the North of the Straights of Messina on the twenty-seventh and meet the fleet just North of Sicily. Marty had the Formidiable sail up to within hailing distance of the Pompée and shouted a report across to Tremayne that the route was clear of enemy ships. He was told to scout out to the horizon ahead of the fleet just in case any had decided to sail down from Rome.

Beware the ill will of Admirals, he thought to himself.

The landings were unopposed but further North than Marty expected, by an old tower that must have been a lookout post in times gone by. Stuart got all his men and his supplies ashore and set up a base camp from where his campaign could begin.

The Formidiable was again sent out to act as a picket, patrolling out to sea to spot potential threats. Then on the third of July they were summoned back to the fleet and replaced by one of Smith's own frigates. Marty was signalled to attend the Admiral and as soon as they anchored, he was rowed to the Pompée.

"Sit down Captain, make yourself comfortable," Smith said as he was ushered into the cabin and after the usual pleasantries continued,

"I would like you to accompany Major General Stuart on his campaign."

Marty was surprised to hear that but held his tongue and waited for Sir Sidney to continue, after a moment he stood and turned to stare out of the transom window.

"The army doesn't appreciate the interference of Admirals in their operations and I cannot go ashore personally to observe his movements."

Marty had a glimmer of what was to come. "But you, with your peculiar role could offer the assistance of your marine sharpshooters without causing him offence."

"And provide you with an unbiased report of what goes on?" Marty concluded.

"Quite," Sir Sidney replied and waited expectantly.

"A squad of twenty marines and teams of gunners with some smaller Navy pieces that can be transported easily?" Marty offered.

"Why yes, that would be perfect!" beamed Sir Sidney.

Marty thought for a minute and then added,

. "Four six-pound guns should be enough. I saw a couple of old four wheeled waggons on shore, we can take the wheels off them to make field carriages

Sir Sidney's smile got even broader. "Absolutely! I would be obliged if you would make it so, Captain Stockley."

"I will send a message to General Stuart immediately; can I impose on you for paper and a pen?" Marty asked.

Thirty minutes later the message was on its way to the General and Marty was talking to Tremayne about borrowing four of the six-pounders he had on the quarterdeck of the Pompée.

"You only have carronades?" he asked in surprise when Marty told him why.

"Apart from the main battery of eighteen-pound longs we carry; four sixty-eight pounders on the quarterdeck and two more on the fore."

"Remind me not to get into a fight with your ship at close range," laughed Tremayne.

The midshipman who had carried Marty's message to General Stuart returned with a written reply. Marty was more than welcome to join him as were his sharpshooters and guns.

There followed an intense period of activity where the guns were barged over to the shore and several ships carpenters and their mates turned them into field pieces by building improvised carriages with wheels from the carts. Yeovilton came over to oversee the whole operation and was like a mother hen with a clutch of chicks.

A pair of handcarts were 'borrowed' from the Army to be converted into limbers to carry the powder and shot. The guns and the ammunition would be hauled by the gunners under the command of Lieutenant Trenchard. The Marines would join the Army skirmishers and were resplendent in their red coats and gleaming pipe clayed belts. Captain la Pierre took the opportunity to get some shore time and took personal command of them.

So it was on the fourth of July when scouts reported that the French Army under General Reynier was advancing down the North bank of the River Maida. The Army, a Special Operations Flotilla contingent of Marines and a battery of four, six-pound cannon, marched to confront them.

They followed the coast south fording the two small rivers between the camp and the Amato, *the marines have gotten the better of it,* Marty thought as he watched his gunners hauling the guns and ammunition along at the rear of the column.

Ropes were attached and were run out behind the gun and limber for the men to haul on. The big wheels made it easier, but the dust kicked up by close to five thousand troops was making their lives miserable.

Marty was better off as he was riding a horse loaned to him by the General and was with General's command party off to the side of the column. Blaez trotted along beside him. He was more than impressed with the performance of his men who manoeuvred the guns as if they did it every day and would make sure they would be rewarded when they got back aboard...

A scout arrived and reported that the French were about three miles inland on the same side of the river then turned and dog trotted back the way he came. He was dressed in an odd uniform and when Marty asked about it was told that he was a member of the Royal Corsican Rangers a light infantry unit that specialised in skirmishing.

"Damn fellows do everything at a trot," Stuart observed.

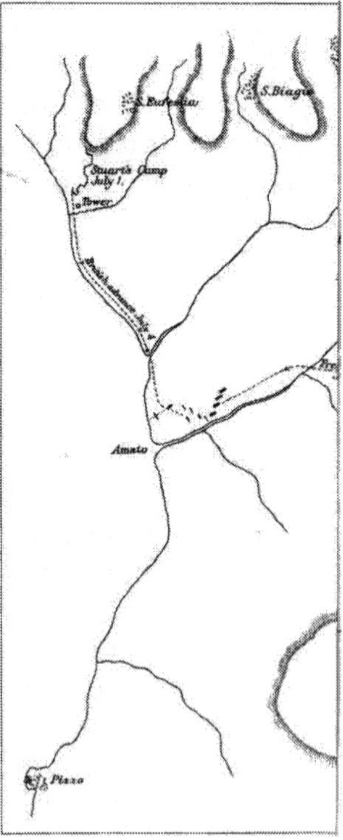

The battle of Maida
Courtesy of Wikipedia.

Stuart had chosen his ground carefully and ordered his units into echelon left formation as soon as they caught sight of the French. The French formed up in a similar formation but unlike the British, who were formed up in line, they formed up in columns with their light infantry leading on their left.

Marty scanned the field with a small pocket telescope he had brought with him. He could see the skirmishers advancing ahead of the main body of troops and exchanging fire with the French Voltigeurs. He looked for his marines but couldn't see any red coats, but then he spotted the familiar figure of Paul la Pierre dressed in a nondescript grey jacket and black marine hat. It looked like the boys had taken a leaf out of the Corsican's book and dressed for the occasion.

The skirmish turned into a hand to hand brawl as the two groups made full contact. There was evidently no love lost between the Corsicans, Sicilians and Marines on the one side and the French on the other as they fought with a savage intensity.

A command must have been given as the allied skirmishers suddenly fell back in an orderly retreat supported by elements sent forward from the Advanced Guard who held the British right flank. Marty scanned the line with his telescope and saw that the forward French column of Light Infantry was advancing on the British right.

His guns were positioned on the British left flank with the First Brigade and opened with their first salvo of the day. The echo of the shots was dying away when the French opened in reply.

"Damn, but they have us outnumbered!" General Stuart exclaimed after scanning the French formations with his telescope.

"Keep steady we can thrash them yet!" he shouted, but Marty wasn't sure anybody in the line could hear him.

Stuart turned in the saddle to look to the rear. "Where the hell is the 20th Foot?" he asked

The 20th had been sent out on a diversionary raid earlier and had failed to get back in time for the main event.

The French light regiment had advanced to within one hundred and fifty yards when the British, under Colonel Kempt, opened fire with their first volley. The front two ranks fell but the column reformed and kept marching forward, stepping over the wounded and dead.

At eighty yards the British fired their second volley. More troops fell and through the smoke Marty saw an officer who was obviously wounded urging his men on. He raised his Durs Egg Carbine and took aim; the range was about one hundred and twenty yards. His horse fidgeted throwing his aim off and he patted its neck to calm him and tried again.

The French were just over twenty yards from the British line when he pulled the trigger just before the British fired their third volley. Now there was so much smoke he couldn't see if he had scored a hit or not.

The third volley was all the French could stand, the column broke and started to run away. The British charged, bayonets glinting in the sun, howling and hollering their challenge and blood lust. Marty expected them to stop once the French left the field, but they just kept going; their commander had lost control.

It wasn't over yet! The two French columns to the right of the defeated light infantry were advancing on the British 2nd Brigade under Colonel Acland who fired their first volley at around three hundred yards and kept up a withering fire after that. The French knew their left flank had run and, disheartened, stalled in their advance. The French commander realised what was happening and ordered the next two elements, that Stuart told Marty were Polish brigades, up in support.

But it was to no avail the Poles were routed by a bayonet charge and the French Cavalry were sent into the fray along with the Swiss. The British immediately performed a parade ground evolution and went from line into square which was good against the cavalry but not so good against the French artillery that took its opportunity to make a real nuisance of themselves.

"Can your pieces target the French guns?" Stuart asked Marty, "if you can silence them, the 20th Foot are approaching and can flank the French."

"Aye Aye Sir!" Marty replied and spun his horse to gallop over to the left flank and the battery. Blaez ran along beside him enjoying every minute.

"Mr Trenchard, General Stuart would be mightily obliged if you would target the French artillery and stop them annoying our boys fighting those Chasseurs," he shouted as soon as he reached them.

"Aye Sir!" came the reply and the crews levered the pieces around towards the enemy right flank.

"Five hundred yards Sir?" Ackermann asked as Marty had the advantage of the extra height from the saddle of his horse.

Marty stood in the stirrups and stared as the French position for a few seconds.

"More like five hundred and fifty," he replied.

Trenchard made the adjustment and the guns roared. Marty was surprised that they didn't sound as loud as they did on ship, but the smoke was just the same. When it cleared he reported,

"Short twenty yards."

No adjustment was necessary as now the barrels were hot; they would throw a little further. The guns roared again.

"Oh! Good shooting, that landed right in the middle of them. Give them another!"

Meanwhile, the 20th Foot had made their ground and were pouring flanking fire into the French who broke and ran. It was all over.

Marty sat with the other commanders and General Stuart enjoying a celebratory meal.

"Damn fine shooting by your men, I will mention it in my report," he congratulated Marty.

"Thank you, sir, I will be in your debt," Marty replied.

"Not at all my boy!" Stuart laughed and slapped him on the shoulder.

"What was the butchers bill in the end?" Marty asked.

"Not that bad at all!" Acland replied, "forty-five dead and two hundred and eighty-two wounded."

That still sounded like a lot to Marty, but the Army fellows seemed to think they had gotten off light.

"We estimate the French lost around five hundred killed and another thousand or so wounded," Stuart explained with a satisfied grin.

That puts it into perspective, Marty thought.

"Where have the French run to?" Marty asked, wondering where the majority had gone as they had only captured around seven hundred and a few cannons so far.

"Scattered to different towns," Stuart replied, sipping his wine and looking thoughtful.

"I say, Captain, would you do me a final favour?"

"If it's in my power, of course Sir." Marty replied.

"I've had a report that that part of the Polish Brigade has buggered off down the coast and is holed up in some town called Tropea. Do you know it?" Stuart asked.

"Why yes Sir, its south of here," Marty replied.

"Don't suppose you could run down there in your ship, put the fear of god into them with your guns and persuade them to surrender, could you?"

Marty grinned at him. "It will be my pleasure Sir."

Stuart raised his glass, which had been discretely refilled by his stewards along with everyone else's,

"A toast! To the Navy, may their winds be fair and their aim straight and true!" he proposed.

"TO THE NAVY!" shouted the rest and downed their glasses to heeltaps.

Marty had his men barge Tremayne's guns back to the Pompée. As they were being lifted aboard, Tremayne invited Marty up to the quarterdeck.

"His Lordship would like to speak to you. I will take care of getting my guns back where they belong, unless you want to trade your sixty-eights for them?" he said with a grin.

"Not a chance," Marty replied as he set off for the Admiral's cabin.

"Captain Stockley Sah!" bellowed the marine crashing his musket but on to the deck where the timbers showed signs of a lot of previous abuse.

"Come," called the brisk voice of Sir Sidney.

Marty entered to find the Admiral pacing up and down in front of the transom windows reading a letter. Marty stood in the centre of the room with his hat firmly under his arm.

"Damn the man, what does he think he is doing?" he finally blurted out in exasperation.

"My Lord?" Marty asked.

Sir Sidney stopped pacing and looked out of the window.

"Against my advice, General Stuart has decided not to liberate Naples but to consolidate his hold over Calabria by taking a few minor fortresses in the area and then maybe having a go at Capri! He feels he needs to ensure the protection of Sicily!"

Marty felt there was more to come, so just waited, then the Admiral spun his top half around so he could look at Marty over his shoulder.

"Did he discuss it with you?"

"Not at all Sir. Never mentioned it," Marty replied.

The Admiral sighed, walked over to his desk, and slumped down in the chair. His honours glinted in the sunlight on his uniform jacket.

"Please, take a seat," he said and waved at one of the comfortable chairs.

"His report of you and your men's conduct is exemplary. He said you managed to wing the commander of their 42nd Infantry?"

"I took a pot-shot at him at around one hundred and twenty yards, didn't see if I hit him as the front rank gave forth with a volley at around the same time. The smoke you know."

"Hmmph, well at least you got to see action. Do you have your report?"

"Aye Sir." Marty said, and handed over the packet.

Sir Sidney read it from end to end. `

"Are you normally this modest? You will never get a mention in the gazette writing like this," he remarked as he finished it. "You don't even mention shooting the French colonel."

"Didn't kill him Sir, so didn't think it worth mentioning," Marty replied.

Sir Sidney looked at him and remembered what Collingwood had told him. This unassuming young man was a renowned killer, merciless in pursuit of his mission, had been behind enemy lines more often than any other member of the Navy and had run up more prize money than most of the other frigate captains in the fleet.

He was frankly jealous of him if he was honest with himself. To make matters worse, he had an independent command, he wanted to bully him but had the distinct impression that wouldn't work, a gentle touch was probably the best idea.

Marty was watching him carefully, reading his expression and body language. He saw the conflict in him and saw him force himself to relax.

"Collingwood informed me you report to Admiral Hood; how does that work?" he asked in the end.

"The Flotilla is independent from the Navy proper," Marty explained and went on to tell him that they had general orders and cooperated with the Foreign Office intelligence branch to identify targets and missions that would disrupt and otherwise inconvenience the enemy.

"You also carry out missions at the request of the local commander?"

"If it doesn't conflict with an ongoing mission," Marty explained, "and they usually ask us to do something that the regular Navy won't or doesn't have the skills to do."

"And those skills are?"

"Oh, the usual things for undercover and 'dirty' jobs. Subterfuge, assassination, robbery, that kind of thing," Marty said with a smile.

"I shall bear that in mind," he replied with a shudder. "Sounds thoroughly dishonourable. What will you do next?"

Marty ignored that; he didn't give a fig for the overblown and, in his opinion, overrated honour code that most 'gentlemen' adopted when it suited them.

"General Stuart has asked me to drop into Tropea and have a look at a couple of Polish companies that ended up there after running from the field."

"Good lord! And what will you do when you get there?"

"Ask them to surrender," Marty smiled gently.

"And if they don't?"

"Then we will have to persuade them," the smile turned feral.

The Admiral dismissed him and after he left turned around his chair so he could see the Formidiable through the window, his brow creased in thought. He couldn't help but like Martin even if he was unfathomable to him at the moment. He obviously had his own honour code that was very different from the norm and was everything that Collingwood told him. He sighed; he would make a point to get to know him better. He turned back to his desk and wrote a note inviting General Stuart to visit him for dinner.

Marty was greeted in the prescribed manner when he got back to his ship and by Blaez in his way with paws on chest and an overactive tongue.

"Mr. Ackermann, is everyone back on board?"

"Aye sir, the last of them came on just fifteen minutes ago."

Marty looked up at the pennant and saw the wind was from the Northeast.

"Let's get the ship underway, take us out of here and get us down to Tropea. We have some Poles to talk to."

He left Ackermann to up anchor and get the ship away from the fleet. They fired a salute to the Admiral and managed the manoeuvre without bumping into any of the other ships.

It wasn't far to Tropea, and three hours later they were anchored off the beach. Marty studied the coastline; it was lined with cliffs and the main part of the town was built at the top. There was a small fishing port in a cove and what looked to be steps cut into the cliff leading up to the town and a track that wound its way up as well.

There were a lot of men in grey uniforms visible at the top of the cliffs who were watching them in return.

"Bring around the barge Sam and have the boys man it. They need to be fully armed and ready for a fight if we need to. Have Franco bring that volley gun he is so fond of and something to fly as a flag of truce."

"Do you want them dressed in their best?" Sam asked.

"No, I want them to look like killers," Marty replied.

Sam smiled; they were back to business as usual.

"Mr. Ackermann, if we are not back in the barge in an hour, I want you to demonstrate our fire power against that building on top of the cliff there," he said, pointing to a large building built close to the edge of the cliffs. The carronades could be elevated high enough to hit it.

The barge rowed up to the dock and pushed in between two fishing boats and tied on. Four of the men and Blaez jumped ashore and made a show of checking that it was safe. Marty stepped onto the dock followed by the other two shadows. They were fairly bristling with weapons, Franco was carrying a nine barrelled Nock volley gun and looked like he was looking for an excuse to use it.

Marty had his weapons harness with his two Manton double barrelled pistols clipped on, his fighting knife on his right side and his hanger on the left. He also had knives very visibly in the top of his high boots.

Blaez stood on his right, fully attired in his battle collar with its one-inch spikes, Sam on his left armed with a short broad headed spear he had the armourer make him, and a pair of Sharpe's pistols that Marty had gifted him clipped to his belt.

They left two men with the barge and the rest formed up behind Marty as he walked off the dock. The fishermen who were mending their nets decided to go home for lunch at the sight of them.

As they got to the area where the steps led upwards and the track started off inland, a mounted group of nine men in grey uniforms trotted to meet them.

The leader saluted when they pulled up. "*I am Lieutenant Pietrzak, who do I have the pleasure of greeting?*" he said, haughtily in French.

"Captain Stockley, Royal Navy, I wish to talk to your commanding officer," Marty replied, standing casually with his hands behind his back.

"What do you wish to discuss with the Colonel?" Pietrzak asked, looking disinterested.

"Do you always talk to a superior officer from horseback?" Marty replied in a dangerously low voice.

"I think I can talk from wherever I like as you have foolishly come ashore with so few men."

Marty's hand flashed forward as he threw the knife he had ready behind his back. The blade sunk deeply into the lieutenant's shoulder with a wet thud and suddenly the Polish troops were confronted with a dozen cocked pistols and a volley gun.

"If you would all kindly dismount," Marty asked with a wave of one of his pistols. *"We don't want any more misunderstandings, do we."*

They disarmed the soldiers and the two officers and mounted their horses. There were enough for them all to ride and one spare they put the wounded lieutenant on after Sam retrieved Marty's knife. Blaez walking behind the Polish soldiers; herding them forward with the occasional growl, they started up the track. It was slow going, and it took fifteen minutes to get to the top where they were confronted by a double rank of grey uniforms with their muskets at the ready.

At the centre stood a man that Marty assumed was the Colonel. He stopped his horse, dismounted, stepped up beside the Lieutenant and indicated he should dismount.

Once he was down, he took him by the arm and led him forward until they were a scant five yards from the Colonel.

"You are the commanding officer?" Marty asked.

"Colonel Warovzki, 19th Polish Infantry," he replied in strongly accented English. "Do you always assault officers sent to greet you?"

"Only if they offend me by being rude. You should get him to a surgeon."

"Alas ours was killed in the battle, we only have a number of orderlies to tend our wounded," he replied.

"If we can continue in a civilized manner, I will have my physician come over from my ship, he is very skilled," Marty offered and put away his pistol.

The Colonel looked at him and decided he actually liked what he saw and nodded. He gave a command in Polish and the troops lowered their muskets to parade rest.

Marty waved a hand to his men and there were clicks as hammers were returned to half cock and the pistols hooked back on belts.

"Sam and Antton, stay with me, the rest of you get back to the ship and bring Mr Shelby, his assistant and his medical chest back here," he ordered and then to the Colonel,

"Can we impose on you for the use of the horses?"

"Certainly. Come, we will go to my headquarters to continue in a 'civilized' way," he replied, inclining his head and holding out his arm in the direction they would walk.

He snapped some orders at the Lieutenant, who looked miserable and gave orders that dispersed the men.

"If I hadn't agreed and taken you prisoner, what would have happened next?" he asked in a conversational tone as they walked.

"My ship would have demolished this town one house at a time until you released me, if you were still alive that is," Marty replied without a hint of a smile.

They continued in silence through the narrow streets until they came to a square with a tree in the middle of it where a half dozen cats loitering around as though they owned the place. There was a large house at the back that had been commandeered as the headquarters.

Blaez tensed then shot forward, chasing cats was one of his favourite sports. The cats scattered; some went up the tree others headed to the houses. Blaez followed the ones that went up the tree and stood on his hind legs with his front paws on the tree trunk with a look that said, "Look what I dun boss!"

"Is your dog grinning?" Warovski asked Marty as he eyed the dog curiously.

"Yes, he is enjoying himself, makes a change from chasing midshipmen up the mast," Marty joked.

They sat around a large dining table while drinks were served. A plate of bread with some kind of meat paste spread on top was placed in the centre of the table. It had a distinct red colour and Marty eyed it suspiciously.

"A local delicacy," the Colonel explained, "it is nduja, a type of sausage the locals make with hot pepper in it. I like it but it may be too hot for you."

Sam stepped forward and took a piece before Marty had a chance to taste it for himself. His eyes widened after he put it in his mouth and then he grinned.

"That's some good stuff Captain!" he grinned as he picked up another piece before stepping back.

Marty picked a small piece and took a bite; the heat of the peppers in the cured meat hit him and got hotter.

"Strewth Sam! You must have a mouth made of old leather!" he gasped, his eyes watering. He gulped a glass of wine but that just seemed to make it hotter.

Warovzki looked amused and said,

"It's an acquired taste, you get used to it."

Marty waited a minute or so until the fire damped down to smouldering embers and then continued.

"The main body of our Army will catch up with you soon and I have been sent ahead to offer you terms for surrender. There has been enough bloodshed and we would like to prevent any unnecessary casualties if they can be avoided."

"Like my Lieutenant?" Warovzki asked pointedly.

"I needed to make a point."

Warovzki looked at him with a flat stare and Marty prepared himself to react if needed, but then the Colonel sighed and said, "allying ourselves with the French was always a matter of necessity rather than choice. We have done our duty, what are your terms?"

The discussion was simple after that. The terms were:

Lay down your arms and you will be allowed to march back to the North under parole. You agree not to take part in any more hostilities towards the British or their allies.

It was agreed. Shelby arrived, set up a field hospital and went to work. Marty sent a message to Stuart by the ship's cutter and midshipman Longstaff and the marines came ashore to collect the Pole's weapons. Marty never did get used to nduja, but Sam got his hands on a string of twenty or so and took them back on board as private stores. He let some of the men try it when they asked, and the result was a queue at the heads and some sore backsides.

Back in Gibraltar, Marty reunited with his team and was impressed at how well they had settled into their new home. His own quarters had been set up for him by Fletcher and were comfortable with a suite of rooms that included a bedroom, sitting room and a dining room. His Lieutenants had even adapted one room to be a communal bathroom but where they found the tin hip bath he never did find out.

He paid his respects to Admiral Collingwood who read his report and thanked him for his assistance. He said he would buy in the corvettes as they were always useful. Even so he seemed distracted and worried about something and as Marty was about to leave asked,

"By the way, how were General Stuart and Sir Sidney getting along when you left?"

Marty sat back down and looked the Admiral in the eye.

"To be frank, they were disagreeing on what the next step should be in the campaign. Sir Sidney believed they should go on and liberate Naples, but General Stuart wanted to consolidate his hold on Calabria and mop up the rest of the French garrisons, then maybe take Capri to exert some control over the bay of Naples. I think he is more concerned with defending Sicily."

"Which of them do you think is right?'

Marty sighed; he had been afraid he would be asked this,

"it is my belief you should not leave an enemy behind you unless they be dead or demobilised, and I think Stuart has the right approach at this time."

Collingwood looked at him for a long moment and Marty braced himself for a roasting for not supporting a senior officer, but the Admiral smiled and replied.

"that was also my thought and that, as the General on the ground, Stuart would have a better overview of the situation." He paused, and then continued. "I have had a letter from General Stuart asking that I relieve Sir Sidney from command due to unremitting interference in the land battle that is the sole responsibility of the Army."

"Unresolved frustration and a desire for a grand gesture on one side and a lack of tolerance to suggestions on the other," Marty observed.

"Quite, but as the General has formally made the request I don't have any choice but to replace him," Collingwood concluded.

"May I make a suggestion?" Marty ventured.

"Please speak your mind, Captain."

"They are scheduled to return to Sicily soon, anyway, so why not leave Sir Sidney there until they do and then 'find him' something else to do. That way you satisfy General Stuart and save Sir Sidney from a loss of face."

"Are you sure I cannot tempt you into becoming one of my Flag Officers?" Collingwood asked.

Marty took that as a rhetorical question and held his peace. Collingwood took the hint.

"Thank you for your assistance, I will let Mr. Ridgley know if I need your assistance again," he said in dismissal.

Marty had one last question.

"May I ask Sir, if a regular source of information would help the defence of Sicily?"

Chapter 12: A Spanish Cruise

A visit to 17B Devils Tower Road planted the suggestion that they could probably set up a similar method of infiltrating agents into Spain and Italy as they had for France. Ridgley agreed to look out for likely organisations they could work with or take over. He informed Marty that he was already setting up a network of agents and this idea fit into his plans very nicely, thank you.

"In the meantime, could you and your boys run up the East coast of Spain, disrupt their semaphore operations and burn any boatyards along the way? Oh! And by the way, Fox will be moving to Sicily to take over the defence of both there and Malta."

"Who will be taking over here then?" Marty asked.

"Don't know yet, but I should be informed in the next set of dispatches."

Marty wasn't happy with his latest task, it smacked of a lack of imagination or even an attempt to get him out of the way for a while. He looked down at Blaez, who strolled along beside him.

"Well, idle hands get into mischief. Let's see what we can stir up while we are out there."

When he got back to base, he called an all-officers meeting.

"Gentlemen, we have orders to go up the east coast of Spain, destroy semaphore towers and burn boatyards," he looked around saw disappointment on their faces. "But as these 'orders' were couched as more of a request I intend to give the entire flotilla an outing and cause as much mayhem as possible." That brought back the grins he noted.

"I want everyone except a guard detail on board their ships and ready to go on the turn of the tide tomorrow morning."

Shelby approached him on the Formidiable that afternoon as he watched Ackermann finalizing the provisioning with Fletcher.

"Permission to visit the flagship before we leave Captain," he asked, "I would like to have a look and see how the Admiral is fairing before we leave and to make sure he has enough medication."

"I don't suppose you will tell me what is wrong with him?" Marty asked, knowing the answer.

"Patient confidentiality prevents me saying, but I can say he should not be here and would be better off at home."

Oh lord, he's that bad is he, Marty thought but said.

"Take the gig and please give him my compliments."

The Eagle was first to leave as she was their scout and Marty wanted her an hour or more ahead of them to spot potential targets. The Formidiable led the rest with Frasier, commanding the Hornfleur a cable behind him and the Alouette out to windward.

They kept to a gentle pace of around eight knots and Marty had them running the usual practice exercises. They didn't expect to see any French or Spanish country ships as they cruised along the South coast.

He had it in mind to have a look into Malaga. The city was prosperous and had a history that went back centuries, he had also heard that the Granadans particularly hated the French. They cruised leisurely into the bay at around six that afternoon, flying Spanish flags.

Marty couldn't believe his eyes! There was a French third-rate anchored right in the middle. She looked like she had gotten the worst of some weather and pulled in for repairs. There were a plethora of small boats running back and forth from the beach and her main mast was missing its top two thirds.

"Well, well, well," he said to Wolfgang Ackermann, "the sun is shining on the righteous today. Please go to quarters, but do not run out, and signal our consorts to do the same. Take or burn do you think?"

"It would make more of an impression if we burnt her," Second Lieutenant Trenchard suggested as he studied her through his telescope.

"But the blast if her magazine goes up would flatten half the docks district and that is not what we want. If we sink it in the bay it won't block the port and it will be a permanent reminder that the French can be beaten."

He pondered for a minute.

"Double shot the guns and load the carronades with smashers. I want the carronades to concentrate on her waterline and shoot the bottom out of her. The main batteries to wreck her upper works. Low charges so we don't shoot all the way through, we don't want our shot landing in the town! Don't run out until we raise our own colours."

They had fifteen minutes to wait before they would be in position as they cruised along at less than four knots under topsails.

Marty planned to anchor beside the sixty-four towards the bow, attach springs then begin. He trusted James to try and position the Alouette across her stern and the Hornfleur to pass him so they could rake the French bow from ahead. He would begin as soon as everyone was in place.

James did exactly as he expected, veering to larboard to anchor behind the sixty-four. The Hornfleur, however, showed all the signs of staying directly behind them. Marty went to the rail and waved his hat at them and when Frasier appeared at the bow, he waved to indicate he should pass him and pointed to the bow of the Frenchman and made a 'T' of his hands.

Frasier ran back to the wheel and the Hornfleur turned to pass the Formidiable. On his larboard side.

Marty gritted his teeth as the whaler masked his guns from the Frenchman while sailing past. If they twigged what was going on, they were in trouble.

It seemed to take forever for the Hornfleur to clear them and then it was time to anchor. It was risky, but he dropped a stern anchor first. They had lashed one to the starboard quarter with its cable looped around to come up their stern and through the transom so all the had to do was cut it loose letting the cable run out before backing the top sail and dropping the best bower anchor as they came to a halt. Then use the capstan to haul back on the stern anchor to get them in position.

The French who were watching jeered this evolution and Marty imagined there were plenty of comments about the ineptitude of Spanish sailors.

The time had come, the springs were set.

“Raise the colours!” Marty called. “Run out! Make every shot count!”

Marty had schooled his men in aimed broadsides and they quickly trained their guns on the gundecks of the Frenchman. He wanted as many of her guns out of action as soon as possible.

As the colours ran up and the union flag streamed out in the breeze a shout went up on the Frenchman, hopefully too late.

The eighteen-pound mains roared, and the big sixty-eight-pound carronades coughed. On the Alouette, James had swung her around as they anchored and gotten right across the stern. His carronades were loaded with a dozen four-pound shot each.

On board the Frenchman chaos ruled. They had been taken completely by surprise thinking that the British fleet was in Sicily and believing that the visiting ships were Spanish. It hadn’t helped that their captain had been hurt during the storm and an inexperienced second lieutenant was in command as the first was with the captain, on shore, at the hospital.

The sound of gunfire in the bay roused the two men from their conversation, the captain lying in bed, his broken leg stretched out, splinted and heavily bandaged.

"Mon Dieu! The British are in the bay!" shouted the first lieutenant as he stared out of the window. He could see his ship, L'Argon, shudder as she was hit by a second broadside from the frigate moored a cable off her starboard bow.

Cunning that, it seriously limits the guns that can fire back, he noted. Was that a French corvette raking the stern? No, she was flying the hated British flag as well, as was the whaler that had gotten across L'Argon's bow.

"What the hell is whaler doing in the Mediterranean?" asked the Captain as the first described the scene.

They shot the poor L'Argon to pieces with only a few shots in return. The carronades blew huge holes in her waterline and she soon started to settle as the sea flooded in. It took scarcely more than an hour for her to become nothing more than a pair of masts sticking up out of the water. Marty ordered the boats into the water to fish out the French survivors.

In the quiet that followed the last gunshot, Marty became aware of cheering coming from the shore. Then as the smoke blew away, he could see that the dock was lined with a large crowd of people cheering and waving the Spanish flag. Now he regretted sending the Eagle ahead as Ryan Thompson and Matai were the only ones to speak Spanish. Matai had gone with Ryan to replace his captain of the mainmast who had broken his arm.

"They are chanting 'death to the French' and 'long live the British'," Midshipman Jonathan Williams told his usual partner in crime, Midshipman Eric Longstaff, as they stood side by side at the rail of the quarterdeck.

Marty gave him a sharp look.

"And how do you know that Mr Williams?" Marty asked from directly behind him.

Williams nearly jumped out of skin at being addressed directly

"My mother is Spanish Sir!"

"Is she now."

"Yes, she still is," the panicked youth stammered and then went bright red when he realised what he had done.

Marty looked at him and grinned.

"Mr Williams, I would be obliged if you would have my barge brought around and manned, we are going on a short trip ashore. Put on your best uniform, we need to put on a show!"

Sam helped Marty into his number one dress jacket which was adorned with his badges of office. Then he buckled on his dress sword and handed him his best hat. Marty had gone the full mile with gold buckled shoes and solid gold buttons. He was out to impress.

A knock at the door and Midshipman Longstaff was pleased to inform him that the barge was ready and a pair of marines "was all scrubbed up and shiny" and ready to accompany him

A last tug of the coat to straighten it, an adjustment of his dress sword and he was ready. Sam was also dressed in his best and preceded him down into the barge. Between them they had enough concealed weapons to take on a platoon.

The boat pulled up at the dock and the marines stepped up to secure the top of the steps before Marty went up followed by Williams and Sam. Williams had borrowed a clean shirt from Longstaff, the gunroom steward had given his shoes a quick polish and his best uniform a brush.

The crowd were cheering and clapping, and Marty waved and grinned back at them. Then there was a shout and a squad of Spanish soldiers muscled their way through the crowd forming a corridor through which a regal looking man approached them.

He said something in very rapid Spanish to Marty. Williams stepped up and translated,

. "This is Don Andreas Carlos de la Borda, he is the Minister for Justice and has been tasked with welcoming you and thanks you for removing the blight of the French from their bay."

Marty replied and told Williams to translate as exactly as he could,

. "I am Captain Sir Martin Charles Stockley, Baron Candor of Cheshire." If the Spanish could do titles and long names so could he. "I am pleased to be of service in helping our Spanish brethren resist the depredations of their so-called French allies and lend assistance wherever I can."

The exchange of pleasantries was quickly repeated through the crowd and Marty's statement was greeted with more cheers. It was followed by an invitation from the, obviously impressed, Don to visit their local ruling elite in the Ayuntamiento.

They were walking side by side and Marty was getting a running commentary of the more historic buildings when the French first lieutenant appeared with a pair of pistols shouting about treachery and pirates. He pointed his pistols at Marty who was reaching for the stiletto in his sleeve when the man's eyes rolled up in his head and he folded to the ground.

A scruffy looking individual dressed in fisherman's garb stood behind him holding a crude club grinning at Marty with a mouthful of rotting and broken teeth. Marty grinned back and said, "Gracias, senior!"

The Don snapped an order to the sergeant and two soldiers picked the Frenchman up and dragged him away. Marty didn't know, or particularly care, where.

They came to an ornate and ancient building, which reminded Marty of the Moroccan style. Entered by large ornate double doors up a flight of steps and were led to a large meeting room. Seated inside were seven aristocratic looking men and one senior military officer. Marty made a leg and bowed to the assembly.

"These men are the governing body for Malaga and the surrounding area," Williams translated and introduced each man in turn ending with the uniformed man who was the local military commander.

The man who had been introduced as the chairman started to speak and Williams gave a phrase by phrase translation.

"We welcome you in the name of the Kingdom of Granada which is in its entirety is opposed to the infernal alliance between the government in Madrid and the French dictator Napoleon. The French ship in the harbour was threatening us with its guns if we did not cooperate with their repairs and behaved more like occupiers than allies." He paused to gesture at his fellow men. "We thank you for your action. It removed a thorn from our side."

Marty bowed and replied,

. "My lords, it was my pleasure, even though my country and yours be at war over a trifling matter we have a common foe in the French and should put aside our differences to push the dictator back from your borders. Alas, I have doubt that the men in Madrid will see it so clearly as we. May I ask what you will do with the French that are still on shore?"

The military gentleman stepped forward.

"The crew will be disarmed and allowed to walk back to Cadiz, the officers are more of a problem. The captain is in hospital with a broken leg, the first lieutenant is in a cell at the rear of this building and the rest of the officers are under house arrest."

Marty thought for a minute.

"Give them to me," and when he saw looks of alarm he continued, "they will be sent to Gibraltar and from there exchanged for British officers that are held by the French.

They will be told that I forced you to give them up under threat of bombardment."

And interrogated by me in the meantime.

This suggestion was welcomed after a brief debate and after a drink to toast their accord Marty and his men returned to the ship.

They made a show of running all the guns out and threatening the town. The governors made sure the locals knew that it was just for show. The French officers were marched to the dock and handed over to a squad of marines under Sergeant Bright's command. The French Captain was carried on a stretcher and the first lieutenant had to be led, as the blow to his head had rattled his brains. His eyes were most definitely crossed, and he had a confused look about him.

Once aboard Shelby went to work examining the Captain and Lieutenant. Ackermann got them under way. Marty gave orders that the officers must be kept apart and not allowed to talk to each other either before or after he talked to them. He started with the most junior.

Sixth Lieutenant Jean-Phillipe Trudeaus was just nineteen years old and was the third son of a baker from Lyon. He had joined the navy to find adventure at sixteen and all he had seen since leaving the naval college was the Mediterranean from Toulon to Cadiz. They had been one of the few ships to get out and patrol the Mediterranean before that demon Nelson had decimated the fleet the previous year.

Now he was a prisoner of the British and his ship was at the bottom of the Bay of Malaga. Worse, he was kept apart from his fellow officers and was being escorted by a silent midshipman to God knows where!

They came to a door which he guessed must be the captain's cabin. A marine guard knocked the door, opened it a crack and said something. There was a response, he was ushered inside and sat on a hard-wooden chair in front of a desk behind which sat a young man in captain's uniform.

He looked around the nicely furnished cabin as the captain was ignoring him for the moment. There was an elegant but functional sideboard with a decanter set and glasses on the top. Judging by the fact the decanters were almost full the Captain wasn't a drinking man. Hung on the wall above the sideboard was a portrait of a stunningly beautiful woman and on either side of her were portraits of two children.

Beside the sideboard, next to one of the stern chasers that was covered in an embroidered cloth, was an open chest that was full of weapons. He gaped, no one had that many!

He was brought back to attention by a polite cough, the captain was watching him with an amused look.

"I am Captain Stockley of his Majesty's Royal Navy and you are?" he asked in perfect French with a Lyon accent.

Jean-Phillipe introduced himself and waited.

"May I offer you a drink?" Captain Stockley asked him politely and when he nodded a steward, who he hadn't notice come into the room, went to the decanters and poured them both a glass of dark liquid.

He took a sip and holy Mary it was strong stuff! He coughed as it burnt his throat and the Captain laughed and said,

"Navy rum. Not as elegant as French brandy but beggars cannot be choosers."

He waited until Jean-Phillipe had regained his composure and then asked.

. *"Have you been in the Navy long?"*

The interview took an hour during which Jean-Phillipe's glass was refilled twice with the almost one hundred proof un-cut rum. It appeared that the Captain was drinking just as much as he was, but the fiery spirit didn't seem to affect him in the slightest.

Marty had in fact drunk none of the rum he had been served but had used sleight of hand to empty his glass into another concealed in the top drawer of his desk. In the hour he had watched the young lieutenant get increasingly comfortable in his surroundings and a flush had risen in his cheeks as the alcohol did its work.

He chatted to him as if they had known each other for years and slipped questions into the conversation about their mission, where they had been and where they were intending on going next.

The next lieutenant in seniority was brought in and Marty went through the same process with him, confirming what the sixth had told him and adding to it. By that evening as he sat eating dinner with Shelby, he knew that L'Argon had sailed from Toulon a month ago and was cruising with a frigate in attendance down towards Corsica when a storm had hit them, and they got separated. A squall had taken out a third of their mainmast and two thirds of their mizzen and they had limped into Malaga bay to make repairs having been driven Southwest.

The captain had been worried about using that particular bay as the Granadans were belligerent towards the French and were at odds with their national government. The French hadn't thought to pay for anything either which had further aggravated the locals.

They had kept the town under their guns as their men acquired the necessary for the ship to be repaired. That was why Marty had such an easy time sinking her as all her available gun crews were manning the guns on the landward side and by the time they got the starboard battery ready it was too late.

It was time to talk to the first lieutenant, Shelby said he was still confused and was suffering from something called concussion.

"Hello, how are you?" Marty asked him as he lay in his cot.

"My Captain! The British!" the lieutenant gasped and tried to sit up.

Marty pushed him back down onto his pillow and made comforting noises.

"It is alright, Steffan you are safe now, all is well," Marty reassured him; he had gotten his name from one of the other officers.

"Our ship, they sunk it! What of the mission?"

Marty needed to know what that was, he had gotten hints from the other officers, but they wouldn't, or couldn't, elaborate on it.

"I have been ordered to complete the mission, but your captain has been sent back to France to recover from his injuries. I need you to help me, his written orders are at the bottom of the bay, sunk by the bloody roast beefs," Marty lied.

The man struggled to focus his eyes on Marty then grimaced as a shaft of pain ran through his head.

"Please, I need to know the details, it is too important not to complete," Marty pleaded.

"We must make the rendezvous at midnight on the tenth of August."

"Yes, we know that" he lied, *"but the exact location?"*

"Marsalforn, Gozo, you must get the agent off before the British discover him! He will be watching for the signal."

Marty assumed he meant a recognition signal.

"What is the signal?"

"A red light over a white which is flashed three times."

"A red light over a white light that gets, flashed three times?"

"No! No! The red light is flashed three times!"

The strain finally overtook him, and he collapsed back onto his cot, his eyes closed.

Well, well, well, Marty thought, *a French agent on Gozo, and therefore in Malta.*

Chapter 13: The Gozo Deception

Marty left the Alouette and the Hornfleur to continue the mission up the East coast of Spain and gave written orders to James that gave him the freedom to do what he thought was necessary. They would rendezvous again in around ten days' time.

They parted company on the fifth of August with the Formidiable heading East to make the three-day trip to Gozo. Marty had the second, third and fourth lieutenants) transferred to the Alouette. He kept the two most junior on board and tasked them to care for their captain and first lieutenant who were under guard in the brig. It was a little crowded with four men, but they were secure. The two junior officers had given their parole so were able to exercise on deck which eased things somewhat.

The trip started out routinely, they neither saw any enemy ships nor experienced any bad weather. It was steaming hot though; with temperatures hitting in excess of eighty degrees Fahrenheit. To make matters worse the wind was on their stern so there was hardly any apparent breeze over the deck. All the crew took to wearing shoes to protect their feet from the hot tar seeping up from between the deck planks.

Gradually the wind dropped to nothing, and they were becalmed. The temperature, which had felt high before, now soared as the sun beat down making the tar melt and drip from the rigging. Lacking anything else to do Marty let those that could swim go over the side and cool off.

At the Master's, suggestion they pulled the barge around and moored it to the bow, tied the gig off towards the stern slung ropes between them so those that couldn't swim could take a dunk by pulling themselves through the water by the rope.

It soon dissolved into chaos as the swimmers started jumping from the deck, with their legs tucked up and arms wrapped around their knees, to splash the non-swimmers like cannonballs dropping from on high. It almost ended in a brawl and Ackermann had to restore order by banning it. Even then one particularly eel-like swimmer scared the life out of a Bosun's mate by swimming under him and grabbing one of his legs. The poor man thought he had been attacked by a denizen of the deep and screamed like a girl to the amusement of the rest of the crew. *Retribution will follow,* Marty thought.

They lost a day and a half before a lookout spotted a wind devil scurrying across the sea towards them. It filled the sails for a few seconds and then died, but another followed and then another until a light breeze had developed and they were making steady way. If they were lucky, they would just make it.

They approached Gozo late morning on the tenth. The weather had turned, and a summer storm had passed over the island leaving it shining and wet. They stayed well out to sea so as not to spook the agent if he was keeping a lookout.

As it got dark, they closed in on the shore to about half a mile and Marty ordered the cutter brought around, a mast rigged, and the lamps mounted.

At just about a quarter before twelve they started in and looked for a signal. They weren't disappointed, a light was shown and flashed three times long and two short. Marty ordered the lamps un-shuttered and made the reply.

As they got to the beach the clouds broke and the moon illuminated a figure moving quickly down towards them.

"Allez vite!" Marty called as if he had spotted someone coming and beckoned the man forward. As he approached something struck Marty as strange in the way he moved. As soon as the bow touched the sand he jumped up and climbed in, gesticulating for them to get out to sea as soon as possible.

Once the boat had turned and was past the surf line the agent worked his way down the cutter to be next to Marty.

"Captain La Fontaine?" said a decidedly feminine voice.

"Yes," replied Marty making a show of concentrating on steering the cutter as he hid his surprise.

"Thank you for being on time. The British were very close to capturing me."

"It is my pleasure, madame. Have they discovered you were spying on them?"

"They suspected, there is a new intelligence officer on the island, and he is very tenacious, we will have to deal with him."

The ship came into view as a silhouette, the spy didn't seem to realise it wasn't a two decker and continued to chat.

"I have the plans; we must get them to Naples so they can plan the retaking of Malta."

Have you really! Marty almost said aloud.

"I had that stupid brigadier eating out of my hand, so it was worth it even if he made love like a pig."

Aah the old honey trap. Marty grinned to himself and swung the tiller to bring them up to the side.

"Will you need assistance to board?" Marty asked politely.

"I can manage, I am wearing trouser," she replied.

They hooked on and Marty shot up the side to warn off the reception committee he had arranged to be waiting at the top.

When she made the deck there was only a minimal side party in evidence and Marty quickly invited her to his cabin, ushering her away before she could look around the deck.

Inside the cabin Marty stripped off his coat, slumped into one of his armchairs and indicated she should do the same. She took off her hat, revealing a shock of long, silky, red hair, and slipped off her coat. She was a looker! With bright blue eyes in a classically beautiful face and even the man's clothes she wore couldn't hide her curves.

"You have me at a disadvantage, you know who I am, but I cannot call you Madam for the entire voyage." Marty grinned at her.

She had been looking at the portrait of Caroline on the wall of his cabin and a small frown creased her brow.

"You may call me Claudette," She replied still looking at the painting.

"Is that your wife?" she asked.

"Yes, it is and my two children," Marty answered with a proud smile.

"That necklace must be worth a king's ransom; did you give it to her?"

Marty looked at the picture and the diamond necklace.

"Yes, I had some good luck in the Caribbean and that was one of the rewards."

I bloody hope the French have a prize system like us he thought a little worried his deception had been rumbled.

Claudette, however, gave him a calculating look and sat a little straighter to display her wares a little more and served him a dazzling smile.

"Have you ever thought of taking a mistress?"

"I might," Marty grinned at her, *"but first the plans? I would like to get them into a safe place before we discuss other possibilities."*

"Tease," she replied with a flutter of her eyelashes and started to unbutton her shirt. She treated Marty to a view of her ample assets before she fished a packet of papers out.

Marty took them from her hand, brushing it with his fingers, making sure she saw him looking. He looked her in the eyes and smiled then went to his desk to examine them. He was surprised to see that there was a detailed plan of Malta with all the fortifications and defences marked with the number and calibre of the guns, regiments, strengths of the troops and ships in the harbour.

He folded the papers, put them into his desk and locked the drawer.

"Let us celebrate with a glass of brandy and you can tell me all about how you seduced the brigadie,." Marty smiled.

Just then there was a knock at the door and Matai came in when Marty called enter.

"Captain you are needed on deck," he announced.

Marty made a disappointed face and gave a gallic shrug as he took up his coat and followed him out of the door.

Claudette went straight to Marty's desk and tried the drawers which were all locked, she then went to the sideboard and started searching that. She was surprised when she heard a splash and the sound of a cable running out, then she realised the ship had stopped.

She was alarmed and redoubled her efforts and found an unlocked drawer with a pistol in it, took it out and cocked it.

"My, my you didn't waste time did you."

She spun around and saw Marty leaning on the door frame. He had changed and now wore his regular uniform.

Her mouth made an O of surprise and her eyes were wide as she recognised it. She raised the pistol and pointed it straight at Marty's chest.

"Who are you?" she asked in almost accent less English.

Marty sketched a bow.

"That would be telling," he grinned at her, "you can call me Captain." He stepped forward until the pistol was only six inches from his chest.

"It's not loaded?" she asked.

"No, I never leave loaded weapons lying around in drawers."

She sighed, shrugged and let it spin around her finger. Marty reached up, took it and returned it to the drawer. The sun was coming up outside and began to shine through the transom windows. Claudette looked through the glass and gasped as she saw they were anchored in Valetta harbour.

Sam came in and stood beside her. She looked him up and down appreciatively,

"If you ever want another job . . . ."

Sam said nothing.

"Search her, she might have a hidden weapon." Marty instructed as he put the finishing touches to his uniform.

Sam grinned and proceeded to thoroughly search her from head to toe extracting an outraged squawk as he made sure he didn't miss anything.

"He's very thorough!" Claudette commented when Sam stepped back.

"I trained him myself," Marty quipped in return, "come we are expected ashore.

"That will be my death warrant," she cried.

"That all depends on you now doesn't it," Marty smiled.

As they reached the dock a reception committee of soldiers and two civilians awaited them. Marty touched his hat in return to the salute from the sergeant in charge of the squad and held out his hand to the civilians.

"Artimus Chadwell," the first introduced himself, "your midshipman said you have a package for us."

"Absalom Jarrett, Commissioner's Assistant," said the second.

That makes you the intelligence officer, Marty thought as he looked over Chadwell a second time.

"Shall we proceed to the residence?" offered Jarrett. "It will be getting damn hot soon and it's much cooler there."

They strolled down the dock to where a carriage waited. Sam climbed up on top while the other three men and Claudette stepped inside. Marty told Sam he could ride inside out of the sun, but he just replied that from on top he could cover both doors.

"The soldiers aren't really necessary she won't get away from Sam." Marty told them.

"Oh, they aren't to stop her running its to stop her compatriots from attempting a rescue," Jarret replied.

"How many of them are there?" Marty asked.

"We know of four, but there may be more." Chadwell informed him.

"Put one up top with Sam and one on the back," Marty suggested, "we can handle four or even a couple more."

Jarrett went to the sergeant and after a brief exchange one man went up on the back of the coach, the sergeant climbed up beside Sam after dismissing the rest of the men. Both were armed with muskets.

They started out and Marty chatted merrily with the other passengers while keeping an eye on what was going on outside. They had travelled about a mile and were coming out of town through a more run-down district when he reached inside his jacket and pulled out his Manton pistols.

"Gentlemen, if you are carrying weapons, I suggest you ready them," he grinned as he cocked the pistols against his forearms.

"If you try and run," he told Claudette, "I will shoot you in the arse," he smiled and winked at her. She knew he meant every word.

Things happened very fast after that; there was a shout, then a shot from above followed by a scream. Marty dove out of the door, rolled up onto his knees, pistols levelled and snapped off two shots. He cocked his second barrels against his forearms and spared a look and a grin for Claudette. There were more shots from the roof of the coach.

He brought his right gun up, aimed carefully and squeezed off a shot. There was a scream. He waited for a full fifteen seconds then stood, his empty gun disappearing inside his jacket.

In the space of a minute, three men died, and another was wounded. The soldier suffered a near miss when a bullet hit the action of his musket, knocking it out of his hands. A shard of the shattered ball left a wound in his forehead which bled profusely but was shallow and not life threatening.

Marty brushed himself off and walked forward swapping his remaining pistol to his right hand and pulling his fighting knife from its sheath behind his back with his left. He looked to the roof of the coach, saw that Sam and the sergeant were reloading. He waited until they were ready then walked forward until he saw a pair of boots protruding from behind a wall. Cautiously he advanced until he could see the body, the face of the man had been ruined by a seventy-five-calibre ball hitting him in the bridge of the nose. Definitely dead, his mother wouldn't recognise him.

He looked up at Sam who pointed with his Sharp's pistol at the corner of a building. Marty again moved carefully and silently until he found the second corpse. This one had taken two bullets through the chest and was lying face down showing the wreck of his back where the balls had exited after flattening out on their way through.

He crossed the road to where he could hear moaning. Through a garden gate in a wall, behind which was a third corpse and a man sitting, holding what remained of his left arm.

He put away his gun, pulled a large handkerchief out of his pocket and applied a tourniquet to the man's bicep above where the ball had shattered his arm just above the elbow.

Chadwell's head appeared over the wall,

"A survivor?" he asked. "Francis said you were deadly, but I had no idea—"

"He was lucky. I wasn't the one who shot him," Marty replied grimly.

They got the man into the coach. Claudette gave a gasp as she recognised him and pulled him onto the seat beside her, cradling him in her arms as the coach rocked and moved on.

"What is his name?" Marty asked her.

"Jerome. Jerome Gasquet," she said through tears.

"He will live, I will have him moved to my ship and our surgeon will treat his wound, but I am afraid his arm is lost."

They reached the mansion. Marty dispatched the coach with the soldiers and the wounded Frenchman to the docks with a note to Shelby. The rest entered, went straight to the drawing room and settled into chairs with relief. It was at least ten degrees cooler than outside. A servant brought cold lemonade which Marty drank with relish. Sam sipped his, and sat in a high-backed chair by the door, obviously guarding against unwanted visitors and the chance that Claudette might bolt. Marty gave him his pistols to reload.

Claudette was in a state of shock; her skin was pale, and her hands shook. She had witnessed the professional violence meted out by Marty and his men to her would be rescuers and that had frightened her. There was far more to this young captain than met the eye and she was terribly afraid of what he might do next.

Marty on the other hand was the most relaxed of the three men and sat drinking his lemonade looking around the room taking in the fine art on display.

Claudette watched as a servant came in and offered to clean his coat. He took it off revealing the weapons harness he had under it. She had never seen anything like it before. It looked to be based on a set of infantry cross belts; the shoulder straps crossed behind his back and attached to his belt but instead of crossing at the front, as the army's did, came straight over his shoulders to attach to his belt just in front of his hips.

Straps ran under his arms from midway up the front vertical straps to the crossing point at the back. His pistols were clipped to these horizontal straps, so they hung down his sides with the buts facing forward slightly forward of his armpits. He had had it made by a master saddle maker, after trying different configurations, the stitching was exquisite and left not a bump to give away the harness's presence.

His fighting knife was in a sheath on his waist belt that was angled across the small of his back, so the hilt was easy to reach with his left hand. His hanger hung over his left hip for a right-hand draw. The position of the knife meant he had to sit erect but that was his natural stance, he wasn't a sloucher, so it didn't matter.

His shirt and jacket cuffs were cut looser than was fashionable to allow access to the stilettoes sheathed on his forearms and, to finish the ensemble, throwing knife hilts protruded from his boot tops which were calf length and laced. What she couldn't see was the laces could be used as a garrotte and lock picks were hidden in the uppers of one boot and the blade of a cutthroat in the other.

Jarrett eyed Marty with a newfound respect. Chadwell had warned him that the young captain of the Formidiable was no ordinary Navy man and was attached to the Intelligence Service, but to see him in action was quite something.

Chadwell was excited, he had only been on the island for six months and had ruthlessly tracked down the many French spies that they had left behind when they left. The elimination of this cell was a major coup.

The door opened and through it walked Rear Admiral Sir Alexander Ball, tall elegant with grey hair tied in a Navy cue with a black silk ribbon. Marty stood, along with the others and bowed.

"You are underdressed captain, if somewhat over-armed." The Admiral commented as he shook Marty's hand. Just then the servant returned so Marty excused himself, retrieved his pistols from Sam, replaced them on his harness and put his coat on after thanking the man.

"I think that's better my Lord," Marty grinned as he tugged his coat back into place.

The Admiral nodded in approval. "Collinwood wrote to me about you and your excellent physician, he omitted to mention you are a walking armoury."

"Just the tools of the trade sir."

"Quite, a special unit attached to Naval Intelligence, I believe."

Marty coughed and inclined his head to Claudette which brought the Admiral up a little short and a chagrined look on his face.

Chadwell stepped in quickly. "Thanks to the good Captain we have neutralised another French spy cell," he interjected making a point of not mentioning Marty's name and putting the emphasis on his rank.

The Admiral looked down his long nose at Claudette. "A hanging, then," he scowled at her.

"If I may Sir, I believe this presents us with a unique opportunity," Marty opened, "if Mr. Chadwell and I are permitted to interview Madam Claudette and extract what information we can before any trial, we may be able to come up with an option that will benefit us more."

Admiral Ball looked at the two of them and frowned.

"I hope that process will not involve any ungentlemanly conduct! You can have two days," he concluded and turned to leave.

"My ship will be the perfect venue where I can guarantee we won't be overheard," Marty offered.

"Perfect!" said Chadwell, and Claudette fainted.

Back on board the Formidiable, Marty and Chadwell sat Claudette on a hard-wooden chair in the middle of Marty's cabin. Marty had Shelby examine her before they started to 'make sure she was fit to be interrogated.'

"We can't have her dying under interrogation and cheating the hangman," he had said cheerfully as he handed her over.

Now Marty sat behind his desk, while Chadwell leant against the door frame out of her line of sight. He had taken the fighting knife out of its sheath and laid it on the desk alongside his two stilettoes. He prepared a pen and carefully laid out a piece of paper to take notes.

"Shall we begin?" he asked Chadwell.

Chadwell stepped silently across the checkerboard canvas that was laid over the decking.

"What is your full name?" he said quietly from just behind her right ear.

She jumped, not expecting him to be so close.

"Claudette Fremont."

"Where were you born?"

"Nancy."

"What are your parents' names?"

"Why do you want—"

"Answer the question," he gripped her shoulder and squeezed.

"Eric and Madelaine," she winced.

"Do they come from Nancy as well?"

"Yes."

Claudette was confused. *Why are they asking me this?*

"Are they still alive?"

"What?"

"Are they still alive? Are they dead?"

"No! I mean, yes, they are still alive."

"When did you arrive in Malta."

"Three years ago."

"Why."

"I was sent by the D.I.A."

Marty raised his eyebrows the dreaded Department of Internal Affairs was something he was very familiar with.

"Why you?"

"Because I spoke English with hardy any French accent."

And so, it went on with Marty switching to take the lead and asking the same questions in a different way and order. After three hours they had all the information they could squeeze out of her. She was exhausted and weeping when Marty asked who her controller was.

"My what?" she replied, confused.

"What is the name of the man in Paris, who gives you instructions and knows who you are?"

"He is not in Paris; he is in Italy."

"And his name?"

"Jean-Christoph Messier."

"And where in Italy is he located?"

"Naples."

"He is the only member of the D.I.A. who can identify you?"

"Yes, he recruited me and has kept me to himself."

Marty knelt in front of her on one knee and looked her in the eyes. "If I can remove him would you work for us to save yourself from the hangman?"

"My family!"

"Will be quite safe. I will guarantee that."

The next morning, they were in Rear Admiral Ball's office making a report.

"She seduced Brigadier Du Mort of the Froberg regiment and managed to get all that information out of him?" he gasped incredulously.

"Yes, she is extremely skilled," Marty replied.

"And you say you have turned her to our side?"

"With the guarantee I will kill the only man in the French Government who knows who she is."

"Then I can't hang her?"

Marty let that pass as a rhetorical question.

"You could hang Du Mort for treason," Chadwell suggested.

"Damned if I'm not tempted, but I will have to leave his fate to his superiors."

Chapter 14: To Spring a Trap

Marty made the rendezvous with the rest of his ships and was pleasantly surprised to see they had picked up a couple of prizes on the way. As the S.O.F. went by the rule that every prize belonged to the flotilla, not just the ship that captured it, everyone was happy.

They returned to Gibraltar and Marty sent a message to Ridgley that he wanted to talk to him.

"How do we explain that she no longer needs to get off the island?" Ridgley asked after he had read the letter from his colleague Chadwell.

"We don't, we use her to bait one big operation that will seriously damage the French's ability to cause trouble in the Mediterranean. Then I will kill her controller and she will be free to work for us."

"A right little mercenary," Ridgley huffed.

"Just a survivor," Marty smiled.

"Well then, how do we proceed?"

Jean-Christoph Messier sat in his office and tried to ignore the dead fish stink that came off the clothing of the man stood the other side of his desk. The Maltese fisherman was a regular messenger between him and his, every shrinking, set of spies on the Island and the message he bore was more bad news.

The ship that was supposed to pick up Claudette and get her off the island with the information she had screwed out of the royalist pig of a Brigadier, had gotten itself shot to pieces in the bay of Malaga.

"Tell her to be ready, we will find another ship and get her out within a month. I will send a message as soon as we have the details."

The fisherman left with a gold Louis clutched in his grimy fist leaving the door open behind him.

He got up to cross the room to close it when a voice said,

"It's so touching that you think so much of me that it takes a message to get you to organise a replacement ship to come and get me," said Claudette as she stepped through the door.

"How?" he started to say. *"The fisherman!"*

"His boat stinks as bad as he does. It will take a week to get the smell off my skin."

He stepped forward to embrace her and crinkled his nose at the smell.

"You need a bath and a change of clothes, but first what news?"

"The plans for the defences of Malta," she pulled a packet from the shoulder bag she was carrying and handed them over.

"The English captured me. These are a second set I had made just in case of an instance such as this. They think I am passing you the fakes they produced which would get any invading force annihilated.

There is a new force in the Mediterranean, a flotilla attached to Naval intelligence. It is operating independently to the Commander in Chief and is run by a, rather attractive, Captain who is very clever and a deadly fighter. From snippets I overheard he has a number of boats and they are based in Gibraltar."

"Did you hear his name?"

"No, they were very careful not to mention it, but he has a beautiful wife and two children, his ship is the Formidiable."

"Hmm, that is a Spanish version of the name, I wonder...."

Messier went to a cupboard, took out a sheaf of papers and sorted through them.

"Ah Ha! I thought so. There was a report of a battle for a Spanish treasure fleet in the Caribbean last year and it was reported in the British newspaper the Gazette. Captain Sir Martin Stockley, Knight of the Bath and Baron of Candor,

captured two Spanish galleons and two Frigates one of which was the Formidiable."

"A Lord? He doesn't act like an aristo," Claudette commented thoughtfully.

"Forget it, Claudette. He is married to the infamous Baroness Caroline Candor, she has a reputation that eclipses even you and is even more ruthless. They are inseparable."

"Well he thinks that he has turned me to the British side and will use me to trap and destroy a significant French fleet, but we can trap and destroy him instead. He killed my men, I want his head in repayment."

"What we need to do then is provide him with the right bait and get him somewhere where we can spring a trap," he sorted through some more of the papers, *"and I think I know just who."*

Claudette reported back to Chadwell as soon as she returned to Gibraltar and he, in turn, sent a report back to Ridgley. Marty sat in Ridgley's office and read it.

"She handed over the fake plans and we now know where her controller's office is and what he looks like," Ridgley commented, "your idea to follow her and that Maltese fisherman worked a treat."

"What's this about the French sending a new force into the area?" Marty asked.

"They are sending in a frigate and a couple of corvettes to try and re-establish a presence in the bay of Naples. A chap by the name of le Bonne, is the Captain of the frigate, he is not long back from the Caribbean. Apparently walks with a cane and has lost his left arm." Ridgley read from a page of the report he hadn't handed to Marty yet.

Marty felt a shiver run down his spine, it couldn't be, could it?

"That cannot be a coincidence," Marty murmured.

"What?" Ridgley asked.

“Thinking out loud,” Marty replied, “I think I smell a rat. But let’s play the hand and see what happens”

Marty took the Formidiable and Eagle back to Malta and after giving the requisite salute moored in Valetta harbour. He took Ryan with him when he went to visit Chadwell in his rooms.

“How is the plan progressing to feed the French with information to pull them into a trap?” he asked the agent.

“Good, good,” Chadwell smiled. “Claudette delivered the maps and planted the fake information about the supply fleet.”

They had come up with the idea of letting the French know that a fleet of merchant ships escorted by only a minimal Navy force would be delivering fresh troops to Malta to replace the resident force to allow them to return to England. The destruction of such a fleet would be a major victory for the French Navy.

“We know where her contact is based,” Chadwell continued, “we had an agent on the fishing boat who ‘offered’ to escort her and act as her bodyguard.”

“Does she know?” Marty asked.

“That he was an agent? No of course not.” Chadwell confirmed in a slightly injured tone.

“This new Navy commander, what of him?”

“Experienced chap, not long back from the Caribbean,” he looked at Martin as a thought struck him. “I say! You were there last year, weren’t you?”

“Yes, but I’ve never heard of him,” Marty dissembled causing Ryan to look at him out of the corner of his eye.

“Where is Claudette now?”

“At her house.”

Marty got up, walked to the door to Chadwell’s bedroom and opened it.

“I say!” Chadwell squawked in outrage.

Marty sniffed and closed the door with a grin.

"And when did she leave here? Your room stinks of her perfume and she's wrecked your bed."

Back on board the Formidiable Marty called an informal officers meeting. Blaez objected to the crowd and went up on deck.

"Gentlemen it would appear that our old friend de Faux or le Bonne as he is now known is back on the scene. This time with a frigate and a couple of corvettes."

"Oh good! Can we can get to blow him up again?" asked Yeovilton, the Gunner, with a laugh.

"It's all too convenient that they chose him for Naples," Ryan interjected, "we think they may have identified the Captain. The treasure fleet action was posted all over the Gazette after all. The man is highly motivated to kill us all."

"Well that's what we will assume, and we can also assume that Claudette hasn't turned as far as Chadwell thinks she has. I will lay good odds; the bitch is playing a triple cross. Which also means that the trap we have been planning isn't worth a farthing." Marty concluded."

He went to his drawer and took out two packets of drawings and held one up. "The drawings we found on her when we captured her," he held up the second pack, "and the duplicate set we found in her house when we searched it. I replaced this with a set of the fake plans we came up with for the deception."

Marty sat on the edge of his desk and recalled the sequence of events. After the interrogation of Claudette, he had John Smith make a very convincing replica of her drawings but change some key details. He had gone ashore to her house that night with John and searched it, found the plans and replaced them with John's fakes. If the French believed them, they would be annihilated if they tried to invade.

"We need to know if le Bonne and his ships have arrived yet. It's only a couple of days sailing from Toulon to Naples with a fair wind." Marty continued and then ordered.

"Ryan, take the Eagle and go and have a look, don't take any chances we need information, not prizes," he ordered, and Ryan immediately left.

". Mr. Fletcher, I would appreciate it if you can procure us a serviceable fishing boat big enough for seven men," Blaez walked in through the door as Ryan left, "and a dog."

He thought for a while longer then grinned.

"le Bonne seems to have a vendetta against us, I think I should reciprocate and there is a Sicilian tradition when you declare a vendetta on your enemies."

A message was sent on the regular packet to get the Alouette and Hornfleur to Palermo where Marty would meet them later. He didn't want Claudette to know his real strength. Then he set off to meet with Chadwell.

He entered Chadwell's rooms and picked up Claudette's scent immediately. He had Blaez with him who gave a violent sneeze as the cloying odour got up his nose.

"She can come out of the bedroom Chadwell, I want to talk to her as well," he said to the spy who was making out he had been sat at his desk all along.

The bedroom door opened, and Claudette came into the room dressed in a silk robe and not a lot else. Blaez went to her and promptly stuck his nose up under the robe in the vicinity of her groin, making her squeal.

Marty laughed, "he's just checking you for fertility."

"His nose is cold!" she complained, "and there is nothing wrong with my 'fertility'."

Blaez returned to Marty's side and sat with a doggy grin and his tongue hanging out the side of his mouth.

"I have some questions," he opened and sat down in Chadwell's comfiest chair. Blaez immediately climbed up so he could rest his chest on Marty's lap with his back feet on the floor.

"Excuse my dog, he is just a big softy. Oh yes, the questions. Did your contact, what's his name again? Look at the plans?"

"Why yes, he examined them very carefully, and his name is Jean-Christoph." She replied, thinking *He was very happy because they were the real ones.*

"He wasn't suspicious that they could be fakes?"

"No, not at all."

"Excellent! Will he inform you if they will act on them?"

"Yes, he will not want me caught up in an invasion."

"Very considerate."

"Now, what do you know about this new Naval commander and his force?"

"His name is le Bonne; he will command a frigate and two corvettes to replace what was lost. As far as I know he spent the last year in the Caribbean where he was wounded and lost an arm. He also walks with a cane as he was wounded in the legs as well."

"Sounds like an unlucky sort of chap to me," Marty laughed, "or damned careless."

"Have you never been wounded?" she asked, sounding just a little annoyed at Marty's jest.

"A few times," Marty admitted.

Blaez got too hot, slid to the floor, found a cool piece of uncarpeted wood and lay down, farted, sniffed the air like it was something someone else had done, and moved to the other side of the room.

"What does 'Jean-Christoph' want you to do now?" Marty said wondering what smelt worse, her cloying perfume, or Blaez's fart.

"I am to find out when the supply ships are due and send the information so le Bonne can attack them."

"Well that's what you should do then," Marty stated as he stood to leave. He looked at Chadwell, "make sure you mix genuine information with the fake to keep it believable."

Chadwell looked like he would protest but the look in Marty's eye stuck it in his throat.

"She will make sure that 'Jean-Christoph' only takes note of the real information, mate," he said to Blaez as they walked back to the docks.

Blaez would have agreed but at that point a stray dog walked into his path and a minor war broke out about who had the right to set foot on the path. The stray was out of his league and soon left yelping with his tail between his legs. Blaez followed for a few steps, stopped to scratch the ground stiff legged to mark his victory then anointed the street as his with a steaming stream of piss.

"Can't take you anywhere without you either getting in a fight or finding some poor bitch to bang on," Marty told him as they resumed their walk, "and I bet you haven't noticed that bloke following us either."

Their tail followed at a respectable distance and to the untrained eye would appear to be just travelling in the same direction, but Marty knew all the tricks and varied his pace, stopped to look in shop windows and knelt to give Blaez some fuss. The man stayed the same distance behind.

Just before he got to the docks, he saw Antton leaning nonchalantly against a wall as if he had never seen Marty before in his life. He had spotted the tail as well. His gaze slid across Marty who gave the smallest of shakes of the head and signalled 'follow him' in the sign language they had developed over their years together.

Two hours later in Marty's cabin, Antton reported that the tail had hung around the docks for about thirty minutes before walking to Claudette's house.

"Our double agent seems to have found some more men to make up for the ones we eliminated, or she had more men than she admitted." He thought for moment and then ordered, "I want a watch on her, her house, Chadwell, and his rooms."

"You think she has turned him?" Antton asked.

"A wise man once told me, 'Sex will drag you further than gunpowder will throw you,' so I would not be surprised. Let's leave a sixteen-man team ashore when we sail for Palermo, I want them working in pairs and rotated every four hours to keep both targets under surveillance full time. If she humps, I want to know who with and for how long. If she leaves, one man is to follow her the other stays with the house. They are not to take action unless they are attacked and then leave no witnesses." It went without saying he thought his men could win any fight they got into.

The orders given he went on deck to check on the provisioning and their preparedness to sail.

Antton decided he would lead the shore team himself and selected his men carefully. Every one of them had done gaol time in England for burglary, pickpocketing or some other suitable felony. They slipped ashore after dark and made for an empty building they had identified as a potential base on a previous excursion. The first four men faded into the dark to start their four-hour stint.

Unusually, every man had a pocket watch, a few sheets of paper and charcoal to write with. Marty had been encouraging his men to learn to read and write ever since he was a midshipman and Antton had only picked men who could.

The Formidiable left port on the morning tide, with a conspicuous roar of cannon as they saluted the Admiral. They slid past Fort Saint Elmo, a great star shaped citadel on the Sciberras Peninsula and on out into the Mediterranean. Marty was going pirating.

They met up with the rest of the flotilla at Palermo and immediately got a report from James. There was no sign of any frigates or corvettes in the Bay of Naples.

Well he wouldn't waste time worrying about le Bonne he had a couple of things to do and wanted to get on with them. First, he had them sail north up through the Tyrrhenian Sea looking for a merchantman. It took two days, but they found one that was out of Olbia on the island of Sardinia. The crew gave up without a fight, so he let them take their ships boat and sail home.

Later that day the merchantman sailed into the Bay of Naples, moored up near the dock and the captain went ashore with his first mate. The mate went to a merchant to see who would give him the best price for his cargo. The captain went further into the town carrying a bloody sack.

The ship was gone the next morning, taking its cargo with it. It was if it had never been there.

Jean-Christoph Messier woke with the dawn and noticed his bedroom window was ajar, which was strange as he never slept with it open. He rolled over and became aware of a large mound under the cover on the pillow the other side of his large double bed.

He sat up and pulled the cover back.

The dead eye of a horse's head looked back at him and attached to it by a knife through the cheek, was a piece of paper with a drawing of a skull with a knife driven through it from top to bottom above a pair of crossed pistols.

He knew what this meant – someone had declared a vendetta against him in the Sicilian fashion!

He met Le Bonne later for lunch. He had travelled down from Rome, where his ships were based, by coach, for a briefing on the information Claudette had been passing them.

"A horse's head?" le Bonne exclaimed when Messier told him of his discovery that morning. "Do you still have the paper?"

Messier dug the blood-stained sheet out of his pocket and passed it over. le Bonne looked at it and swore as he crumpled it in his fist in fury.

"What is it? Do you know this symbol?" Messier asked, surprised at the furry boiling in the man across from him.

"It is the bastard son of a pox ridden whore who cost me my arm and ruined my legs. It is Captain Stanwell, the privateer, who is also known as Captain Sir Martin Stockley of the British Royal Navy."

Messier slumped back in his seat, the man must have been stood over him in his sleep and hadn't slit his throat.

"What does this mean?" he eventually gasped as he recovered enough to speak.

"He is giving us warning that he will offer no quarter," le Bonne spat, "the drawing is in red. This is not just aimed at you my friend but all of us."

Marty now put the second part of his plan into play. To cause devastation and disruption to trade to the ports up and down the Italian coast and the French run islands. Eventually the military commander would have to order the Navy to stop him.

They sailed Northeast up the Italian coast and looked in at every cove and fishing village. They had the flotilla spread out to sea in line abeam with the Hornfleur nearest the coast with the Alouette next, then the Formidiable and last the Eagle. They were in no hurry and swept up every ship they saw, no matter how small, unless they were fishing boats. If they were big enough or the cargo valuable enough, they kept them, everything else was burnt. They flew the red jolly roger over the British colours.

The Hornfleur came up on the town of Terracina. They could see a boatyard with two large hulls almost completed and what looked like warehouses behind the harbour wall. The amphibious team went to work. The boats were launched, and the marines stormed ashore. They were a little rusty but only a practised eye could see that. Within twenty minutes the boatyard was in flames and then the warehouses.

The boats returned loaded to the gunnels with cheeses, hams and sausages with the mark of the French Army on them. The warehouses had been commandeered by the French and there had been a platoon of French infantry guarding them which the marines had run off. They had only expected to have to guard against theft from the locals not a concerted attack by a well-trained force.

Onward they sailed like Vikings on a mad rampage looting and pillaging, every port they came upon. Marty had banned rape to the disappointment of some of the crew Nettuno, Fiumicino and Civitavecchia all suffered in turn. Messages flew to the French commander in Milan who sent orders to the Navy to stop the scourge and destroy the raiders.

le Bonne got back to Rome just in time to receive the orders he had been hoping for. He boarded his ship and looked out at the other two frigates one French the other Italian, that formed his squadron. His own, the Hermione, was a new forty, the second French ship was the Indienne an older thirty-eight, the Italian was the Sibilla, also a thirty-eight.

If Messier was correct the British were expecting a frigate and a couple of corvettes not three much larger Frigates and now with his new orders, he could commandeer the two Italian Navy Xebecs across the harbour to add some extra firepower.

"This time it will be me that has the advantage, you bastard!" he spat with crazed eyes, a hint of drool running down his chin as he stared at the flag drawn on the piece of paper. He could still feel pain in his missing left arm, reminding him of the woman who had shot him from an impossible range. Once he had killed him, he would go after her!

Marty kept raiding until he had to return to Palermo to rid himself of the prizes. While he was there, he went to pay his respects to Admiral Collingwood who was in port and was surprised to see Fox there as well.

"I hear you have been doing your best to annoy the Italians as well as the French," Fox commented after the formal greetings had been shared.

"It's a plan to draw the French and Italian ships out so we can destroy them." Marty smiled and went over his plan with the two senior men.

"I think I would like to help," Collingwood said with a faint smile.

"I would be grateful of any you can give," Marty replied with a bow of the head.

"I would like you to take Sir Sidney along. With his ships of course. He is upset about being relieved of command of the Calabrian campaign and a brisk action will put him to rights."

Marty was shocked and amused at the same time!. The infamous Sir Sidney could be a renowned pain in the ass, but he was also a man of action. He would have to be extremely careful in his dealings with him.

"Aahh, exactly what would my relationship be to the Rear Admiral?" Marty asked, hoping Collingwood knew what he was getting at.

"Don't worry you will still be in command of your flotilla," Collingwood reassured him, "Sir Sidney will be there to offer you support, to close the trap, as it were, in a joint operation."

"Will he only have the Pompée?" Marty asked, seeing a problem where the Admiral was only in charge of a single ship and he four.

"By no means! He will have two sloops of war and a cutter under his command, he will need their nimbleness to cut off the French and Italian's retreat." Collingwood reassured him.

"Good that will work well," Marty confirmed. "However, I have been informed by Intelligence in Malta that the commander is an old adversary of mine from the Caribbean and I would like to be the one who finishes him off."

"A personal affair?" Collingwood responded in surprise.

"Very much a professional one, he is my opposite number, and it won't end until my sword is through his heart," Marty snarled.

Marty met with Admiral Smith and was surprised at how well he was received and how well they got on.

"I have been burning boatyards and warehouses along this stretch of coastline," Marty informed him as they poured over a chart. "I've also taken or burnt every merchant ship sailing in that stretch of water I could find."

"I presume you have been methodical so the French will know where you will hit next?" Sir Sidney observed.

"That was the general idea, that and aggravating them into having to do something to stop me, Sir."

"Oh, please call me Sidney and I will call you Martin," the Admiral laughed, "I like you; you think like I do!"

Marty almost choked on the wine he was sipping.

"Well, Sidney, the next target is Porto Santo Stefano it's here in the straits between Corsica and the Mainland. We have just over seventy miles of sea room to play with there to the East."

They had been informed that the bulk of the French and allied Italian ships were in the North near Rome so assumed they would come from that direction, following the coast down to intercept the Flotilla moving up the coast. The plan was for Smith and his ships to stay to windward out of sight, over the horizon and circle around to take the French from the rear or flank as soon as the trap was sprung.

"If I was commanding the French I would try and catch you on a lee shore and pin you up against the coast," Sir Sidney commented.

"Yes, so would I, and if I let him, it will give you a good chance to be the hammer to my anvil." Marty responded.

"Damn dangerous, Martin! You could get pounded before I can get there."

"Yes, but he knows he can't get too close or my carronades will smash him. So, it will come down to the nimbleness of my Sloop and Clipper and the strength of the Formidiable's hull."

Sir Sidney looked at the young man sat beside him and saw himself twenty-five years before but with an extra core of steel. This was one determined and brave young man.

Chapter 15: The Battle of Giannutri Bay

The flotilla set sail in the morning and headed up the coast towards Porto Santo Stefano to continue their reign of destruction. Sir Sidney followed on a few hours later.

Marty sat in his room absently scratching Blaez's ears. He was troubled by something that occurred to him as they left port. What if le Bonne didn't have just a single frigate and a couple of corvettes? The man was no fool, and he couldn't imagine he would let himself be out gunned as he was in the Caribbean. No, he should expect that he would arrive armed to win and that meant either bigger or more ships. Hopefully not both.

He looked again at the map and had an idea.

"Please give Captain la Pierre my compliments and ask him to come to my cabin and signal the Hornfleur for her captain to report aboard."

Thirty minutes later, after a short heave to so that Angus Frasier could be rowed over, they sat around a chart.

"We can expect the French to show up with more and heavier firepower than we have been led to believe and we need to counteract that." Marty said in introduction. "However, the Hornfleur is not a warship; her sides are too thin, she is chock full of marines and I will not put her in harm's way unnecessarily." Frasier spluttered and went red, ready to defend his ship and his men. Marty grinned at him and held up his hand.

"Easy now Mr. Frasier. Your ship has, what, sixteen twelve-pound longs and you can only bring eight of them to bear at any one time. My plan is to enable you to bring all sixteen into action at one time and surprise the hell out of the enemy."

He pointed to a dot on the chart.

"That is the island of Giannutri, it is about ten miles from this headland," he indicated a bump off of the mainland. "We will raid here at Porto Santo Stephano and make as much noise as possible to attract le Bonne and his ships. When we see the French coming, we will sail around the headland to the south side and set ourselves here," he pointed to a bay formed by the crescent of the island.

"We will have taken the guns out of the Hornfleur by then and installed them on this hill with a strong redoubt and ovens to heat the shot. My intention is to lure the French into this killing zone and for you to burn the bastards. Do you understand?"

Both la Pierre and Frasier barked, "Aye Aye Sir," and grinned evilly at the thought.

They went to work on the logistics. They had ample boats and men and soon had a working plan of what they would do.

When they reached the island, the Hornfleur broke away from the rest of the flotilla and commenced the invasion of Giannutri.

An amphibious landing was carried out, much to the surprise of the fisher folk who lived on the island, and a beachhead established. The marines then surveyed the land between the beach and the top of the headland some hundred feet or so above sea level for the easiest path to drag the guns up.

The rest of the Flotilla anchored in the bay and ferried extra manpower over to help with the work. It wasn't going to be easy; the island was volcanic in origin; the ground was rough and had a lot of ridges. They mapped out a route and started making a road by smashing rocks and packing them into the volcanic ripples to smooth the way.

The Hornfleur's guns were taken off their carriages and swung over the side to be slung between a pair of whalers. The boats were kept apart by cross beams lashed between them. This meant that they only needed oars on the outboard side of each boat giving them a crab like appearance.

Once a gun was close enough to the shore it was hauled out of the water by an A-frame and reunited with its carriage. Then a large team of men hauled it up the road to the gun positions on the headland. The small wheels of the naval carriages didn't make that easy. Redoubts were made by making rough, but thick drystone walls and ovens were constructed out of the local rock.

After three days they were exhausted, but ready.

The Formidiable and Alouette up anchored and sailed around to the northern side of the headland where they enthusiastically began pillaging the port of Santo Stefano. Marty wanted time for a signal to be transmitted by the semaphore towers the French had installed along the coast, so he took his time and had his men be far more methodical than usual.

Smoke was soon boiling into the air as boatyards and warehouses were put to the torch and a nasty little pitched battle with a reinforced guard left most of the French dead and three marines wounded.

The Eagle sailed North to give early warning of the French ships approach. Marty didn't want to be surprised! Once she had spotted the enemy and passed their details by flag hoist, she was to sail at full speed to warn Smith that they were coming, give him their disposition and numbers and lead him to the bay.

At the end of the second day the Eagle appeared over the horizon, all sails set. Ryan ran her down to two miles from the port firing a double gun every fifteen minutes warning Marty that they had spotted the French. Marty immediately ordered the men to withdraw to the boats and re-embark.

He was on his quarterdeck when a grim-faced midshipman handed him the signal.

"Oh, Christ!" he said under his breath as he read.

"3F. 40, 38, 38, two X. Good luck."

Ackermann came and looked at the note,

"Meine Gott! Smith better get a move on or we will be fish bait!"

Marty could only agree.

He called a quick council of war.

"We are going to be heavily out gunned and we have to hope the battery on the island can even the odds somewhat. We must lead them into the killing zone before we engage so that Mr Frazier and Captain la Pierre can pound them and hope that Smith arrives in time to close the door. I plan to anchor here as planned," he pointed to the large-scale map of the island they had made while moving the guns, "under the cliffs and use springs to point the guns. It's not the usual way we fight but we need to hold them until Admiral Smith arrives. We will be sitting ducks, but we will just have to take it for the hour or so that he will need to get here.

James you keep the Alouette out of the slugging match with the frigates, your job is to use your agility to take the Xebecs out of the fight then, if you are able, harass the frigates and try to distract them.

The warning had arrived at midday having taken just a couple of hours to travel up the coast. le Bonne has set sail immediately and was heading South as fast as he could. They had sighted the Eagle and Ryan had made sure that he had gotten close enough that le Bonne would recognise his ship and the flag. Marty wanted him in no doubt about who he was facing.

le Bonne watched as the Eagle sped south and made a signal. Then, to his surprise, it turned west and headed away from the mainland.

"Ha! He knows when he is beaten, look at him run!" He gloated to his First Lieutenant.

"But Sir!" the lieutenant tried to interject as he sensed something wasn't right, but all le Bonne was aware of was the Formidiable and Alouette making sail and beating around the headland, leaving the smoking port behind them.

"Go on! Run, you miserable dog! I am coming for you and this time it is I that has the advantage!" he shouted to the wind.

"Make all sail! We will catch them and send them to hell!"

His First protested that something wasn't right again.

"Do as ordered! Or I will have you shot as a traitor!" le Bonne shouted, spittle flying from his mouth.

Marty was watching the approaching ships as they came up over the horizon. He wanted to keep the French in sight so there was no doubt they were following. He had removed his uniform coat and had the red version of their pirate flag flying from the mizzen. The challenge was made, there was no going back now.

Sam arrived, helped him into his weapons harness and put Blaez's fighting collar on. The dog knew what was coming and was excited. He looked at Marty and gave an expectant bark/yip.

"Steady, boy," Marty reassured him, "you will get your chance."

le Bonne had a junior lieutenant calling out the range almost constantly. The poor man stood on the quarter deck measuring the angle to the top of the Formidiable's main mast and working out the maths. As soon as he announced the result he was back on the sextant for the next measurement. When he announced they were at two thousand meters le Bonne ordered the chasers to fire.

The French only carried twelve-pound chasers, putting more value on the eighteen pounders in the main battery, so this was at extreme range to hope for a hit. But blast away they did in the hope of a bit of luck.

Marty saw the smoke and watched the black dots of the balls fall well wide.

"Keen, isn't he," he grinned at Ackermann, who laughed and shouted orders to bring them to quarters.

They were now sailing a little east of South and Marty increased sail to reduce the closing rate. He needed time when he sailed into the bay to anchor to set springs. Third Lieutenant Stamp and Midshipman Hart had the range measurement duties and were calling out the numbers every fifteen minutes.

He saw yet another puff of smoke from the lead French ship which looked like a forty. The other two frigates moved out into an echelon formation with the Xebecs in line astern behind the centre ship forming what he imagined was an arrowhead.

"Wolfgang, what do you make of that?" he asked his First.

"Odd Sir, I've never seen anyone do that before."

"Do you think he is planning to engage us with the lead ship and get the others to try and flank us?"

"With the Xebecs going after the Alouette? Maybe." Ackermann replied. Marty chuckled, that would only work if they were caught in open water.

They were flying the 'enemy in sight' signal, which Captain la Pierre had seen and was preparing his cannon. As the more experienced and senior he was in command of the battery on the hilly headland. The shot ovens were at full temperature and the shot was as he wanted it. All he needed now was for Marty to lead the French in, but when he saw the French ships come over the horizon, he was worried. Could they hold out long enough?

They approached the island, Marty looked through his telescope but couldn't see the battery to start with. *Are they ready?* he thought worriedly.

"Smoke, Sir!" announced Hart, who was measuring the range to the island and had substituted a telescope for his sextant for a moment.

"Where?" Marty asked as calmly as he could.

"There, Sir, just above that big rock that sticks out like a pimple." The boy replied.

Marty scanned along the coast until he saw it and then he picked up the faint haze of the smoke.

"Good! They've got the ovens going. Range to the island?"

"One- mile Sir."

"Be ready Wolfgang, we will hit the lee of the island soon."

The island was shaped like a crescent with a bay on the East side. The wind was coming from the Northwest so as soon as they rounded the headland, they would fall into the wind shadow.

Marty wanted the French in the bay between the land-based guns and his ship's battery in that wind shadow. He didn't want them to be able to easily set sail and get away. He steered his ship close to the headland and rounded into the bay. They had enough momentum to let her drift in under no sail until she was under the cliffs and drop the best bower anchor. A boat crew rowed out to pick up the buoyed cable attached to the stern anchor they had dropped when they had been landing the guns. It was a sandy bottom with good holding, and they could attach springs to swing the ship to allow then to bring their guns to bear as required.

The Alouette steered out to sea to give her room to fight a running battle.

"Signal from the Battery Sir." Hart reported, "enemy in sight, engage more closely."

"Guns ready, double shot loaded as ordered," Ackermann reported.

"Get phase two underway," Marty ordered.

le Bonne was puzzled. He saw the Formidiable and its escort round the headland but only the escort was visible as they reached the point, and they looked like they were running away.

When they cleared the headland, he saw the Formidiable in the bay with men all over the foremast as if they were frantically trying to repair damage. Yes! The fore topmast was being taken down!

"Reduce sail to fighting topsails. Order the Xebecs to destroy that corvette and steer us into the bay. We will anchor so we can bring the mains to bear and close off his exit!" he ordered, eyes fixed on the Formidiable and its cursed red flag.

"You cannot escape me!" he cried, *"I have you now, you bastard!"*

His three frigates swung into the bay and their sails started to flap as they entered the wind shadow, but he didn't care, they had enough way on to get them into position. They were three cables away from the Formidiable and just starting to turn when she opened with a broadside.

Marty knew he had to get in a couple of good punches before the French ships got into position to use their broadsides. He targeted the forty-gun frigate and gave her the benefit of everything they had. Given the stable platform and close range his gunners could hardly miss. He had a faint hope the smoke might confuse their gunners as well.

Paul la Pierre waited until Marty let loose with his first broadside and ordered his guns to fire as soon as they could get the red-hot shot loaded.

He was pleased to see that the nearest ship to them, which was flying an Italian flag, take half a dozen hits, the others going wide or just missing. As the shot was coming down at an angle it was smashing through her deck and lodging inside her hull. Perfect for starting a fire.

He swore at the gunners to improve their aim and reload as fast as they could.

le Bonne cringed as the first broadside from the Formidiable smashed into his ship. Given the angle most hit forward, and his fore mast gave a nasty shudder as it was hit low down. However, the impacts pushed her bow around a little quicker and his guns started to fire as they bore. He swore at his men as he saw the shot going high.

"Do not aim for their rigging, you idiots, she isn't going anywhere!"

Marty heaved a sigh of relief; the French had wasted their first broadside firing high and the cliff took more punishment than the ship did. The Italian frigate on the left was catching it from the shore battery and didn't seem to have understood where the fire had come from.

Then he heard the second French frigate open up. She had sailed around the big forty-gunner to get into position and had the benefit of being on the Formidiable's quarter. She didn't aim high. Shot crashed into the hull and caused the deck planking to jump, men screamed and died.

His gunners fired again and knew they had to keep up a steady three shots every two minutes until they were all dead and burning or Smith arrived, and the French were beaten.

James saw the Xebecs turn to give chase. They moved up so they were abeam of each other looking to catch him and put him between their broadsides.

"Time to test their seamanship Mr. Davidson," he said to his midshipman, "wear us around to reverse course and steer right for the middle of them."

James had studied every crazy manoeuvre that Marty had ever pulled in ship to ship combat and he was relishing the chance to pull one himself now.

The bow came around and they were soon going head on at the two ships.

"Ready to tack!" he called, "guns aim for her bow!"

If this works .... he thought as he measured the distance to the Italian ships. Three cables, two, one and a half,

"Larboard tack! Fire as you bear!"

The Alouette pirouetted through the wind right across the bows of the Xebec to larboard. Her carronades roared one after the other until all fourteen of her starboard battery had fired.

The bow of the Xebec shattered under the onslaught of one hundred and twenty-six, four-pound balls delivering five hundred and four pounds of iron. Her captain panicked and swung his wheel to larboard causing the other Xebec to have to veer away. He was doomed, his bow was shot to pieces and his foremast crashed over the side in a tangle of rigging.

James tacked back to starboard to bring them broadside to broadside to finish them off. To give the Italians their due they did get some shots off, but they were largely ineffective. The broadside from the Alouette was divided between round shot and smashers every other gun, an innovation James had thought up. The Xebec's side grew huge holes at her waterline and star shaped holes along her side. She was sinking and her flag came down.

The second Xebec seeing what had become of her sister ship decided discretion was better than valour and made off with the wind on her stern.

James ignored them both and ordered the helmsman to sail for the bay, he had to help Marty.

The Italian frigate was out of the fight, Paul's guns had pounded her, and she was burning, but to his dismay the guns had overheated forcing them to cease fire. He had to let them cool down before he could help with the French frigates.

Marty knew he was losing the battle of attrition. They were doing damage to the forty-gunner, but she was still firing, and the other frigate was pounding him at will. All he could do was serve him with his stern carronades but that wasn't enough no matter how big they were. They were still floating but a third of his main battery was out of action and the list of wounded and dead was long and getting longer. He had picked up a splinter in the thigh, which, though painful, wasn't life threatening, yet. It was getting desperate! Then the mainmast snapped about halfway up and, thankfully, fell to the landward side. It must have taken a direct hit further up and snapped where it had been damaged earlier. They were shooting him to pieces!

Paul was frantic and even had the men piss on the barrels to try and cool them. In the end, he ordered the guns loaded with cold shot, it would still be dangerous but not as much as with hot shot.

"Target that frigate and don't miss!" he ordered as he ran up the battery cajoling the men to work faster. Frasier was sat off to one side his leg broken when he had gotten too close to a recoiling gun, but he too was shouting encouragement and refused to lie down.

The guns roared and kicked so hard they jumped off the ground and when the smoke cleared, he could see that they had scored but the frigate was still firing. Two guns had turned on their side and the rest would have to be man handled back into position. It was taking too long!

Eventually the men were able to sponge out, carefully, steam from the red-hot barrels curling into the air. They were in danger of the charges going off as they rammed them home and they knew it.

"SIR! SAILS!" a lookout cried pointing to the Northwest.

He grabbed a telescope and looked at the approaching ships. It was Smith and he had every stich of sail he could set on the big sixty-four. She was a fast ship and was flying. The sixty-fours could give a frigate a run for her money with their long hulls making them hydrodynamically efficient, her consorts including the Eagle were spread out behind her.

Another fifteen to twenty minutes and they would be there but could the Formidiable hold out!

James could see the Italian frigate was well ablaze, so he was steering towards the French thirty-eight to try and distract her from the fight. He drove his ship mercilessly and fired his first broadside at three cables range. As the smoke cleared, he could see that they were opening the gun ports facing him. "For what we are about to receive!" he said to the helmsman and shouted, .

"Everybody down!"

Marty saw the men on the smaller frigate rushing to their seaward battery and could see the Alouette getting into firing position. Having to face only the bigger ship's guns bought him time but wouldn't change the long-term outcome. He looked around the deck and knew at some point soon he would have to save what men he could. He was thinking when to give the order to abandon ship when midshipman Hart, who had a bandage around his head, cried,

"Signal from the Battery! Engage the enemy more closely!"

"What the hell?" Marty wondered and then. Then it struck him, Smith must be here!

"Keep firing you bandits! We offered no quarter and we can still finish that French bastard off! Smith is coming!" There was a ragged cheer and the gunners went back to work.

It took another fifteen minutes for the Pompée to round the headland her guns roaring as she served the French a full broadside. It was hurried and most of the shot missed but it served to distract the French. The gun crews were well schooled, and a second more accurate broadside soon followed. By this time the Formidiable was more wreck than ship, down to half her guns still operational. The Eagle and the rest of Smith's ships targeted the second Frigate in support of the Alouette. It would soon be over.

Except for one thing.

Marty took a boat manned by the shadows across to the now quiet frigate and climbed the side. Sam carried Blaez on his shoulders as he refused to stay behind. Marty limped, Shelby had taken out the splinter and bandaged the wound, but it still hurt.

He walked to the quarter deck and as he got to the steps signalled his men to stay back. Matai held on to Blaez's collar and the dog whined anxiously.

"le Bonne," he greeted the one-armed man standing holding a sword in front of the wheel.

"Captain Stockley, you have come to gloat?"

"No, gloating is the pastime of fools," he responded. *"I have come to kill you."*

"Really? Doesn't that go against your gentleman's code of conduct? We have struck."

"You are still holding a sword and you are mistaken if you think I am a gentleman. I have declared vendetta and there is only one possible outcome to that."

"One of us must die!" le Bonne shouted and lunged forward with his sword hoping to surprise Marty before he could draw his.

Marty drew his knife and parried the blade with his left hand then flipped the knife to his right, dropping into a knife fighter's stance. Knees bent, weight on the balls of his feet, shoulders over his toes. The knife held blade down pointing forward. His wounded leg dragged a little and hampered his movement. There would be no fancy footwork in this duel.

"What, no sword?" le Bonne sneered.

"I won't foul its blade on a dog," Marty replied with a grin.

That grin! le Bonne remembered it as Marty had tossed the hissing grenades into the centre of the room. He exploded in rage and threw himself forward, slashing down at Marty's neck with all his strength.

Marty stepped forward inside the swing and came up against le Bonne chest to chest. From a distance it looked like he was holding him in a lover's hug as he was looking directly into his eyes, which were wide, his mouth open in a silent scream. He was vaguely aware of Blaez barking and a shriek of pain in the background.

He continued to hold him, looking into le Bonne's eyes, as he twisted the knife that was embedded in his gut until the edge was uppermost. Then ripped it up through his heart.

Le Bonne's eyes rolled up and dimmed as his last breath rattled in his throat. Marty held him for a while longer until he was sure he was dead then dropped him to the deck. He leant over, using the dead man's coattail to clean his blade before sheathing it.

"Remind me never to get on your bad side," a voice said from behind him.

He turned to see Sir Sidney stood at the top of the quarterdeck steps.

Marty grinned at him then looked down at le Bonne, and said,

"I don't know about you, but I could do with a drink."

He looked for Blaez and saw that he stood beside two of his men who were holding the French first lieutenant between them. His arm was torn and bleeding and there was a pistol lying at his feet.

Chapter 16: Vendetta

The repairs to the Formidiable took a week just to get her seaworthy enough to get to Palermo. Sir Sidney guarded her like a mother goose and had his smaller ships running up and down the coast continuing the work Marty had started. Incidentally, running up a nice score in prize money. The two men dined together every night and a friendship blossomed.

They couldn't be more different. Smith came from a military family; his father was a Captain in the Guards. He was educated at Tonbridge and had been in the Navy since 1777. He was a contemporary of Nelson and had a distinguished career only blighted by his ability to piss off his superiors.

Marty, on the other hand, was a son of the soil (or under it in his case) only had a junior school education, plus what he had learnt aboard ship and had come up through the ranks. He had earned his promotions by doing what no one else would.

But there were more than enough common points for the two to get along.

"So, once we get your ship back to Sicily the job will be done," Smith observed over the port and cheese.

"Not quite," Marty corrected him, "le Bonne has been taken care of but there are a number of loose ends that need to be tied off."

"By loose ends, I suppose you mean his associates."

"Yes, and some characters on our side who need to be tested."

Smith's eyebrows rose in surprise.

"Traitors?"

"Some, and misguided souls who have been led astray," Marty replied.

"Will there be a public enquiry?" Smith asked.

"No, this needs to be dealt with quietly," Marty stated firmly.

"Dash it! I can't pretend to like that side of your 'profession'. It all seems a bit dark and . ." he searched for the word.

"Dishonourable?" Marty added for him.

"Well, yes, but it's a contradiction! You are one of the most honourable men I have met!" He thought for a moment.

"Ruthless, but honourable."

Marty snorted a laugh. "I will get them to put that as my epitaph."

"You know you have more power than even an Admiral," Sidney observed thoughtfully.

"How do you figure that?" Marty asked curiously

"Well as an Admiral I have the power of life and death over the men under my command, but you not only have that but hold the lives of many others in your hands."

Marty was a little surprised at the insight and waved it off.

"We buried the last of the men that didn't survive their wounds today," he said changing the subject.

"What was the butchers bill in the end?"

"The Formidiable lost twenty-three men; one was a follower of mine, Franco, a Basque, who had been with me since India, two others were men I rescued from the slave pens in the Caribbean. We had another fifty-two wounded, forty-six of which can get back to light duties. The Alouette took damage to her rigging and had two marines killed when they were shot out of the tops plus a few walking wounded."

"Did you include yourself in that count?" Smith asked not entirely surprised at the compassion Marty had for his men.

Marty gave an ironic laugh,

"No, we should make that fifty-three." He was lost in thought for a moment.

"They are all volunteers you know and most of them have enough prize money to stay ashore and lead happy lives. I don't know why they keep coming back."

Smith looked at him, *I do,* he thought.

A slow sail back to Palermo and the Formidiable was put into dock for repairs. Marty left her in the hands of Ackermann and, along with the remaining shadows, went back to Malta on the Eagle.

They went ashore quietly and met up with the surveillance team they had left behind.

"Here is a list of all the people that visited Claudette since we have been watching her; their address's and occupations."

Marty looked down it; there were a couple of government officials, an army colonel, a sergeant of marines and a Navy lieutenant. The rest were an odd mix of civilians.

"We raid her place tonight; with a bit of luck, we will pick her up there. I want another team to pick up Chadwell. Then we round up every person on this list, including the tradespeople. I want every one of them secured in the cellars of Fort Elmo by dawn."

He looked around at the grinning faces of his men.

"I want all of them held bound, hooded and apart from each other. Make them as uncomfortable as possible. It's time to clean house."

He organised the team into three-man snatch parties and divided the individuals he wanted collected amongst them, then he went to the docks and got the Eagle's marines and ten sailors. Wilson and Ryan invited themselves along, leaving the ship in the hands of Midshipman Archer.

Lieutenant Griffin of the marines was briefed and took his men to the fort to organise things for the arrival of their guests. In case of opposition from the fort commander he was armed with a letter of authority from the Commissioner which Marty had acquired the last time he was in port.

The night was long and the cells in the fort were gradually filled with surprised, confused and very frightened individuals. Marty stayed up all night. The team that had raided Claudette's house returned and reported that it looked like she had left in a hurry, leaving a lot of papers and notes behind. She had either realised that Marty was on his way back or heard that le Bonne was dead and decided to run.

Marty spent the night going through the papers they had found and making notes. He went to sleep at five AM and slept for two hours.

The first candidate to be interrogated was an army colonel from the Second Brigade of Grenadier Guards. He was dragged into the interrogation room with his arms tied behind his back and a hood over his head. He was pushed into a kneeling position and a rope, strung through a pully on the ceiling, was hooked onto the binding that held his hands.

"What is your name?" Marty asked in a quiet voice.

"Colonel Thomas St John, who the hell are you? Why am I being treated this way?" His voice muffled by the hood he still wore. He tried to stand but Wilson kicked him in the back of the legs forcing him to stay knelt on the hard stone.

"What was your relationship with Claudette Belloc?"

"What business it is of yours?" he blustered.

"Answer the question."

"Fuck you."

Marty nodded to Wilson who was holding the rope. He pulled and lifted the colonel off the ground, so he was suspended with his arms straight out behind him. The colonel yelled as his weight stressed his shoulders painfully

"She was my mistress!" he sobbed, and Wilson let him down to kneel on the stone again.

"Did you tell her about the plan to expand Fort Elmo with a musket parapet?"

"We talked about a lot of things. Please who are you? What have I done?"

"You have committed treason by passing military information to a French spy."

"I've done what?" he squawked.

"Did you tell her about the parapet?"

"Yes, I might have, but it's common knowledge!"

"And the new magazine?"

The Colonel slumped as he realized what he had done.

Marty signalled to Wilson to return the man to his cell, he was to be kept in a kneeling position, hooded and not allowed to move. He would be interrogated again.

Each of the prisoners were treated in a similar way, some, mainly the tradespeople were returned to their homes without more than a short questioning. Severe physical coercion was only used if necessary. Then he only had one more person to talk to.

Chadwell was brought in but instead of being made to kneel he was sat in a chair and Marty removed his hood and untied his hands. He wrinkled his nose, the hood hadn't smelt good, but the room smelt of piss and fear and was worse.

"You know that your career is over," Marty stated, "she played you like a violin."

Chadwell rubbed his wrists and looked around the room. Then at Marty.

"How many?"

Marty looked at him in question.

"How many men did you lose?"

"Twenty-three dead, she lied about the force we would be up against, but we expected that."

"We heard you killed le Bonne, she said you would come after her next, something about a vendetta."

Marty didn't answer, but instead looked directly at Chadwell.

"Why?" He asked.

"I love her, I can't help it, I love her." The man sobbed, breaking down.

"That is no excuse for betraying your country," Marty snapped.

He pulled a short-barrelled pocket pistol from his pocket and put it on the table in front of him. He felt sorry for Chadwell; he had been a fool and she had used him mercilessly, but he was a weak link.

"You have a choice," was all he said as he stood and walked to the door.

He left the room, the marine guard closing the door behind him, and went to go and get something to eat. He didn't miss a step at the sound of a single shot.

In the next two days the colonel was removed from his post and sent back to England. The parapet and magazine weren't the only things he had told Claudette. He would face a quiet courts marshal and be kicked out of the Guards. His body would be found in a rented room in London a week later hanging from a beam.

The sergeant of marines was sent back to his unit where he was reduced to a private, the Navy lieutenant was removed from his ship and sent home, never to step on the deck of a Navy ship ever again.

Several men, who they positively identified as active agents, never left the fort, and two government officials were found dead after they were released, apparently due to accidents. One fell out of a window and the other was run over when he fell in front of a cart carrying barrels of beer.

"Is my island secure now?" Admiral Ball asked when Marty reported to him. Like Smith, he didn't entirely approve at how it had been achieved and the measures Marty had taken to close things off, but he also didn't want it public that the spying had been on his watch.

"As we can make it. I have sent a report to Ridgley and he will arrange for a new man to be sent out."

"Oh! that reminds me, I have some letters for you." The Admiral reached into the top drawer of his desk. "Came in the government mail bag."

Marty looked at them and saw there were a half dozen from Caroline, two from Hood and one from Collingwood, which he opened.

"I must conclude my business in Italy." Marty said as he folded it.

Ball was curious, but if this intense young man didn't want to tell him what the letter was about then he wouldn't ask.

They shook hands as Marty left.

"Please ask Mr. Shelby to attend me in my cabin at his earliest convenience," he instructed the first mid he came across. Blaez was very pleased to see him as usual and jumped up, grabbing his hands in his jaws but never closing. Marty knelt and scratched his neck fur causing one of his back legs to make scratching motions and thump the deck. He noticed grey coming into his muzzle fur.

"You wanted to see me?" Shelby asked from behind him.

"Let's go to my cabin," Marty said as he led the way.

"You need to go back to Gibraltar; Collingwood has taken a turn for the worse," Marty told him and handed over the letter.

"I expected as much. I am ready to leave immediately," Shelby replied, looking grim.

"Is it bad?" Marty asked

Shelby sighed. "He is slowly dying and there is nothing I can do to stop it."

"Does he have long?"

"If he gets rest then he could live another ten years. As it is, I don't know."

"The Alouette will take you; they are provisioned and ready to go. Please give the Admiral my best regards."

Marty watched the Eagle leave port, James piling on as much sail as he could. A premonitory shiver ran down his spine.

The Formidable was going into dock the next day for the Navy yard to refit her. She needed new masts and a lot of new planking in her hull. Marty packed a small bag and moved over to the Eagle. Sam and Blaez went with him along with Antton and Matai.

It was nice being a passenger; it gave his time to read his mail. He read the one from Hood first, it was mostly about developments in the Government and news that Wickham was going to retire. No one had been nominated to take over from him yet, but he would let him know once he knew.

"You will be next, old friend," he said to himself.

Next, he sorted Caroline's letters into date order and started with the earliest. They talked about the children and their latest adventures, how young James had managed to find his way into the kitchens and distribute a half a sack of flour all over the place before he was discovered. Beth had decided she wanted to be a warrior prince 'like mummy' and was nagging Tom to teach her to use a sword. The last one informed him she would be sailing to Gibraltar; the baby was due in October and she wanted him to be near when it was born.

He looked at Blaez,

"We had better finish this up quickly then, hadn't we?"

Blaez butted his hand for a rub in agreement.

Marty, Ryan, Antton and Matai went ashore in the bay of Naples in the middle of the night in the fishing boat Fletcher had acquired. They were dressed nondescriptly and moved quietly as they made their way to the town. By morning they were positioned near the entrance to Messier's rooms. No one showed up so Marty decided to take a look inside.

He strolled confidently up to the door and knocked. No answer. He tried the door; it was unlocked, and he slipped inside.

The rooms were empty, just bare furniture and dust. The floor creaked and he spun around going for his knife but relaxed as he saw it was Ryan.

"Our chickens have flown," he said unnecessarily.

Ryan nodded as he scanned the room.

"I know I got talking to the old lady in the shop next door; they left two days ago." He paused.

"And?" Marty said, impatiently.

"Oh, they went to his villa on the outskirts of Pompei," Ryan continued looking at his fingernails. "You know, I've broken a nail!"

Marty decided he was being teased and gave him a look that said talk or regret it. Ryan coughed and continued,

"She overheard them arguing. The girl wanted them to leave for Paris immediately and he told her that he needed to set things in order at the villa and not to worry as no one knew where it was."

"And do they?" Marty asked.

"What?" Ryan replied.

"Know where the villa is?" Marty almost shouted.

Ryan grinned. "Absolutely!"

"Why me?" Marty asked as he stomped out of the door.

That evening at dusk they arrived outside of a walled plot with a large ornamental garden. Fancy iron gates closed the entrance and a guard stood on the inside. The top of the wall had broken glass embedded in it. They didn't welcome visitors.

Matai was wearing a leather cape that he took off and with an expert flick of the wrist sent up so it landed athwart the top of the wall. Then Antton made a cup with his hands for Matai to step into and be boosted up. At the top he took a quick look around then silently dropped down the into the garden.

The rest of them moved quietly back to the gate and found it open with Matai bowing them through. Each of them bowed in return as they stepped through thanking him grandly in whispers. The guard's feet stuck out from under a bush, they didn't move.

They split into two pairs; Ryan and Matai circled around to the back of the villa, Marty and Antton went directly to the front.

Marty waited until he had counted sixty and then tried the door. It was locked, of course, so he took out his picks and went to work. It was an expensive lock and took him all of thirty seconds to pick. The door opened silently, *when will people learn that squeaky hinges are the best form of alarm?* Marty thought, thankful that no one did.

The four of them met at the bottom of the very ornate double staircase that led up to the bedrooms on the first floor after checking the ground floor for occupants. They had found a couple of sleeping guards who would wake no more but apart from that it had been easy so far.

Marty and Antton took the left staircase and Ryan and Matai the right. All four of them took great pains to test each step before they moved on to it, but Ryan didn't see the trip wire halfway up and was totally unaware he had broken the fine thread.

That is, until the door of one of the bedrooms burst open and Messier came through it with a pistol in each hand. He saw Ryan and Matai, aimed and fired the left in one motion. Ryan let out a yelp as the ball hit him and Messier raised the second to take aim at Matai with his right. That is when Marty's knife, thrown with great force, entered his body under his right armpit. Messier gasped and looked across at Marty in surprise.

He tried to raise the unfired pistol to bring it to bear, but his arm wouldn't cooperate. Marty wondered how he was staying on his feet; the wound must have pierced his right lung and the wide blade must have caused severe bleeding internally.

Marty stepped up to Messier, took the knife hilt in his right hand, placed his left hand on his shoulder and pulled the blade out with a wet sucking sound. There was a gush of blood, which he stepped to the side to avoid. The stricken man fell to the floor. Marty knelt by him and said,

"Vendetta on you complete."

Messier tried to say something, but blood gurgled out of his mouth as his lungs filled, and he died, drowning on his own blood.

Marty stepped away and went to see how Ryan was. Matai waved him away as he was already working on the wound which was in Ryan's abdomen.

Marty and Antton moved up to stand either side of the door that Messier had come out of. It had swung shut behind him. Marty took the knob, stayed under cover behind the wall and rattled it.

Nothing.

He turned it and pushed.

The door swung open.

Again, nothing.

He took a breath, knelt and stuck his head around the door frame.

There was a shot and he ducked his head back as plaster rained down on it.

Antton nodded and launched himself through the door at an angle, Marty followed knife in hand and dived in the opposite direction. He came to his knees to see Claudette knelt half naked on the bed frozen in the act of loading a pistol. Her eyes were wide as she looked at Antton and the pistol he had trained on her and then at Martin.

"I told the fool you would find us here," she sighed and tossed the gun onto the covers on the bed. *"Will you take me back to Malta for trial?"*

Marty sat on the bed next to her after putting his fighting knife back in its sheath, "I don't think so, you might get away again," he told her his hand coming down a little hard on her shoulder."

She looked at him and started a little pout but was surprised as her eyes fell on the stiletto in his hand. She noticed it had blood on it and it looked very sharp.

I'm so tired, she realised, *that's so strange,* and let herself slump down onto the bed.

She looked at Marty, he was very handsome she thought. The world slowly and gently closed in until she could only see his face, and then it went dark.

"It's done," Marty said as he checked her neck for a pulse, "let's see how Ryan is." He ran his hand over her eyes to close them before standing. He gave a last look at the still body; she looked as if she was sleeping, then turned away putting her out of his mind.

"We have to get the bullet out now," Matai said. "If we try and get him back to the ship with it in, it might split one of his intestines."

He explained that the bullet had passed through Ryan's leather belt before entering the abdomen. He couldn't smell any corruption so guessed it hadn't hit any of his guts, but as it had penetrated the belt it would have flattened, possibly with sharp edges. That had saved his life as it hadn't gone through anything vital, but the last thing he needed to do was walk with it still in.

They carefully carried him down to the kitchen where there was a well-scrubbed oak table and laid him on it. Matai searched and found a bottle of brandy and a pair of silver sugar tongs. He had watched and assisted Shelby extract bullets from all different parts of the body, and the physician had explained what he was doing as he went along. Matai was nothing if not a quick learner.

He got the others to strip Ryan and carefully cleaned the area around the wound with neat brandy, making Ryan gasp. He was washing his own hands when Ryan looked at him.

"Jesus! You miserable pirate, are you trying to kill me as well?" he groaned.

"Bite on this," Matai said and placed Ryan's belt between his teeth.

He took one of Marty's razor sharp stilettoes, washed the blade in Brandy and then flamed it. Taking a deep breath, he cut an incision to extend the hole where the bullet had entered.

Ryan groaned but couldn't move as he was held firmly top and bottom by Marty and Antton. When he had a hole big enough, he slid his finger in and gently felt for the bullet. At first, he couldn't find it, but then he felt a hard edge against the side of his finger. He traced it with his fingertip until he knew how it lie, its shape, size and where it was relative to the entry hole.

He took up the tongs, cleaned them, then gently as he could inserted them in the wound. He got hold of the ball, but the tongs slipped off as he pulled. He went in again, this time getting a tighter grip on it. He gently pulled and Ryan arched his back in pain as the squashed ball very slowly came out.

"Almost done," Matai reassured him as he dropped it in a china dish with a clatter.

He slipped his finger back in and methodically searched the wound again, then took the sugar tongs and went back in. This time he pulled out a piece of cloth layered with a piece of leather. That went into the dish as well.

"All out!" He proclaimed and saw the look of relief on all three faces. He grinned and took a needle and a length of cat gut from his pouch,

"Just got to stitch him up now."

Ryan spat out the belt. "You're enjoying this, you mother fucking son of a bitch!" he groaned as Matai dunked the lot in brandy before pinching the wound together to make the first stitch. As Shelby had taught him, he first closed the muscle layer using a special stitch that could be pulled out from the loose end left outside the wound. It also helped the wound drain and reduced the chance of infection. That would be followed by a row of stiches to close the skin

Five, painful, minutes later all Ryan had to show for the whole misadventure was a very neat row of stitches just to the left of his navel with a two-inch-long length of gut hanging out either end.

Marty looked at his watch and said,

"As much as I would like to give you time to recover, we have to go. Dawn is in an hour and we want this place burning and us as far away as possible by then."

Antton had noticed some buildings at the back of the house and after a short absence, turned up at the front door with a hand cart as Marty and Matai helped Ryan out. They loaded Ryan in it and made him relatively comfortable before Matai and Antton set off down the drive leaving Marty to finish up.

Some more brandy, lamp oil and curtains started a merry blaze that soon spread. Marty left happy that the funeral pyre was well and truly on its way. Then he remembered the guard at the gate. He quickly went to the body, slung it over his shoulder, deposited it in the kitchen, then rushed to catch up with the others.

He heard voices ahead, Ryan swearing at whoever it was in Italian. He slunk closer and could see a pair of night guards who had confronted his three compatriots. It would appear they were asking what they were doing wandering around at this time of the night and Ryan was playing the part of a drunken noble and berating them for their impudence.

Marty snuck up behind them and hit the first on the back of the head with his knife hilt. Matai swung a haymaker of a punch and felled the other with a crack of his jaw breaking.

“What was stopping you?” he barked and gestured them to get a move on.

“We were waiting for yous, boss.” Antton grinned, imitating Sam.

Marty shook his head; he was working with a bunch of comedians all of a sudden. Then he grinned, *that’s not such a bad thing.*

Chapter 17: Double trouble.

The Formidiable was ready for sea by the third week in September and they set off in convoy for the trip back to base. It was relatively uneventful with just a moderate storm to slow them, and they sailed into Rosia Bay on the third of October.

A lot has happened in the last nine months, he thought as he watched Ackermann and his other lieutenants bring the ship to anchor, *nine months!* It hit him! It was this month the baby was due!

He scanned the shoreline and spotted a carriage pulling up at the dock. Shelby got out and helped a very pregnant Caroline to step down. She walked over towards the edge, stopped and waved a scarf. Marty waved back and then became aware his barge was being pulled up at the side. When he looked around, he saw Sam leading a crew to man it. The rest of the men were grinning at him and Ackermann approached with a salute.

"With the crew's compliments, Captain, but would you kindly bugger off and go and see your wife before she gives birth." He grinned and put his hand on Marty's shoulder.

"We can manage without you."

"Watch it, or I will have you at the grating," Marty grinned back and slapped him on the shoulder in return as he bolted for the side and his waiting boat.

As it turned out he got back just in time. They got to the house that Caroline had rented and an hour later she went into labour. Marty was all in a dither; his mother wasn't here! Who would look after the birth!

Tom, who had come over with Caroline as she had wanted his wife with her, took Marty to one side, told him Shelby had everything under control, gave him a glass of rum and asked about his latest adventures. That sent Marty off into another direction, Ryan! He needed to be seen by Shelby, Matai had stitched him up and he seemed alright, but Shelby must see him.

Tom rolled his eyes. It was strange how a man who could face the sternest of tests facing the enemy and was normally as cool headed as you like could turn into a gibbering wreck at the hint of childbirth.

"Shelby is overseeing the birth," he told him again as if he was taking to a child, "he will check Ryan over when he gets done here."

Marty slugged back the rum, and gradually calmed down as Tom kept talking to him. In the end Tom persuaded him that he should take a bath as the stink of the ship was on him and he should greet the new-born clean.

It only occurred to Marty that he hadn't seen his other children since he had arrived once he got into the bath. Tom, who wasn't about to leave him alone for a minute, explained that they were out with Mary, their nanny, visiting the Barbary monkeys.

Marty hadn't even notice that the bath had already been filled by the time he got to his room and that some of his clothes had been brought from England. His steward had also miraculously appeared and helped him undress and shed his weapons.

While he was in the bath Sam turned up, having returned to the Formidiable for his sea chest. He and Adam unpacked his uniforms, sorted out what needed to be cleaned or repaired and had a clean suit of clothes laid out ready when Marty had finished his bath.

Calmer, now, and more in control Marty went with Tom and Sam to the drawing room. The house was built high on the slope of the hill where it could get a cool breeze. The windows were open, and he could see Rosia Bay below them. His ships looked neat and tidy; their yards crossed perfectly with the sun glinting on their brass work.

Shelby came down and sat with them for a while.

"How long do you think it will take?" Marty asked.

"This isn't your first, you know they take as long as they will," Shelby answered.

"I wasn't home for the first and we were in India for the second and I had a lot on my mind,"

"How long did she take for the first?" Shelby asked.

"That un was quick," replied Tom, "well less than a day. The second was a bit longer."

Marty looked at him in surprise, he hadn't realised Tom had paid so much attention.

"Then I expect she will take around the same for the first and the other will come out soon after."

Time stopped.

"What did you say?" he finally whispered.

Shelby looked at him in surprise and looked at Tom who suddenly found something to look at out of the window.

Sam started to laugh as what Shelby had said sunk in,

"You be having twins boss!"

Marty was mad at Tom for not telling him and madder at Caroline for not even mentioning it in her letters. He took Blaez out and walked it off before he trusted himself back in the house again. It was early October and the weather was grey which suited his mood.

The children were back when he got home and Blaez went into paroxysms of joy at meeting them again. Beth was now six, going on eight or nine as far as Marty could tell; had his mother's strong will and knew her own mind. James was three and showing a mischievous streak.

"Uncle Tom has been teaching me to use a sword," she proudly announced.

"Really?" Marty said, "and why do you want to learn that?"

"'Cos I am going to be a warrior pwincess when I grow up and have a ship like mummy and fight piwates!" she said seriously.

"And how do you know about mummy fighting pirates?" Marty asked, casting a gimlet eye on Tom.

"Mummy told me in a bedtime stowy!" Tom looked smug and gave him as innocent a look as the old rogue could manage.

It wouldn't do but she showed him her skills, resulting in him getting bruised knuckles as she whacked him with the wooden blade of the sword Tom had carved for her.

Luckily a maid rushed in and announced that the first of the babies had arrived and the second was on its way out! Which saved his knuckles but sent his nerves in a spin. She rushed back up the stairs before anybody had a chance to ask if it was a boy or a girl!

Another half hour passed, and Shelby walked into the drawing room rolling his sleeves down and looking satisfied. He was heralded by the joint lusty calls of the babies from upstairs.

"You may go up and see them Martin, mother and babies are doing well."

He didn't need a second invitation and hared up the stairs two at a time. He slowed down at the bedroom door as he realised the crying had stopped, eased open the door and entered quietly. Amara, Tom's wife, was sat beside the bed sewing a, something, and Mary, the children's nurse, was watching from the foot of the bed.

Caroline, looking beautiful, sat propped up in the bed holding a baby to each breast, feeding them simultaneously. Marty, eyes wide in wonder, stepped forward and sat on the edge of the bed. Caroline watched him with a happy smile and love in her eyes. The pain of childbirth forgotten in the moment.

"Girls?" Marty asked as he gently sat on the edge of the bed.

"They didn't tell you?" she asked mischievously.

Marty gave her a pleading look.

"One of each, a boy, the eldest, and a girl," she relented. "and damn, are they hungry!"

"We will have to get a wet nurse," Amara said in her deep Indian accent, "there is no way that mistress can manage with two babies like that on her own."

"Where do you find one of them?" Marty asked.

Domestic bliss was short lived; the twins seemed to be always hungry and Mary had to find two wet nurses in the end to keep them fed. Until that time, Caroline was permanently tired and made it clear if Marty came within ten feet of her with an erection, she would chop it off!

After a week of that Marty found an excuse to go to the base and check that everything was alright with the flotilla. Everything was fine, of course, and he found Ridgley sat in his office.

"Take-over bid?" he snarled as he walked through the door.

"Now that's a nice way to greet an old friend. Twins getting you down?" Ridgley smirked.

Marty hmphed and plonked himself down in one of his comfy chairs.

"Any missions that will take me away for about five years?" Marty growled.

"You know I once had a friend whose wife gave birth to twins who volunteered for a polar expedition." Ridgley said thoughtfully.

"Did it work?" Marty asked.

"Don't know, he never came back." Ridgley quivered with laughter.

"Very funny."

"Well, you will have to put up with it for a few weeks yet, your officers tell me the men need a rest and you need to recruit some replacements. How's the thigh by the way?"

"It's healing well enough. I don't suppose there are any reports on that desk for my attention?"

"What, these?" Ridgley smirked as he tossed over several brown cards folded around sheaves of papers tied together with black ribbons. "I was about to bring them to you at the house. The folded cards are my idea, keeps things from getting mixed up."

Smart! Marty thought, but wasn't about to say anything of the sort to Ridgley, he would be insufferable.

"I also wanted to tell you that London are sending out a new man for Malta."

"Do we know him?" Marty asked.

"No, unfortunately not. His profile reads well, though, been to Oxford, trained in a seminary, thrown out for duelling. Has mixed parentage, his father was an English officer in the Indian regiment and his mother a high caste Indian woman. Apparently makes him look somewhat Mediterranean, by all accounts."

"Fit right in, then." Marty commented off handedly.

"Listen," Ridgley leaned forward intently, and Marty took notice as he sensed something coming, "how well do you get on with Sir Sidney Smith?"

"Friends I think," Marty replied honestly. "I like him, he just needs to be a bit more diplomatic when dealing with his superiors."

"Yes, quite, he called General Stuart an ass," Ridgley told him. "That's what got him taken off the Sicily station."

"Yes, I can imagine him doing that," Marty laughed at the vision that created.

"Do you think you could rein him in?"

Marty looked at him sharply.

"What are you getting me into?" he asked bluntly.

"Nothing yet, but there are plans in the making and having a part of the task force that wasn't directly under his control, led by someone who could influence him might be an attractive option."

"And if he fails dramatically?" Marty asked.

"Then you and your flotilla will never be named in any of the reports. As usual."

Chapter 18: Falling on deaf ears

After a well-earned break, Marty was introduced to the infamous Enreekaay that he had heard about when they first got to Gibraltar. His name was Enrique Castell, a Catalan who had some distinct prejudices against the French. He needed someone to get him back into Spain close to Madrid and the S.O.F. was given the job and Marty chose to do it himself.

To be honest, he could have tasked Ryan or James to do it. He used the excuse that the Formidiable was Spanish-built and therefore less likely to attract attention than the others, which they all knew was hokum. He just needed to get away from the chaos the twins had turned his home life into, and the job would only take a couple of weeks if all went well.

He tasked Ryan to sail back to England and see if he could recruit some more volunteers. James was left in charge of the shore base and would handle anything else. Marty borrowed twenty of his men to get the Formidiable back up to strength.

It was cold, rainy and miserable weather when they set sail with the wind veering between due North and Northeast which made getting out of the bay tricky. They had a nasty time getting into the straits and just made it into the Mediterranean before dark.

The plan was to sail up the coast and put Enrique ashore at Alicante, which was a fishing village halfway between Cartagena and Valencia. There was a well-travelled route to Madrid from there directly Northwest which Enrique could take by horse, to get him into the city in two days.

It was close to three hundred and eighty sea miles and should only take a day and a half if the weather gods were kind. But they weren't, the barometer dropped when they were just off the coast of the Gulf of Almeria and a storm hit from the North. The gale force wind spinning around the concentrated depression first blew west shooting them along their course then swung more to the North giving them no option but to run before it towards the North African coast.

They had, maybe, ninety sea miles of sea room before they would come up on a lee shore so Marty steered as much East as he could to try to gain a bit more. Enrique was as sick as a man can be without dying. Shelby had him down in the sick bay and was trying to feed him fluids, but the poor man just couldn't deal with the crazy corkscrew like motion the Formidiable was making.

They ran out of sea room and ended up anchored off the coast of Algeria in a bay near Oran, pinned down by the North-north-easterly wind. They had to sit it out for two days. That gave Enrique time to recover somewhat before the next trial.

The wind eventually swung to the West and they were able to sail out of the bay. The seas were still up, and they headed North with the sea on their beam towards Cartagena. Enrique got sick again and he sat in the sickbay with Shelby and his loblolly boy, Henry Ford, the ship had started rolling badly as soon as they had set sail again.

"You really would feel better up on deck you know." Shelby told him.

"That may be, but I would be a mass of bruises. How do the men in the crew stay on their feet when the ship is rolling like this? Captain Martin looks like his feet are nailed to the deck no matter what it does."

"He has been at sea since he was twelve years old, he has more trouble walking on dry land," Shelby laughed

"Is his wife as beautiful as they say?" Enrique asked to keep the conversation going.

"Probably more. She has an inner light and energy that shine through as well as being physically beautiful."

"They must make a striking couple!"

"That they do."

"And he is a Baron?"

"Well, technically she was a Baroness when they got married and he got his title that way, but he is also a Knight and he got that all on his own," Shelby explained.

Just then, the rolling lessened noticeably as they felt the ship turn.

"Mr. Enrique?" Midshipman Williams enquired sticking his head through the door.

"Captain's compliments sir, but we will be putting you ashore in about an hour."

"Si! Tell him I will be ready!"

It was dusk as the Formidiable hove to and a boat was brought up and manned. Marty shook hands with Enrique and bade him a safe journey. Once he was ashore, he didn't look back but walked quickly up the beach and disappeared behind the dunes.

"Time to go home," Marty said to Ackermann as they set the foresails to pulling and moved away.

It was hard to make progress with long tacks to make headway against the westerly wind. It was during a southerly leg that the squall hit. The lookout caught sight of it when it was only one hundred yards away and he barely shouted a warning before it slammed into the ship from the starboard side dead in line with the mizzen mast.

The subsequent chain of events unfolded at phenomenal speed. The back of the ship was driven around by the force of the wind and the quartermaster and his mate were thrown from the wheel as it was ripped out of their hands. Marty, who had the watch, was also thrown from his feet. He was just getting up when he saw that the mizzen gaff sail boom had ripped loose and was falling towards the quartermaster who was struggling back to his feet. He didn't think, just launched himself across the deck to push him clear.

Then it all went dark.

There were several moments during which he felt like he was waking up, only to hear a gentle voice murmuring and a sweet liquid pass his lips. Then it all went comfortably black again.

He finally woke up in a bed and the first think he noticed was it was very quiet, the second thing was he had a hell of a headache. Caroline's face appeared and she said something to somebody behind her and then her lips moved as if she was saying something to him.

He couldn't hear a thing!

Caroline looked down at the man she loved more than life itself. He looked confused then frightened and she said,

"It's alright, my love, you are at home, you will be fine."

His look turned from fear and confusion to concern and he said in an odd voice,

"I can't hear you! I can't hear a thing!"

The door opened and Shelby came in, he sat on the bed and checked Marty's eyes and pulse. Then he gently felt around his head, which Marty realised was bandaged.

"Get me a slate and some chalk please," he said to Caroline.

Once she left, he looked at Marty and winked, pointed to his head and mimed hitting it then made a motion with his hands as if they were being pushed apart. Lastly, he pointed to his ears and stuck his fingers in them.

Marty couldn't suppress a laugh as the normally serious physician looked ridiculous. But he thought he got the gist of what was being said.

He had been hit on the head, something had swollen up and that had blocked his ears.

Caroline arrived with the slate and chalk.

"How is your head?" Shelby wrote.

"It hurts like hell," Marty said.

"You were hit by the boom that fell onto the quarterdeck," Shelby wrote after wiping the slate clean.

Marty frowned and replied,

"I don't remember anything after leaving Almeria

"Bad wind. Squall, boom fell, hit you on head," Shelby wrote.

"Is the ship alright?" Marty asked.

"Ship fine, no other casualties." Shelby assured him after cleaning the slate again,

"You saved the quartermaster."

Marty shook his head, gently, he didn't remember any of it.

"How long?" he asked as he realised he must have been out for quite a while.

"Four days sailing and two days here."

"Six days?" then….

"OUCH!" as pain shot through his head as he tried to sit up.

They left him to sleep. A little while later the door was pushed open and Blaez slid silently in. He gently climbed on the bed and lay beside Marty so he could lay his head on his chest. He was still there when Caroline looked in to check on him later.

Shelby had told her when they had gotten him home that the blow on the head from the boom had caused a swelling of the brain. He had drugged Marty to keep him unconscious for the trip home and the two days after, as from experience, and everything he had read, total rest was the best cure. They had fed him water through a tube down his throat; he thought six days was enough.

Now, Marty was hungry, but they only allowed him thin chicken soup to start with and he was ordered to stay in bed. Over the next four days they gradually increased the number of solids in his food. Blaez hardly left his side and it was a great relief when he was finally allowed to sit in a chair in the drawing room and look out over the bay at his ships.

His first visitor was the quartermaster whose life he had saved, Tim Green, a tough Londoner.

Tim was ushered into the drawing room by Caroline and stood looking worriedly at his Captain. The bandages had been removed but you could still see the scab on Marty's scalp where the boom had hit him.

"Hello, Green, you look well." Marty greeted him.

"All because of you Sir, I wants to thank ye for saving my life," he replied.

Marty had become slightly adept at lip reading and got the gist of what he was saying, although he could only hear a dull mumble.

"You are welcome," he replied with a grin. "I wasn't quick enough to get myself out of the way though. Tell me what has been happening on my ship while I have been gone."

Tim started to tell him as he stood there but Marty made him pull up a chair and when he couldn't follow his description of the damage got him to draw it on the slate.

Eventually he tired, and Caroline put a stop to the chat with the promise that someone would visit every day to keep him informed of what was going on.

It took another month for his hearing to return and even then, he still had ringing in his ears. Shelby advised him to put wax in his ears and to bind a bandana around them when the guns were firing. He didn't need to damage them anymore than they were.

Even better, his forced inactivity meant he got to know the twins and they chose their names together. Edwin George Arthur and Constance Willow Mary. The wet nurses took over the feeding and he and Caroline got back to being how they had been in bed, which improved his wellbeing immensely.

Over the winter things were quiet in as much that he didn't receive any orders for specific missions, instead the flotilla trained and honed their amphibious landing skills on the West side of the Rock at Sandy Bay.

Starved of entertainment in the winter months the locals started turning up to watch. The audience grew as the word spread and people decided this new form of entertainment was better than just sitting and watching rain run down the gutters. Inevitably, elements of the army started coming down in groups and shouted insults and advice in equal measure.

la Pierre's reaction was simple, he saw an opportunity to exercise his snatch squads. These were specialist teams who were there to infiltrate enemy territory and kidnap individuals who they were interested in 'talking' to. They had used them in the exercise on Malta and now they were busy developing the idea and the techniques involved.

He would point out individuals who were regular spectators and amongst the most vocal, task the teams to snatch them from their barracks at night and deliver them to headquarters, where they were put through a mock interrogation.

That led to some complaints, especially when a lieutenant of artillery was snatched mid-dalliance with his mistress and unceremoniously bundled in his nightshirt through the town. It wasn't the fact that he had his hands tied and a hood over his head, more than the fact that his night shirt only came down to his waist and his 'equipment' was on show to all and sundry, that upset the worthy.

After that Marty reverted to making wagers with the Army commanders that his men could infiltrate their bases and capture an agreed item or person. . This had two effects; first, it improved security everywhere because they didn't know when or where they would make an attempt, and second, Marty's teams got to be as sharp as they could be.

Chapter 19: Omega and Alpha

Marty was in his office on the first of March nursing a slight hangover from his birthday party the night before and watching the rain lash down the windows when there was a knock on the door. A very wet, very young ensign stepped in and saluted.

"Captain Stockley, I have a dispatch for you," he said and held out a packet wrapped in oiled canvas.

Marty took it curiously and went to his desk to open it. He unwrapped the canvas and saw a letter inside with his own seal.

He felt an empty pit in his stomach as he opened it to see it was dated just two weeks before.

Dear Martin,

I'm writing becus mum has taken a turn for the worse. The winter has been specially wet and cold and she has suddenly got much older. If you can get home as soon as you can, it wood be good as we don't know how long she have got.

We had a visit from Captain Turner, and he said he would get this letter to you as fast as possible.

Your lovin sister, Helen

He thanked the ensign and sent him on his way with a silver guinea.

"Ryan! Get the Eagle ready to sail," he yelled into the office that Ryan and James shared and bolted out of the door heading to the house.

He crashed through the door and Caroline looked up from her embroidery in surprise. He thrust the now soggy paper into her hands and ran up to their rooms.

He was throwing clothes into a sea chest when Caroline walked in and sat on the bed.

"When will the ship be ready?" she asked

"What?" Marty said, still emptying a drawer.

"When will the ship be ready?" she repeated.

Marty stopped and looked a little sheepish. "Several hours," he replied holding a pair of drawers.

"And when is the earliest it can sail?"

"Tomorrow morning."

"Right, well send a message to . . ?"

"Ryan."

"Ryan and tell him that we will all be going back to England tomorrow morning. I am sure he will want to set the ship up in the right way to make us all comfortable." Sanity restored, Caroline mobilised the household and got the bare minimum packed.

Ryan had men working all night to convert part of the Eagles cargo space into cabins to accommodate the family, servants, wet nurses etc. It wasn't the easiest or tidiest of constructions, but canvas and a lick of paint hides a lot and they were all in and ready to go when the tide turned.

They sailed straight into Poole and as the wind was favourable out of the Southeast, they took the barge under sail up to Wareham, hired a couple of coaches and were in Church Knowle less than two hours later.

They were met at the door by his sisters, Jane and Helen, and went straight to his mother's room. He was shocked to see how old she looked. Her skin was almost translucent and grey, her eyes were closed, and her breathing laboured. She opened her eyes as they entered.

"I knew you would come," she said in a soft voice, "my Marty would never let me leave without saying goodbye."

"Don't be daft, mum, you aint goin' nowhere," Marty told her, grief making his Dorset accent come out.

"Hello, mum," Caroline said, stepping to the foot of the bed. She held the twins in her arms.

Annie smiled when she saw them. "Twins! They run in the family you know. Great-grandpa Absalom had two sets."

"Do you want to hold them?" Caroline asked.

"Prop me up, boy," Annie instructed Marty with a burst of energy and Marty helped her sit up so they could pile more pillows behind her.

Caroline passed Constance to Marty so he could help Annie hold her in one arm while she helped on the other side. They were asleep but then one at a time they woke up and looked up at their grandma.

"They be alike as two peas in a pod!" she exclaimed.

Then Beth and James decided they wanted in on the party as well, and climbed on the bed,

"Well that be just fine," she said, looking around at them all.

It was the last time they saw her alive. She died quietly in her sleep that night. She had had her last wish to see her Marty and his children once more and went with a smile on her face. They were woken to the news by Blaez howling mournfully outside her window. Marty wanted to join him but kept his grief in a ball in his chest.

Annie May Stockley was buried in St. Peters church two days later and almost everybody who had ever known her turned up to say goodbye. The vicar asked whether one of her children would give a eulogy. It would normally be given by the oldest, but they all decided Marty should be the one. He stood in front of her coffin,

"My mum was the kindest person I knew; she never had a bad word to say about anyone."

There was a general rumble of agreement through the congregation.

"She looked after us kids and did her best to make sure we all went to school and learned to read and do our numbers. She wanted us to have a better life than her and Dad and it was my greatest joy to be able to help her realise that."

He took a deep breath to steady himself, this was far harder than talking to a crew from a quarterdeck.

"When Miss Turner and her brother, Captain Turner, came to get me the day I went into the Navy, she said to me, 'No matter what is asked of you or what you come up against, remember as long as you be brave and do your best no one can doubt you.' That was the best advice anybody ever gave me and I hope I lived up to her expectations.

"She had to live through the deaths of my eldest brother, Thomas, and my Dad, but she only despaired because of what that did to my brothers and sisters."

He paused again then squared his shoulders.

"She was our rock, our foundation, our strength and our inspiration, and will be forever in our hearts."

He had tears running down his face as he ended, turned to the open coffin and kissed his mother goodbye.

The wake would be remembered for many years, as they sent her off proper, in the Dorset way.

That evening anyone walking by the cemetery would have seen a figure, with a dog by his side, kneeling by the freshly closed grave. The dog had his head pressed into the man's chest and gently licked the tears away as they ran down his chin.

Marty, Caroline and the children stayed in Church Knowle for another week before leaving to re-embark on the Eagle and sail around the coast to their company berth in India dock. They had sent messages ahead so there were enough coaches waiting to transport them, Ryan and the servants to the London house.

Marty sent a note to Admiral Hood informing him he was in London and why. He was expecting Hood to contact him but was amazed when out of the blue the Prince Regent plus entourage descended on the house.

"My dear Marty!" the Prince greeted him as he hurriedly straightened his coat. "My deepest condolences on the death of your dear mother!" he continued, giving him a hug and then holding him at arm's length while he looked deeply into his eyes in sympathy. "I met her at your wedding you know. She was a lovely forthright woman; told me I should lose weight!" he laughed sadly.

Caroline glided into the room and curtsied, the Prince went over kissed her hands and told her she was looking magnificent.

Nothing would do but they settle down for tea. The entourage were encamped in the library and they sat with the Prince in the drawing room. When he found out that Caroline had given birth to twins, he just had to meet them and even laughed when one puked milk over his shoulder.

The next morning a note was delivered from Hood inviting Marty to meet him at White's, his club, for lunch. Marty was greeted at the door by a servant and escorted straight to the dining room where Hood was already at a table.

"Martin, my dear boy, how are you? I am so sorry to hear the news about your mother," Hood greeted him and shook his hand.

Marty sat and replied that he was fine and thanked him for his concern.

"Let's order first and then we can talk, I recommend the whitebait, followed by the trout and then the beef and kidney pie," Hood smiled. "We can wash the fish down with an excellent Hock and the pie with a Burgundy." Marty agreed, wondering what was coming next.

The whitebait was served and came with tartar sauce and wedges of lemon. It was extremely popular in London and there were a couple of pubs down near the Palace of Westminster that specialized in it.

"How do you get on with Sir Sidney Smith?" Hood asked around a mouthful.

Marty swallowed the forkful he had just taken and thought, *why is everyone interested in how I get on with him?* but answered,

"Fine, we have become friends after a fashion. He is a very interesting man."

"Excellent, excellent." Hood observed, demolished the pile of crispy little fish in front of him and had the server clear his plate before he continued.

"Portugal is under threat. We have intelligence that France and Spain are negotiating to carve it up between them. We have put Smith on standby to assist them should it be necessary."

Marty still didn't understand why his relationship with Smith was important, so just waited.

"Our man, Castell, is in Madrid and has his ear to the ground, but his position is precarious as his dislike of the French is well known. We want to send in some support."

The trout arrived, swimming in butter with chervil and parsley, accompanied by small new potatoes from the island of Jersey where the climate allowed them to be earlier than on the mainland.

"Linette will join you before you leave to return to Gibraltar. I am sure that will please young Mr. Thompson."

Marty grinned; the relationship between the spy and the lieutenant had developed in the last year or so and they were obviously in love. Not that it would stop her from using her feminine charms to achieve her mission, but her heart belonged to Ryan.

They continued to eat in silence, savouring the taste of the excellent food and wine.

"What else do you want us to do?" Marty asked, knowing that something else was coming.

"We want to ferment dissent in Granada, you have already made contact down there. They are very angry with their Catalan cousins for bowing to Napoleon and are happy to punish any French incursions into their territory. They need training and arming and that's a job for your Marines."

Marty nodded and gently slid the last of the succulent trout flesh off the bone.

"I assume you don't want them to learn all our 'bad habits' as well?" he grinned.

"No, you can tell your men to keep their thieving and murdering ways to themselves, but ambush techniques, hit and run, demolition, that sort of thing, would be very useful to them." Hood frowned and added,

"Have your ships raid the East coast to keep the Spanish occupied over there, away from Portugal."

The second course was cleared.

"There is one other thing you can do in Spain," Hood added and looked around to make sure no one was in hearing range.

"I want you to assassinate the French ambassador in Madrid."

Marty coughed as he breathed in the sip of wine he had just taken and had to use his napkin to cover his discomfort.

Hood waited until he had recovered.

"If we can disrupt the negotiations, it will buy us time and allow Sir Sydney to be prepared for when the agreement is signed, and they act."

Marty nodded, then frowned, and decided to cut to the chase.

"What do you want me to do with Sir Sidney? You have been avoiding that."

Hood gave him a straight look and pursed his lips, his hands held together as if in prayer, fingertips resting on his chin.

"You were ever perceptive. Smith is prone to go off and do his own thing, much to the annoyance of his superiors. We are hoping that when he moves on Lisbon to blockade it, you can accompany him and lend a certain common sense to his actions."

"You think he will listen to me?"

"He has said he respects you and thinks that you will continue to be a great asset to the Navy. I think he will."

Marty was dumfounded, he would never have guessed that Sidney would have made any kind of supportive statement about him.

The beef and kidney pie was served. It had a steamed suet crust pastry and when he opened it, he saw that as well as kidney there were whole oysters and shallots baked into it. It was served with buttered carrots, late season brussels sprouts and creamy mashed potato.

The Burgundy wine was poured by the sommelier for Hood to taste and he grunted his approval as he eyed the plate in front of him in anticipation.

Marty tasted the wine and knew this one as it was imported by the Deal boys and delivered by Caroline's wine distribution business.

Marty picked up the conversation again. "The assassination of the ambassador."

Hood raised his eyebrows over his plate.

"Any particular way you want that done?" he continued as if conversing about the weather.

My god he can be cold blooded, Hood thought.

"An accident or something unattributable preferably."

"You don't want us to make it look as if it were the Spanish?"

"No that might encourage Napoleon to actually take Spain over by force." Hood responded.

The rest of the meal was spent talking about their families and the subject of the twins christening came up.

"You are going to have to do it and soon." Hood observed. It was common to have children christened within weeks of their birth as the infant mortality rate was so high. They had left it very late in the eyes of most people.

"We could get them done in London before we leave." Marty conceded.

"Good idea and invite the Prince to be a godparent." Hood suggested.

Later that afternoon when Marty got back to the house, he found Caroline with Josee, James' wife, in the drawing room.

"Did it go well?" she asked after he had kissed them both, Josee having to bend a little so he could kiss her cheeks.

"We should get the twins christened before we go back to Gibraltar." He blurted out.

Caroline looked at him sideways,

"Hood's suggestion?"

Marty had to admit it was and added,

"He thinks we should invite the Prince to be a godparent."

"Oh, does he?" Caroline replied, but then got a calculating look. "Actually, that's not such a bad idea. When do we have to go back?"

"In two weeks at the latest." Marty replied.

Caroline wrote to the Prince and asked if he would consent to be a godparent to the twins and he wrote back by return that he would be delighted and that furthermore they should be christened in the royal chapel at St. James' Palace.

So it was that a week later, with as many of their family as could be gathered together, they congregated in the Royal Chapel with its soft brown wood panelling dating from the reign of the Tudors.

Marty had repeated second thoughts about having the Prince as godparent as his lifestyle and profligacy hadn't made him popular with the people, but on the other hand, it could only be to all their children's benefit to have a royal patron.

The ceremony was mercifully short. Marty always felt uncomfortable in churches. The Prince gifted the twins with stunning, solid silver baby rattles and christening mugs.

Chapter 20: Like falling off a log

Josee accompanied them to Gibraltar to join James, she was having a hard time coping without him in London as she had no family around her and missed him terribly. Caroline invited her to stay at their house until they could set up their own on the Rock.

Linette appeared for the christening. Nobody asked where she had been or what she had been doing. Prince George made a pass at her and walked away wide eyed and a little pale after she whispered something in his ear.

The planning for her infiltration and the training that the Marines would give the Granadans, took over two weeks before Ridgley and Marty were happy with it. They would gift the Spanish rebels fifty muskets with ammunition, to get them started but they expected them to acquire anymore they needed by capturing them from the Catalans and the French.

Ryan and Marty teamed up to take out the French Ambassador, Linette would join Enrique.

The Hornfleur would stop at Malaga where a contingent of Marines would go ashore and set up a training camp. After they had finished, a select team would stay on as advisors while the rest would return to Gibraltar.

The Formidiable, Alouette and Eagle would range up the East coast of Spain raiding ports and disrupting commerce. Daring the Spanish to try and catch them. Snatch squads would capture French and Spanish officers for interrogation.

Ackermann would command the Formidiable, in Marty's absence, and Trenchard the Eagle in Ryan's stead. James would stay in charge of the Alouette and be in overall command.

"Be careful when you give instructions," Marty warned the Marines in the training cadre during their briefing. "Spanish nobles are incredibly touchy of their honour so request that they do something or couch the instruction as advice."

"Does that mean I can't order them to drop and give me fifty push ups if they don't get summit right?" asked Sergeant Bright with a grin.

"I'm afraid so," Marty grinned back at him, "you will have to use your well-known charm and gentle powers of persuasion to get them to do what you want."

That caused a laugh all around and some good-natured mickey taking.

"Seriously though, do not offend the nobles or gentlemen. I do not want you being called out for duels."

The flotilla set sail in the early morning, slipping out of port without fuss or pomp. Marty had already sent a note to Collingwood apologising for not firing a salute and explaining the need to sail with the minimum of fuss.

Collingwood had been briefed on some of the mission. He knew that they would harass the East coast and were doing something in Malaga. He had not been informed about Enrique and Linette nor about their plans for the ambassador.

They ghosted up the coast to the Northeast in light winds under no flags. Anyone who saw them from the shore would wonder at the strange group of ships, a Spanish built frigate, French built corvette, American built clipper and a whaler.

As they approached Malaga, Hornfleur signalled, 'good hunting' as they peeled off and headed into the bay. The mission had begun.

The remaining ships sailed on, running through sail drills and gun practice without firing until they left the coast of The Kingdom of Granada and entered Mercia where the fun could start.

Following standard procedure, they spread out with the fastest ship to the seaward side. In this case that was the Eagle, but as none of them were slouches and all had reasonably clean bottoms it was more a matter of form than necessity.

Marty, Ryan and Linette were put ashore at midnight near to the village of Alicante and made their way to Madrid as Enrique had, by horseback. Two days later they parted company at the town of Getafe where Linette turned into a lady of means, dressed in the latest Spanish fashion and hired a coach.

Marty would have had a hard time recognising her as she now sported a black wig, piled up high on her head and held in place with ornate combs. Her dress was also flamboyant and fashioned of black and red silk with lace trim and embellishments.

Marty and Ryan were dressed as gentlemen or Caballeros and rode prancing Arabian blood stallions which Marty had bought at great expense. Marty had been learning Catalan and could hold his own in a conversation which took some of the pressure off Ryan. They stayed in the same hotel they had the year before when they had hunted down Linette's sister. The hotelier didn't recognise them.

The French embassy had moved. The burnt-out ruin of the old one was being demolished in readiness for a private house to be built. As they looked at it, Ryan grinned at Marty and nudged him with his elbow,

"All my own work!"

They walked, imitating the other Spanish gentlemen in their manner and attitude, to the new address they had been given and were impressed. The French had used the fire to up their game and make sure they were imposing their presence on the area.

The new embassy was huge and took up the best part of an entire block. The façade was Palladian, was more palatial than ambassadorial and the building was surrounded by a high iron fence. French army guards manned the gates and were checking everyone who sought entry to the building. There were more guards on the door and visible in the foyer.

As they strolled around the block, they could see that the fence extended all the way around and that there was even a double gate to get into the courtyard and stables.

"All your own work," quipped Marty nudging Ryan in the ribs.

They took it in turns to watch the back door of the Embassy to see when the Ambassador left and how. They discovered that while he stayed at the embassy Monday to Thursday, on Friday he would take a coach to an estate that straddled the river Manzanares to the Southeast of the city. The region it was in was very hilly with cliffs and bluffs carved out of the landscape. The Ambassador loved to hunt and the whole area teamed with wildlife.

They followed him that weekend and mapped out the route he took on his hunting trip, for all the good it would do as they seemed to just follow the game and move at random.

Marty was impressed at how good a shot the man was. He rarely missed with either musket or shotgun. His loader was kept busy and he had the Spanish equivalent of a gamekeeper with him who also carried a gun and had a gun dog.

They couldn't kill all three and make it look like an accident, the dog made it almost impossible to get close to them and at their hotel they came up with idea after idea and discarded them all.

"There has to be a way!" Marty huffed in exasperation.

For the lack of any other ideas they decided to follow the hunting party again the next Saturday and had their first bit of luck, there wasn't a dog. That meant they could get closer at least.

They had slunk along staying out of sight in a gulley behind a row of scrubby bushes when the Ambassador brought down a bird that landed a few feet away from them. The gamekeeper said something and walked straight towards where they were hidden to retrieve it.

Marty signed to Ryan to move to one side after passing him the end of a rope they carried to help with climbs. The gamekeeper walked forward, looking for the bird his head moving from side to side. He looked as if he would miss them completely so Marty rustled the bush in front of him as if a wounded bird was thrashing around under it. The man homed in on the sound and didn't spot the rope hidden just in front of the gully until his foot hit it. As he tripped and fell forward Marty stepped in and hit him with his blackjack.

All the Ambassador saw was his man fall forward into a bush with a cry that was cut off abruptly. He left his loader where he was, reloading both barrels of his shotgun, and walked over calling the fallen man's name.

He got to the bushes.

There was a shot!

He fell without making a sound.

The loader didn't look up as he was intent on his task. When it was finished, he looked around and realised he was alone. By then Ryan and Marty were long gone.

Back in his cabin on the Formidiable Marty was explaining to Ackermann what had happened.

"As the gamekeeper fell Ryan grabbed his gun. When the Ambassador got to the bushes, he shot him in the heart at almost point-blank range. I made sure he was dead by slipping a stiletto through the wound while Ryan put the gun next to the gamekeeper to make it look like it had gone off as he fell. We also bashed his head on a rock to make it look as if he had hit it when he had fallen. We were damn lucky that bird landed where it did, and they hadn't brought a dog."

"The lord moves in strange and mysterious ways to aid those he smiles on," Ackermann smiled benevolently.

"Well he helped us on this one. Linette sent a message saying as far as the authorities were concerned it was a tragic accident. They let the gamekeeper off as he couldn't remember anything."

He picked up a sheaf of reports and thumbed through them.

"Looks like you have been having fun. You sent all the prizes to Gibraltar under escort by the Eagle?"

"Aye Sir, only the valuable ones, the rest we burnt."

"The officers we snatched?"

"Taken back in the Eagle for Ridgley to question."

"How are we for men?"

"We are short but expect the Eagle to return in two days, then we will be back up to strength."

There was a knock at the door and Fletcher was announced. He was dressed in his trademark plaid smoking jacket and hat and looked as little like a sailor as it was possible.

"Good afternoon, Mr. Fletcher," said Marty with a welcoming smile.

"Good afternoon, Captain Stockley," Fletcher responded in kind and plonked himself down in a comfortable chair without being invited.

"It's a good job I'm your Captain, any other would strip your back for your insolence," Marty grinned at him.

"If it were any other captain I wouldn't be here." Fletcher retorted.

"The state of the stores?" Marty prompted.

Fletcher laughed and flourished a long list.

"Thanks to all the food and fresh stuff we 'liberated' from our various prizes and ports we are well supplied." He scanned the list, "in fact, we have better food than we get from the port supply office. We can stay at sea for another couple of months easily."

Marty pondered that; they had a list of pick up points where they had to be on particular nights at specific times. Enrique and Linette would be at whichever one was allocated for the day when they needed to get out. He had no option but to stay on this stretch of coast until that time. Well, they would make the most of it.

Chapter 21: Run and Fight

The Eagle returned more or less on schedule and they continued their depredations of the East coast reaching up as far as Perpignan in France. They took out semaphore towers, and kidnapped officers and any French officials they came across, causing the French and Spanish to dedicate more troops to defending them. The Spanish even stationed cavalry units at strategic points to try and ambush the raiders when they struck.

That strategy almost worked the first time the French tried it; the raiding party just got back to their boats in time. However, they had overlooked he fact that the first thing Marty's team would capture was the tower and the extra height that gave them allowed them to see the cavalry coming from a long way away.

The second time they tried it the tables were turned, and the ambushers became the ambushed. Volley guns are devastating against horse, and they deployed a dozen or so grenades to decimate the attacking force.

It was on James' watch that Linette and Enrique returned.

James had taken the Alouette to the scheduled pick-up point for that week and arrived a half mile off the beach at Salou just shy of midnight. As per standard practice, they had a boat pulled around ready to go ashore if a signal was seen.

They were to stay hove to until three AM and then make their way to the rendezvous with the other ships, but James had a strange sensation in the pit of his stomach and an odd feeling of anticipation, so when three AM came, he stayed just where he was.

At a quarter to four they saw a flash of light from the shore followed by the signal. The boat was manned and heading in as he replied with a shuttered lantern.

It was a very dark night with no moon and a light overcast and he couldn't see the shore so was surprised when there were a number of flashes followed by the sound of a volley of shots from close to where the signal had been given, there was a volley of shots in reply.

"Load the guns with cannister if you please, Archie," he commanded his midshipman.

The signal lamp was left un-shuttered to guide the boat back, there were flashes from the beach followed by the report of muskets.

"Note the location of those flashes if you will, Archie, and as soon as the boat is alongside, I would be obliged if you would answer with a broadside." If there was anyone on the beach, they had better have dug a hole as it was swept by a maelstrom of shot.

"Get us underway as soon as that boat is secured," he ordered the master.

James walked down to the entry port to find the boat crew, Linette and Enrique boarding. Two of his men were wounded and being helped. Enrique was slumped against the mainmast, blood coming from a wound to his shoulder, Linette was being held up by his cox, Simon Allen, and had a shallow slash wound across her back.

"What the hell happened?" he asked her.

"We were followed, and they ambushed us on the beach. I was hit from behind as I was climbing into the boat. Enrique was shot trying to help me."

At the rendezvous they transferred Linette, Enrique and the two wounded men to the Formidiable to be treated by Shelby then Marty set a course for home. They were passing through the gap between Ibiza and Valencia when they spotted sails coming from Valencia.

"A ship o'the line and a pair of frigates!" reported Antton from the mainmast. "Headed straight for us with all sail set!"

"Let me know what that liner is as soon as you can!" Marty called up to him, then to Ackermann,

"We better run for it. Wolfgang make as much sail as she can carry!"

It was a half an hour before Antton slid to the deck via a stay.

"She's a new seventy-four, French built," he reported.

"And fast, damn it!" Marty finished for him. The French made superbly hydrodynamic hulls and, when well-handled, were very fast. "What about the frigates?"

"This one's twins, both Spanish-built and -rigged."

"Are they catching us?" Marty asked after taking a long hard look at what he could see from the quarterdeck.

"Slowly. We have about seven miles head start on them."

Marty gathered up the first mate and master and went to the chart table.

"The one ship they will not be able to catch, in any wind, is the Eagle. Ryan is to take Linette and Enrique and get to Gibraltar as fast as possible to hand over the information they have on the agreement about Portugal. We will just have to stay ahead of that liner in a stern chase."

They slowed so the Eagle could sail up beside them and then hove too so they were close together and the two spies could be transferred with the minimum delay. To save time the boat crew stayed on the Eagle as well.

Then all three ships piled on as much sail as they could and sped off a couple of points West of South, as close to the wind as they could sail. It didn't take long for the Eagle to take a lead as she was the better sailor close to the wind and she gradually pulled away.

"God's speed," Marty murmured to himself as he watched their stern disappear into the distance.

"Pump the water over the side, leave only enough to get us home. If the wind stays out of the West like it is, we will take around forty hours to get to Gibraltar."

Staying ahead of their pursuers for forty hours was a very tough call and they would need every knot they could muster. Marty set about lightening the ship even more by dumping all the non-essentials over the side. James on the Alouette was doing the same.

By dark they had almost completed the Southern leg of the trip and were preparing to turn Northwest for their first long tack against the Westerly wind. Their saving grace was that the French and Spanish ships couldn't sail any closer to the wind than they could. This was a true stern chase.

They tacked to the Northwest for the one-hundred-mile leg towards a point South of Cartagena where they would tack again to the Southwest.

There was only one problem.

As dawn broke, they saw sails to their North.

"What the hell?" Marty exclaimed as the lookout called out the sighting.

"What are they?"

"Xebecs!"

Marty realised the French had set a trap and had sent ships out of Cartagena on the expectation that with the prevailing weather conditions they would have to make a tack that would bring them somewhere into that area. Now they had another pair of ships in pursuit that could sail closer to the wind than they could.

"Suggestions, Wolfgang?" he asked.

The phlegmatic German looked at the pennant and then at the two sets of sails closing inexorably in on them.

"Pray for a storm and that those Xebecs are poor shots if they have bow chasers," he deadpanned.

The storm didn't appear, and the gap steadily closed as the made a series of tacks to get them as far west as they could.

Marty was reluctant to throw the guns overboard as every mile brought them further into the British dominated region of the Mediterranean and he was determined not to go down without a fight.

They were almost due South of Malaga off the coast of Morocco and getting close to making their final tack when the first shot was fired. One of the Xebecs had got close enough to try a shot with its single chaser. From the sound it was a twenty-four-pounder.

The shot was well wide.

Fifteen minutes later the second one joined in.

"Another thirty minutes and they will be in range of our stern chasers," Ackerman coolly observed.

"In another hour that bloody seventy-four will be in range of us as well," Marty replied.

It turned into a running fight with neither side able to reduce sail to bring a broadside to bear, and for the French and Spanish their target was tantalisingly close. One lucky shot and they would find themselves surrounded and pounded.

The range gradually closed, the Xebecs got better at shooting and it would be only a matter of time before one got lucky.

"If they get close enough for us to use the carronades, we should be able to take them out of the chase," Marty said, knowing that was a faint hope.

A shot flew above his head cutting some rigging and narrowly missing the mizzen mast.

"Bugger this!" he said, deciding it was time to do something other than run.

"Prepare to wear!"

"Starboard battery double shot and run out. Larboard load and be ready! Wear to starboard!" The men, who were ready and waiting for just such an order, flew to their tasks.

The ship turned and Marty looked across at the Alouette, James had dropped his ship back to a point off their larboard quarter anticipating Marty's move.

"As you bear, fire!" Marty roared.

The guns coughed and fire ripple down the side. The lead Xebec took it on their starboard bow and shuddered as shot hit home and again as the Alouette followed up with their broadside. Her foremast went by the board, taking her out of the chase.

This was satisfying but brought the three original ships into range. Marty continued to wear for a minute or so to make it look like he would take them on head to head and then changed course to the Northeast to open the range.

This caused a small amount of confusion amongst the pursuing ships and allowed him to recover a few cables of distance. It wasn't long, though, before the bow chasers were throwing shot at them again, but at least the Xebecs were out of the game as the second one had stopped to aid its compatriot.

"Sails to the Northwest!" cried a slightly worried sounding lookout.

"Get up there with a glass, I want to know what they are as soon as possible!" He told Midshipman Grey who grabbed a telescope and shot off up the ratlines.

Marty was calculating what he could do to avoid being caught in another trap when a much-relieved hail came down,

"It's a British liner and the Eagle!"

Marty grinned at Ackerman and Trenchard, who had joined him. This changed things completely.

"Fancy a fight?"

The two lieutenants grinned, and Ackermann shouted,

"get those guns loaded," he looked at Marty who decided,

"chain let's go for his rigging."

The altered course slightly to close the gap between themselves and the approaching English ships, Marty had been hoping there would be more than just the two, but it was just the Eagle and,

“Well bugger me, its Smith in the Pompée!” he said as he recognised the ship through his telescope.

“The French have seen the other ships! They are bearing away!”

“Oh no you don’t!” Marty cried. A quick glance showed James was holding station and had his guns run out.

“Helm to Starboard, steer straight for their bows!”

Marty knew they needed to slow the French ship down and the best he could do was to try and get as close as possible to shred her rigging.

“Fire a gun!” he ordered, hoping that a challenge wouldn’t be ignored.

One of the bow chasers barked and they all watched the Frenchman for a reaction.

He ran out his lower deck guns. He could fire those without reducing sail and with the wind on his quarter the ports were well clear of the sea. He eased a point or two to the north to bring his guns to bear.

“Thirty-six-pounders,” Ackermann observed.

“Quite,” Marty replied dryly, as if he didn’t already know. “We will have to take his first broadside to get in close enough to do any real damage.”

The angle was not in the Frenchman’s favour as it would force many of his guns to be trained around to the limit to get even close to bearing. They got a warning as he jinked to starboard.

The French fired before the gun crews could settle their aim and most shots flew wide. Marty could only assume the officer in charge of them was inexperienced.

Marty ducked as a block fell on to the nets, but it bounced and settled without breaking through. Some shots had found their mark. They had also picked up a couple of holes in their sails. He checked the range and ordered,

“Two points to larboard. FIRE AS YOU BEAR!”

The bow slipped around, and the guns barked at a range of four cables. The air shimmered as the chain shot flew across the half mile gap towards the big ships rigging. Then the smoke obscured the view.

The gun crews were calmly and efficiently reloading, the carronades were ready first and about twenty seconds later the mains.

The smoke had cleared, and Marty could see they had shredded his mainsail and there were men frantically trying to splice other damage, but the main thing was they had slowed them.

The Formidiable fired again as the range closed to three cables and this time the Alouette joined in with her carronades. It was at the edge of their accurate range but any hits at all would help.

On the French ship, Capitaine de Vaisseau, Cedric Semillon, looked at the two smaller English ships in wonder. They were barking and nipping at his heels like terriers and doing some damage. Their first broadside was well aimed and even at around eight hundred meters had done enough damage to slow them.

His mouth opened in astonishment when they fired their second in around half the time his big eighteen-kilogram guns could reload. The range had come down to around six-hundred meters and this time the corvette fired as well.

He ducked as chain shot howled through his rigging cutting ropes and stays and causing spars and blocks to fall to the deck.

He looked astern where the two Spanish frigates were – not where they should be.

"Traitors! Cowards!" he shouted at them as they bore away with the wind, abandoning him.

He had no choice he would have to make a fight of it.

"Reduce sail and run out."

Marty saw the damage his second broadside had caused and the Spanish frigates making a run for it.

"Mr. Williams, please signal the Alouette's number and the letter B,"

"Mr. Ackermann double shot and get us in closer, try to stay as much towards his bow as possible."

James saw the signal and knew exactly what he had to do, this was something they had planned and rehearsed. He ordered a wear to larboard away from the Formidiable, a casual observer could think he was abandoning them. He ordered all his carronades to be loaded with smashers. He kept one eye on Marty and saw he was running slightly more sail than you would normally in a firefight so he could stay on the bigger ships bow.

Smoke blossomed from the Frenchman and he saw the Formidiable shudder as she took a hit or two. He continued the wear, swinging around in a great arc that would bring him across the Frenchman's stern. As he rounded the corner, he could see he had four large stern chasers, two on each gundeck.

This wouldn't be painless.

In the Eagle, Ryan put on more sail and was out running the Pompée, such was his eagerness to get into the fight. He had seen Marty's signal to the Alouette and knew his part in that attack plan. He just needed to get there to realise it.

Sir Sydney was urging his flag Captain to go faster but there wasn't much William Tremayne could do; the Pompée was going as fast as she could. They were getting close enough to try the bow chasers. He was impressed with the way that the two smaller ships were harassing the big, two decked, third rate.

"We will get our chance Admiral. Captain Stockley and his men know what they are doing, I believe."

"I know!" Smith barked back at him, "they may finish the blighter off before we get there!"

Marty had no intention of trying to 'finish the blighter off' as he knew the Frenchman would be carrying around eight hundred to a thousand men and even with all three of his ships, he could only muster six hundred. That meant a boarding strength of around five hundred and he didn't like those odds. No, he was happy to harass and nibble at their heels for when Smith arrived and could deal the coup de grace.

He looked over in the direction the support was coming from and saw the Eagle speeding down under full sail. He grinned, *good for you, Ryan.*

James was almost in position astern of what he could now see was the Viala when the stern chasers fired. There were only four, but they were eighteen-pound longs and could do some real damage to his sloop of war.

Two of the incoming balls went wide, one punched a hole in his foresail and the last crashed into his hull about three feet above the waterline.

They fired and the thirty-six-pound balls from the carronades crashed into the big ship's transom, creating gaping holes and upending at least one of the chasers. They created havoc as they crashed down the open gun decks.

James had looked up and seen the French captain look over the stern, when he was slammed to the deck as a musket ball took him in the thigh.

Archie Davidson was summoned from the guns as his captain was carried below. He assumed command without batting an eyelid, this was another of those things they had planned for and rehearsed.

Another musket ball sent splinters up from the deck at his feet and he called up to the marines in the tops,

"Would be obliged if you sorted that chap out, he's making himself a nuisance."

The crew who heard that grinned at each other, they liked the phlegmatic young midshipman who modelled himself after Captain Stockley.

The guns roared again.

Ryan had almost gotten into the fight and was steering to swing around the Formidiable and cross the Viala's bows. The Eagle sailed like a witch and he was making the most of her excellent qualities.

Smith was watching and admiring the way the three ships worked together in such an unconventional way.

"We can learn something from these young men, they are like wasps around a honey pot!" he crowed. "Dammit, man, get in there before that ruddy Frenchman strikes!"

Tremayne grinned and ordered the starboard battery run out. It was time to get 'stuck in'.

Marty looked for the liner as the Formidiable absorbed another few hits from the Viala.

"About bloody time too." he said to no one in particular.

"Get us out of his way, John," he ordered the quartermaster.

"Make more sail!"

Tremayne saw that Marty was moving ahead and swung the Pompée to bring them alongside. It was time for the big boys to play and the two liners exchanged broadsides. The British gunners reloaded much faster than the French and poured a second broadside in. The two giants exchanged blows for another fifteen minutes until Capitaine Semillon knew it was over. He had fought with honour and struck without a conscience.

Chapter 22: The fruits of our labours.

Marty visited James in the infirmary they had set up in the re-purposed barracks the S.O.F. called home on Gibraltar. The ball had hit from a high angle and had broken his femur about a third of the way down. He was lucky the ball hadn't shattered the bone but had snapped it fairly cleanly.

They had transferred him across to the Formidiable as soon as they could after the fight. Shelby had removed the ball and aligned the break before clamping the leg in splints while his assistants held James down.

Now it was a question of whether he would heal cleanly or gangrene would set in. Shelby had taken every precaution, kept his instruments clean and even used sulphur powder on the wound, as there was a theory it would help. If the rot did set in, he would lose the leg, and no one wanted that.

Josee was his nurse and the tall, beautiful Dutch girl made sure that Marty didn't overstay his welcome. Marty had to remind himself she was only eighteen as she was so level-headed.

Marty left the two of them together and went to see the other men that had been wounded in the fight. Shelby was paying a house call on Admiral Collingwood so there was no one who could hurry him along.

He chatted with them and asked if they needed anything. The men appreciated that and knew if that whatever they asked for would arrive sooner rather than later. The other thing that made their confinement bearable is the fact that Lady Caroline and her maids were their nurses.

After leaving the hospital Marty headed down to their prize agents and met up with Mr. Crabshaw, who he had been with since his first year as a midshipman on the Falcon.

"Good afternoon Sir Martin," Crabshaw greeted him as he was shown into the man's office. It hadn't changed much over the years though he did notice a new decanter set on the sideboard.

"Mr. Crabshaw," he replied and shook the proffered hand. "Do you have an estimate of the prize valuations from our last trip yet?"

"An estimation, yes," Crabshaw replied, "but the prize court will not sit for at least another month, so my estimate of the French capital ship is only indicative."

Marty nodded and waited for him to continue.

Crabshaw knew Marty from when he was just thirteen years old and was amazed at the change in the young man. He was still only twenty-six and was calm, assured, and confident. Fatherhood hadn't changed him, either, even though he had four children now.

The dog that followed him around was slightly intimidating as it sat beside Martin and stared at him. He had a thought that this must be how a rabbit felt. The big brindled herding dog was a little grey around the muzzle, but its eyes were intense, and it had enormous canine teeth.

He brought his thoughts back to the present.

"The merchant vessels and their cargo should nett around twenty-four thousand pounds once we have auctioned off everything. The olive oil was very high quality and will attract a premium.

"The Viala is a relatively new ship and even though she took a fair amount of damage should fetch a good price. Then there is the head money for the Xebec as well."

He paused, checked a sheet of paper and seemed to add up the column of figures again to be sure they were right.

"After the Admiral takes his share you will be left with around the value of a frigate to share amongst your ships."

"And that is?" Marty asked.

"Oh, sorry, that's about one hundred and thirty thousand pounds."

That gave a total of one hundred and fifty-four thousand, and if they split it as normal then everyone from Hood down to the cabin boy would make a tidy sum.

His next port of call was Collingwood on the Flagship. He was announced and shown directly in by a beaming, junior flag lieutenant who was shiny new and totally in awe of the young Captain he had heard so much about.

Smith was already there and greeted Marty warmly. Collingwood looked well and shook Marty's hand firmly, but Marty knew better. After they were all settled, he opened the meeting,

"The French and Spanish have signed a treaty to divide up Portugal and to kick out the sitting royal family. Sir Sidney will command an expedition to Lisbon that will either assist the Portuguese to resist the attack or destroy the Portuguese fleet and blockade the Tagus. We would like you to accompany him with your flotilla and lend your special skills to the endeavour."

Marty grinned and shook Smith's hand. This should be fun!

Epilogue

Hood was in his office reading a letter from Admiral Collingwood when his secretary opened the door and announced,

"Mr George Canning, Admiral."

Hood stood and came around the desk to greet the Foreign Secretary of the British government and the successor to William Wickham.

"Hello George, lovely to see you, make yourself comfortable."

The secretary offered coffee or tea and left to prepare what was ordered.

"You said you had some news from Gibraltar." Canning opened without ceremony.

"Yes," replied Hood and held up two letters.

"Our agents have reported that the French and Spanish have signed a treaty at Fontainebleau to drive out the Braganza's from Portugal and divide up the country between them."

"I thought the assassination of the ambassador would slow that down," commented Canning.

"So did we, but they brought in Gerald Duroc and he got it done relatively quickly. We managed to get a copy of the treaty, which was why our ships were pursued as they tried to get back to Gibraltar after the pickup," Hood replied.

Canning considered this for a moment, "I don't believe Napoleon has any real interest in dividing up Portugal, this could just be a ruse to get his troops into Spain without a fight."

Hood nodded,

"I agree, but there's nothing we can do about it now. However, I have also heard from Collingwood and he has tasked Sir Sidney Smith to lead an expedition to either assist the Portuguese or blockade the Tagus and, if all else fails, to burn their fleet as we do not want Napoleon to get his hands on that!"

"Hmmm, Smith. Can we trust him not to go off at a tangent?" Canning frowned in concern.

"Well the man is brilliant if unpredictable, so Collingwood asked Martin Stockley to support him with the Flotilla in the hope he can influence him. They have apparently become good friends."

Canning raised his eyebrows,

"Good grief! Those two working together? Are you sure? That could explode in any number of ways!"

Hood laughed. "Well we can be sure that whatever happens it will be damn uncomfortable and inconvenient for the French and Spanish."

Canning harrumphed and took a sip of coffee,

"Well, at least Stockley and his cutthroats will be in place for when Arthur Wellesley enters Portugal and then Spain to take the war to Napoleon," he commented.

It was Hood's turn to raise his eyebrows.

"You know that he and Martin are friends as well."

Canning smiled,

"Wellesley mentioned that."

Both men just sat and sipped their coffee for a while.

"1808 looks like it will be a very good year!" Hood concluded in satisfaction. He looked at the clock,

"Sun's over the yard arm old chap, can I tempt you with a Brandy?

Author's Note

The incident with the Prince Regent is pure fiction but could well have happened as he was a womaniser and had a sequence of mistresses. It was inspired by something a friend once said, "a wife is expensive, but a mistress is ten times the cost." I guess he should remain nameless!

The years covered by the book were relatively quiet, historically. The Peninsular War was just beginning to fulminate at this time and the British could see the storm clouds on the horizon so moving the whole operation down to Gibraltar made sense.

I was researching that when I came upon the war in Calabria and specifically the Battle of Maida and lo and behold there was Sir Sidney Smith! I have been looking for an excuse to get him together with Marty for ages and that dropped right into my lap!

But the meat of the story is in the counter espionage exercise in Malta and the arrival of de Faux, aka le Bonne, in the Mediterranean. Marty picked up on the horse's head idea in Sicily and I have no idea if it was common practice at that time but it did the job of enraging de faux and setting him off in the right direction, so I put it in regardless.

I tried to put in more details as that's what people have been asking for so this book is 10 – 15% longer than the previous ones and I'm hoping I can beat that in the next one.

I do hope you enjoyed this instalment of Marty's life and I look forward to taking to you again soon.

And now!

An excerpt from Book 7

Chapter 1: Family time

Marty lay in bed and traced the scar that ran across Caroline's ribs with his fingertip and marvelled that she had already started to recover her figure after the birth of the twins. Caroline said she was blessed that even after having them she was returning to her former slender self. She practiced dance and fenced to keep fit and rubbed oils into her skin during the pregnancy which she said helped prevent stretch marks.

He shuddered at the memory of Shelby stitching up the wound that had been the result of a close encounter with a splinter in a sea battle in the Caribbean. An inch further in and it would have killed her.

It was dawn on a wet November morning in Gibraltar and he was relishing the quiet. None of the children were awake yet, Blaez was asleep in his place at the foot of their bed and the only sound, beside his gentle snoring, was the rain on the window.

The previous month the French had signed the Fontainebleau accord that committed them both to kicking the legitimate rulers of Portugal out and dividing up the country between them. Marty's friend, Rear Admiral Sir Sidney Smith, had been given command of a task force to blockade the Portuguese port of Lisbon or destroy their fleet to prevent it falling into enemy hands. The Special Operations Flotilla, S.O.F. was going to be attached to the expedition in the hope that Marty could act as a moderating influence on the mercurial Smith.

But today was for his family, Marty had promised to take the children down to his ship for the morning. Beth and

James were both excited and he knew that his followers, the Shadows, would spoil them rotten.

He leaned forward and kissed Caroline on the stomach, she opened her eyes and reached for him, a smile on her face that promised much. Then the door burst open, Beth and James rushed in and climbed on the bed. *Timing was impeccable,* he smiled ruefully and grabbed his daughter to tickle her, making her giggle.

The Formidiable was tied up at the dock and had a faint smell of sawdust, paint and tar hanging over her as they had just finished repairing the damage caused by their encounter with the Viala a French 74. Sir Sidney had arrived just in time win the battle after the Flotilla had been mercilessly harassing her to stop her running away.

Marty carried Beth and Caroline James; Mary had the twins in a pram. Wilson, a six-foot eight giant of a man and one of the Shadows, strode down the gang plank and walked over to Mary. The big man looked shy and quietly offered to help her get the pram on board.

Caroline exchanged a knowing look with Marty, they knew that Mary had been seeing someone on her evenings off, now they thought they knew who! Mary giggled at something he said then he picked up the pram and carried it up the gangway.

"Uncle John!" Beth cried as she spotted Marty's Quartermaster stood on deck and struggled in his arms to get down. Marty laughed and put her down so she could run over to the laughing sailor brandishing her favourite toy, a wooden sword.

They spent a pleasant morning sat under an awning out of the rain. Caroline took over caring for the twins so Mary could spend some time with Wilson. At the end of the morning he approached Marty and asked permission to have a word with him.

"Well what can I do for you?" Marty asked with a glint in his eye.

"Well captain it's like this, I been walking out with Mary for a while now and I find I have a real care for her." He blushed and rung his hands before he continued, "We have talked, and we would like to get married if that's alright with you of course."

"You don't need my permission Wilson, nor does Mary but I will give you my blessing. I think you will make a wonderful couple." He shook hands with Wilson and clapped him on the shoulder. The two of them re-joined the ladies who were already celebrating.

As the rain had stopped, they decided to walk the half mile back to the house. They were about halfway back when a man stepped out from behind a tree in front of them. Marty immediately recognised the blunderbuss as it was swung up in his direction. He was carrying James and couldn't get to his weapons!

Caroline was walking hand in hand with Beth and saw the man step forward. He was focused on Marty and was swinging the massive, brass, bell mouthed gun towards him. Marty was carrying James and was turning so he had his back to the man to shelter the boy from harm.

The world slowed down.

Her vision zoomed in on the man's face as it contorted to shout something in French.

She let go of Beth and her hand flew to the muff she wore suspended around her neck and the pistol concealed inside.

She thumbed back the hammer as she pushed the gun through the tube of material.

The pistol, a gift from Marty, was a fifty caliber, rifled, four-inch barrelled Manton sometimes called a muff pistol that was preferred by ladies. It packed a punch and she was an expert shot even hampered by the muff.

The Dorset Boy Book 6 - Vendetta

The pistol fired and the bullet smashed into the man's chest, dead center through his sternum, the impact knocking him backwards as he pulled the trigger, jerking the barrel up.

The enormous spread of deer shot flew high missing Marty's back by inches. However, as he ducked, he exposed Mary who was walking behind him pushing the pram with the twins in. A single piece of shot on the edge of the spread sliced through her scalp above her right eye.

Caroline didn't hesitate and stepped over to Marty to reach under his coat. She pulled out his fighting knife and turned to the prone man who lay groaning on the floor. She stepped over to him, looked down at his face then knelt and placed the knife on his throat.

"Who are you?" she asked.

The man looked up into the coldest grey eyes he had ever seen, there was no mercy just cold beauty.

"A patriot." He replied as blood dribbled out of the side of his mouth.

"Why?" she asked, her head cocked slightly to one side.

"He killed my love." He gasped as the life started to fade from his eyes.

"Claudette?"

"Yesss," he breathed with his last breath.

She turned back and saw Marty kneeling over a prone Mary. He was holding what looked like a spare nappy to her head which was soaked in blood. Beth was crying and James stood looking at Mary not understanding what had happened. The dead man was forgotten as she went to care for her family.

The Dorset Boy Book 6 - Vendetta

Made in the USA
Middletown, DE
13 March 2020

86323017R00154